A Mug of Mayhem

The CafFUNated Mysteries

A Mug of Mayhem

Book Four in the CafFUNated Mysteries

By

Angela Ruth Strong

A Mug of Mayhem
Published by Mountain Brook Ink
White Salmon, WA U.S.A.

The website addresses shown in this book are not intended in any way to be or imply an endorsement on the part of Mountain Brook Ink, nor do we vouch for their content.

This story is a work of fiction. All characters and events are the product of the author's imagination. Any resemblance to any person, living or dead, is coincidental.

The author is represented by and this book is published in association with the literary agency of WordServe Literary Group, Ltd., www.wordserveliterary.com

Scripture quotations are taken from the King James Version of the Bible. Public domain.
© 2021 Angela Ruth Strong
ISBN 978-1953957-05-4

The Team: Miralee Ferrell, Alyssa Roat, Kristen Johnson, Cindy Jackson
Cover Design: Allison Phythian

Mountain Brook Ink is an inspirational publisher offering fiction you can believe in.
Printed in the United States of America

Dedication

To Becky, Biceps, and Birdie –
some of my favorite characters.

Acknowledgments

I wrote this book in 2020, an absolutely crazy year. Besides the Covid conundrum, I was also going through chemotherapy. That may sound awful, and it really was, but it also showed me how wonderful people are and made me feel more loved than I've ever felt in my life. If you were a part of my 2020, I can't thank you enough, but I want to try.

First there's my writing group. Every year, Heather, Hilarey, Lisa, Becky, Rebecca, and I go on a retreat into the mountains to help brainstorm each other's books. In January 2020, they rented a house in town so I could be near a medical facility if any health issues arose. They wouldn't let me pay anything toward it either. Then they dressed up in my wigs and helped me plot *A Mug of Mayhem* from beginning to end. But my most treasured memory from the weekend was when Lisa led us in worship with her guitar. I let them sing in the living room while I stood alone in the entryway behind the sofa, offering my praise to God for what a gift He'd given me in them.

There was also a trip to visit my best friend from first grade to whom this book is dedicated. Though I hadn't seen her in three decades, she's been a huge support to me through the trials of life. Her daughter, Birdie, is now the age we were when we met, and their family all began praying for me every night when they heard I had cancer. I got to join them for this bedtime ritual while I was there and experienced another unforgettable moment of worship as we sang together on Birdie's bedroom floor.

I could go on and on from the gifts I received to the meals that were cooked for us, but I'll end with the surprise I had waiting outside the hospital on my final day of chemo. The Sunday before my last treatment was Easter. My husband and I decided to have our own sunrise service in the backyard since churches were closed. We drank our coffee and listened to worship music, which fatefully included the song *I Still Believe* by Jeremy Camp. He wrote it after his wife died of cancer. I started crying, and I couldn't stop for three days. Even though I'd survived, and am now cancer free, I had this ache inside for my family and loved ones to "still believe" in God after I die. I wept for anyone who had ever let pain keep them from seeing beauty in their gift of life.

The good news is that I was able to release all my sadness so that when I rang the bell after my final treatment and walked outside the hospital to find a whole field full of friends and family celebrating with me (in a socially distanced kind of way), I felt nothing but awe. This world is amazing. You are amazing.

And that's the message I hope to impart my readers through my final CafFUNated Mystery. Don't let your pain ever get in the way of loving others. Not even those who might have caused that pain. It may be hard like chemo, but it's what will bring your healing.

Thank you to all who have ever helped me learn this. And to my editor for catching an embarrassingly large number of typos in this manuscript, for which I will make my "chemo brain" excuse only this one time.

Chapter One

Tandy held out the matching Mr. and Mrs. coffee mugs with their heart shaped handles. "I know it's early for wedding gifts, but I wanted to give you these before things get too crazy."

Marissa clutched the gift bag to her heart. She looked every ounce the blushing bride, standing underneath the chandeliers being hung on arched wooden beams. Her groom's family barn was the perfect place for a wedding reception. And the blonde beauty queen would be even more radiant in her grandmother's vintage dress that weekend. "Tandy, I love them. I will drink coffee from mine occasionally. Like when I run out of tea."

"I'll drink coffee from mine every day." Connor stood beside his future wife and wiped his eyes. Having grown up on a farm and currently a building contractor, he was the manliest of men, and at six-foot tall with wheat-colored sideburns and a strong jaw, he looked the part. Usually, anyway.

Tandy frowned at the groom's emotional response. "Connor, are you crying?"

"He has allergies." Marissa patted his arm then turned to face him. "Hon, do you need more medication? I want to know that it's going to work during our wedding. Especially to prevent a bloody nose."

Tandy arched an eyebrow. She wouldn't be surprised if Connor got a bloody nose during the reception, but she would expect it to come as a result of Marissa's clumsy actions. She pictured the bride tripping him on the dance floor or elbowing him in the face as she tossed the bouquet.

Connor glanced at his watch. "I should probably take another pill." He turned toward the barn doors and rubbed his eyes again. "I just hate how moody the drugs make me."

Marissa trailed behind him toward the giant barn doors, though her gaze roved the rafters as if imagining what it would look like when all the white lights and paper lanterns were hung. It was going to be a challenge to get the woman to focus on reality until she was wed.

As maid of honor, Tandy would keep a close eye on her friend to make sure no mayhem broke out before then. Though what mayhem could happen on such a beautiful autumn day?

She followed Marissa into the bright, crisp air, crushing sweet-scented hay under her biker boots. Since it was October, The Farmstead overflowed with students on field trips as well as a shiny, black bus full of residents from a local retirement community. They picked out pumpkins, lined up for the corn maze, and warmed themselves at smoky firepits, but none of this seemed to register with Marissa as she spoke about wedding plans over her shoulder.

"Tables, chairs, and dishes get dropped off Friday in time for the rehearsal dinner. Wednesday morning, I have breakfast with my extended family, so I'll need you to run the coffee shop and tea house without me. You're still planning for pedicures tomorrow, right?"

"Right." Tandy couldn't remember the last time she'd had a pedicure. Oh, yeah. Never. She preferred to be as dark and edgy as Marissa was bright and sunny. At least Marissa had agreed to the black bridesmaid dress and cowgirl boots.

Marissa sighed. "With family coming into town for the wedding and Halloween events at the shop, that's the only spare moment I could find. Hopefully nothing else unexpected pops up."

Connor froze in front of them. Tandy stopped too, but, as usual, Marissa seemed to be more aware of her daydreams than her actual surroundings. She plowed into Connor's backside, dropping the gift bag of mugs.

Connor spun sideways and caught her arm as smoothly as if he had experience with such a move. And he probably did. "Watch out, hon," he said to her but continued squinting his puffy red eyes at something in the distance.

The mugs landed with a soft thunk, and Tandy scooped them up to make sure they wouldn't need handles glued back on the way she'd had to do with many of the mugs in their shop. Nope. For once, excessive cardboard packaging saved the day. She held the cups up triumphantly.

Marissa peered at Connor as if for the first time. "You scheduled your haircut for tomorrow, right?"

Connor shook his head. His hair wasn't very long, but he usually kept it cropped as short as his sideburns. "At the barber, you can just walk…" His spine straightened. He let go of Marissa and lunged forward. "That *is* Hubert. When I fired him, I made it clear I didn't want him back on our property."

"Hubert?" Tandy looked the direction of Connor's gaze. A skinny guy in a hoodie glanced around before disappearing into the corn maze.

"Yeah, he was stealing from the cash box," Marissa explained. "But Connor, what's he going to steal in the corn maze? Corn? Why don't you call Sheriff Griffin on him this time?"

"Not happening." Connor wiped his watering eyes again before marching away. "He could steal from our customers and escape before getting caught. The customers don't know the maze. Sheriff Griffin doesn't know the maze. I'm the only one who can catch him. I'm the left tackle in this play."

Tandy smooshed her lips together. "Left tackle?"

Marissa shrugged. "That's football talk. He's in a fantasy football league right now."

Tandy nodded. She knew more than she wanted to. "Greg's in it too."

Marissa pointed toward Connor's loft apartment above the barn. "At least take your meds first," she called after him. "You're a mess."

"I'll only be a second." Connor cut to the front of the line at the entrance of the corn maze and glowered. "And this time I'll make sure Hubert never returns."

The crowd watched him stride behind the stalks in curiosity. Hopefully, they thought this was some sort of publicity stunt related to advertisements for the "zombie corn maze" featured after dark.

That's what Tandy would have assumed if she'd been a bystander. Connor was usually better than this at keeping his cool. She tilted her head his direction. "He stressed about the wedding?"

Marissa bit her lip. "Wouldn't you be stressed if you'd already had your engagement called off once, not to mention almost losing your fiancée to a homicidal maniac and then to the witness protection program?"

Tandy nodded thoughtfully. "I guess it's been kind of a rough road for you guys."

"Yes, but"—Marissa held up a finger—"we're on the home stretch. The toughest part is going to be keeping my relatives from killing each other after they arrive tonight."

Tandy had only met Marissa's mom, but if her family was all as fake and judgy, murder would be a real possibility. She'd have to try her best not to stab anyone on Marissa's behalf.

She waved a hand to wipe away her friend's worries. "It'll be fine."

"Hey!" Connor's voice carried from the corn maze as if to contradict her prediction.

Tandy looked up to find him chasing the hooded Hubert across a steel bridge that rose above the corn stalks. The skinny guy glanced over his shoulder, still running. Metal clanged with each step.

"Stop, Hubert." Connor lunged, arms reaching to grab him.

Either Connor missed, or he accidentally shoved his former employee down the stairs. They both disappeared from view.

Tandy gasped along with the rest of the crowd.

Marissa watched in horror. Had Connor fallen? He shouldn't even be dealing with the trespasser himself. What if they got into a fight, and Connor sported a black eye or split lip on her wedding day? That would be even worse than the allergies she'd been concerned about.

She took off toward the corn stalks as fast as her chunky leopard print booties would carry her. She should have worn something a little more practical for a farm, but chunky leopard print booties were her favorite part of fall. "Call Sheriff Griffin," she called back to Tandy.

Then she charged through the entrance of the maze with determination. Unfortunately, she only made it twenty feet before hitting a T in the road.

The bridge where she'd seen Connor had been on the right. She turned, jogging once again. Another T. She took a left to go deeper. Dead end.

Backtracking, she yelled for her fiancé. "Connor?"

She stopped and listened. No pounding feet. No shouting. No scuffling. That had to be a good sign.

An elderly man wearing a buffalo checked hunting cap like Elmer Fudd appeared from around a corner, barely giving her a second glance as he passed. And that first glance had been a scowl. "This way."

She watched but didn't follow. Who was this cartoon character? "That's a dead end."

He didn't even slow when he reached the wall of cornstalks. Instead, he parted them and stomped through. Why hadn't Marissa thought of that?

She trotted after him. The stalks he'd parted, snapped back, whipping her in the face. She rubbed at a stinging cheek. What if she was the one with a black eye at her wedding? Hopefully photoshop could fix her portraits. She wanted everything to be perfect.

With a huff, she pushed the stiff stalks to the side and gingerly stepped into a dirt mound that hadn't been trampled solid by customers. She wobbled precariously before catching her balance and swinging her back leg through. "Wait," she pleaded over the rustling of vegetation.

The older man didn't wait, but she was able to spot his red hat before he disappeared around another turn. She followed, only rolling her ankle once. Hopefully, he knew where he was going, and it was the same place she was headed. She called Connor's name again just to be sure.

"Marissa," he called back this time. "Over here."

Her heart fluttered. Whether it was because his voice always had the ability to do that to her or because she'd subconsciously feared he'd been in real danger, she didn't know. Either way, relief ran through her veins at the idea of being reunited with her groom.

She charged past the older man toward the sound of Connor's call. While Elmer Fudd was stealthy and his footsteps sure, she had youth and speed on her side. She rounded one last corner and jerked to a halt.

Connor knelt over a body, elbows locked as he pumped the heel of his palms against the guy's chest in CPR compressions.

Marissa's hands flew to cover her mouth, and her thoughts circled without a place to land. Was the guy dead? Had Connor fought him? Wasn't there a Nicholas Cage movie that started out this way?

Connor looked up, desperation in the wrinkle between his eyebrows. "Call for an ambulance." Blood dripped from his nose. Was that from his allergies or had he been punched?

She scrambled for the phone in the pocket of her turquoise peacoat and only took her eyes off Connor long enough to dial. "Are you hurt?"

"No." He grunted, then dropped lower to blow breaths into the other man's lungs. As he rose to give more compressions, blood dripped from his nose onto the unconscious man.

At least Connor wasn't injured, though with the way Marissa's body had gone numb from adrenaline, his could have done the same, in which case, he might be hurt but not feel his wounds yet. As for the guy on the ground…

She held her breath and listened to the phone ring at police dispatch.

The old man in the hunting cap stepped beside Marissa and stared at the scene before them.

"9-1-1, what is your emergency?" A tinny voice echoed over the phone line.

The old man spoke Marissa's worst fear. "You killed him."

Chapter Two

MARISSA CLUTCHED CONNOR'S CLAMMY HAND AS the EMTs covered Hubert's body in a white sheet and drove him away. Connor claimed to be physically okay, but his face remained pale, and she suspected his eyes weren't only watery from allergies. He hadn't yet said what happened with his former employee, but no matter how innocent he was, he had to feel the weight of being accused of murder even if it was from not being able to resuscitate the man.

Thankfully, Deputy Romero cleared customers out of the farm while Sherriff Griffin joined Marissa and Connor at a picnic table. Though Romero hadn't been the criminal she'd once thought him, she still preferred the sheriff's baby face over the deputy's greasy dark hair and beady eyes.

Griffin sat across the table and studied Connor. The two men weren't exactly buddies, but Marissa had babysat him as a kid and solved a few of his cases for him as an adult. "How did you know the deceased?" he asked.

Connor sat taller from his hunched position. He sent Marissa a quick glance, uncertainty darkening his eyes to the shade of gunmetal gray. "Hubert used to work here. I fired him for stealing from us."

Griffin nodded then looked down at a notepad in his hand. "There are quite a few witnesses who claim you pushed him down the steps of the bridge."

"No." Connor shook his head. "No. I was lunging to catch him, but I missed, and he fell." He motioned to Marissa. "You saw, right honey?"

Marissa's chest tightened. "I..." She had to tell the truth. The truth is what set people free, right? "I couldn't tell what was going on, but I assumed that's what happened because I know you."

Griffin trained his gaze on her. "Hmm."

Connor rolled his eyes. "You know me too, Griffin. You know I wouldn't push someone like that."

Griffin nodded slowly. "What about hitting someone with a shovel?"

Marissa blinked. She looked at Connor to see if he knew what Griffin was talking about because she sure didn't.

Connor's eyebrows arched. "No. Never."

Griffin clicked his tongue. "Come on, Connor. If it was in self-defense that's understandable. But you have to be honest."

Marissa caught her breath. Connor was one of the most honest people she knew. What was going on?

Connor released Marissa's hands and splayed his wide. "I don't know anything about a shovel."

Griffin pressed his lips together for a second. "There's blood on a shovel found not far from your altercation. If it's a match for Hubert's blood, you're going to have more explaining to do."

Connor rubbed a hand over his head. "Hubert had a little blood on his temple when I caught up to him in the maze. I didn't think anything of it at the time. But I guess it's possible someone hit him with a shovel before I got there."

Griffin narrowed his eyes. "You chased a guy into the maze, and by the time you caught up with him, someone else had already hit him with a shovel? Who would have done that?"

Connor shrugged and shook his head. "He's a thief. Maybe he tried to rob someone, and they reacted in self-defense."

Marissa nodded. That made sense. More so than Connor lying about the shovel.

Griffin scribbled in his notebook. His eyes lifted to study Connor again. "If we find your fingerprints on the shovel, is your story going to change?"

"No," Connor blurted. "This is my parents' farm. It's my shovel. You're gonna find my fingerprints, but that doesn't mean I whacked anybody."

Marissa's stomach lurched. She didn't want to think it possible her fiancé could get arrested the week of their wedding, but if Hubert's death really was a murder, all evidence pointed Connor's way. "Connor," she soothed. "Tell Griffin what happened after Hubert fell. How you tried to save his life."

Connor nodded. "Yeah. I gave him CPR."

Griffin sighed. "Which is when your blood got on him."

"Right."

The sheriff shook his head. "If you didn't get into a fight with Hubert, then why were *you* bleeding?"

Marissa swallowed. If only Connor had taken his medication before chasing Hubert into the maze.

"I'm allergic to ragweed," he stated. "I get nosebleeds."

"I can vouch for that." Marissa nodded. "He's even got a prescription, though he doesn't like taking it because they have side effects."

"What kind of side effects?" Griffin paused with his pencil above his notepad.

Connor cleared his throat.

Marissa bit her lip. She knew what was coming. Why did she have to mention side effects?

"They can make me moody," Connor finally answered.

The sheriff glanced up before writing. He drew out the word, "Reeeally?"

Connor huffed. "Yes, really. They make me impatient with wedding planning and irritable about haircuts, but they don't make me attack people with shovels."

Marissa smoothed his hair at the crown where it was starting to stick up from his cowlick. If he went to jail, he wouldn't be able to go to the barber. "Griffin, the blood on the shovel could be from something else. Maybe someone tripped on it and cut their leg. You don't know. All you know is that Connor was on the bridge when Hubert fell down the stairs. Then Connor tried to resuscitate him. He's a hero."

"There's something else," a gruff voice from behind broke in.

Marissa twisted to find the Elmer Fudd guy glaring at them.

"Sheriff," the older man continued. "Before this yahoo entered the maze, he threatened to make sure Hubert never returned to his farm."

Marissa's eyes bugged. She had forgotten that part, but who was this old guy, and why did he seem to hate Connor so much? Didn't he have better things to do than ruin her wedding? "Who are you?" she demanded.

He ignored her, directing his response to Griffin. "I'm Archibald Clack. Veteran and resident of Grace Springs Manor."

Griffin looked the old man over. "Sir, my deputy was supposed to get your statement, and you were supposed to get back on your bus. We're clearing out the farm for our investigation."

"I did get on the bus, but our activities' director is missing." Archibald crossed his arms. "I figured you'd want to know."

Tandy jogged up behind the little bald guy dressed as a hunter. She'd been trying to get the residents of Grace Springs Manor on their bus but loading the big woman in the wheelchair took so long that the other residents had scattered. By the look on Marissa's face, that wasn't their biggest issue at the moment.

Tandy hadn't wanted to consider the possibility that Connor might get arrested for murder since Griffin knew he wasn't capable of such a thing, but Griffin was capable of anything. "I'm just going to help this gentleman back to his bus," she said. "Everything all right?"

Marissa grimaced.

Griffin squeezed the button on the mic of his walkie talkie clipped to the lapel of his uniform. "Romero, are we missing the activities' director for Grace Springs Manor?"

Static crackled. "Affirmative."

No wonder the old folks weren't getting on the bus. They'd lost their leader. Or maybe their leader was lost in the maze.

"I'll find her," Griffin said into his walkie. "You get the evidence back to the station for processing."

Static crackled. "Yes, sir."

Griffin pointed at Connor. "Wait here. I'm going to go find the activities' director."

"Yvette," Archibald supplied.

"I'm going to go find Yvette," Griffin amended.

Connor half stood between the bench and table. "I can help. I know the maze."

"No." Griffin turned his back on them and strode toward the corn. "I need to make sure she's okay, and, if not, I want to keep you from becoming a suspect in another crime."

Tandy's stomach lurched. So Connor *was* a suspect.

Marissa pouted at Tandy. "They found a shovel with blood on it in the maze. Griffin thinks the blood belongs to Hubert, and right now Connor is the only suspect."

Tandy held a hand over her heart. A death in the cornfield was bad but blaming Connor for it made it so much worse. "That's preposterous."

Connor sank back down on his bench. "The evidence will prove me innocent."

Tandy's boyfriend could help too, like he'd defended her when she was arrested for murder. "I'll finish getting the residents rounded up then call Greg for you."

"Thanks." Connor waved at a farm hand as he drove the tractor past the corn to set up for rides to the pumpkin patch. "Hey, Vince! Will you go help Sheriff Griffin find his way through the corn maze?"

The bearded man in jeans and a flannel shirt shot a thumbs up before continuing past. "Sure, boss."

Tandy hooked Archibald's elbow. "Come on, sir. I'll take you back to the bus."

Archibald shook free of her grip. "I fought in Vietnam and led my men to capture two platoons. I hiked for forty-eight hours straight through a foreign land in freezing temperatures with enemy fire. I don't need your help."

"My bad." Tandy raised her hands and stepped away. "I apologize."

"For cryin' in a bucket." Archibald grunted.

He may have been capable of getting back on the bus, but a tiny woman with white hair hobbled after Griffin toward the corn maze like she was E.T. and he was Elliot. If she entered the maze before Tandy could stop her, Yvette wouldn't be the only one lost. Tandy pointed. "I'll go get her."

Archibald's stony expression softened. "Yes. Stop lollygaggin' and go get Birdie." He saluted and marched away.

After a deep breath, Tandy scrunched her nose at Connor and Marissa. "This is not what I'd planned for when agreeing to be maid of honor. I thought, worst case scenario, we'd be stopping one of Connor's nose bleeds with a tampon."

"Ew... I hope not. Though I should probably carry tampons with me just in case." Marissa pressed her cheeks with both hands. "Everything is going to be okay. Griffin will find Yvette, and forensics will find the blood on Connor's shovel doesn't match Hubert's."

And then a pumpkin in the pumpkin patch would magically turn into a coach and whisk Connor and Marissa off to their honeymoon in Costa Rica. Tandy pinched her lips together to keep from saying anything negative.

Connor gripped Marissa's hand in solidarity. "This was simply a tragic accident."

Tandy turned away to catch Birdie. She did believe Hubert's fall down the stairs to be an accident, but even when accidents happened, Griffin still wanted someone to blame.

She jogged to catch up with the old woman. "Birdie," she called.

The woman paused and looked around then returned to pumping her arms in slow motion with every step.

Tandy easily trotted around her and blocked the entrance to the maze. "Hey, Birdie. The farm is closed now. Time to go home."

"My lands," Birdie said in a shaky voice then changed directions to continue past Tandy. "I can't go home without Hubert. He's sweet on me, you know."

Tandy pivoted to keep her eyes on the old woman. From what she knew, Hubert was a punk and definitely not likely to have a crush on someone old enough to be his grandmother. "You know Hubert?"

"Oh, yes. Lovely boy. Lovely. He brings me my medication."

Tandy arched an eyebrow at the woman's back. So Hubert had worked for Grace Springs Manor after Connor fired him. That explained why he was at The Farmstead. Should she tell Birdie what happened to the man? She didn't want to, but how else was she going to get the woman back to the bus?

Tandy gritted her teeth. "Did you see the ambulance earlier, Birdie? Hubert had an accident in the maze, and they had to take him away."

Birdie stopped her trek. She looked over her shoulder, light blue eyes stormy. "It was no accident."

Tandy rocked back on her heels. Had Birdie seen Connor chase Hubert over the bridge? Was she coherent enough to testify against him? "Yes, it was. Connor didn't mean to—"

"Young lady." Birdie's tone lost its tremble.

Tandy stood at attention as if she were the guilty one about to get scolded. The older woman could have been a school principal in her day.

"I don't know who Connor is, but if anything happened to Hubert, Yvette is involved."

Chapter Three

T_ANDY'S LIPS PARTED BUT SHE COULDN'T form words. If Yvette was involved, that might be why she was missing. She could have been the one who hit Hubert with the shovel, and now she was on the run.

"Why do you think she's involved in Hubert's death?" Tandy asked Birdie cautiously.

"Yvette has a thing for Hubert. It's a crime of passion."

Oh, boy. Birdie's words made it sound like they were in a soap opera. The Old and the Restless. Tandy refused to let her lips quirk up in a smile. Because whether or not Birdie was delusional, Hubert really had died. "How about I help you back to the bus, then I can go tell the sheriff your suspicions."

The woman's wrinkles deepened with her smile. "Thank you, dear."

Tandy gripped the woman's elbow the way she had gripped Archibald's earlier, only Birdie didn't resist. She told stories about her grandchildren as Tandy escorted her across the parking lot and up the steps of the bus.

Archibald snorted. "About time."

Tandy bit her tongue to keep from responding.

The large woman in the wheelchair touched her elbow. Her spiky brunette pixie gave her a sassy edge. "Don't let him get to you. He's always a nincompoop."

That was one way to describe Archibald.

"I'm Winifred. What's your name?"

"Tandy."

"Nice to meet you, Tammy," Winifred greeted her. "I'll keep the troops entertained so they don't bother you anymore."

Tandy didn't have a chance to correct the woman on her name before Winifred launched into a song about washing that man right out of her hair. Tandy paused at the door, impressed by the clear pitch and strong tone. It was kind of like she'd walked into a musical with all these crazy characters, but maybe getting old meant these people didn't have to try to be normal anymore. They could sing, scowl, get names wrong, and imagine themselves in musicals all they wanted.

It was the possibility that Birdie hadn't been imagining things about Yvette that had Tandy hopping to the ground and heading toward the cornfield to find Griffin. Though she didn't have to look far.

The sheriff charged around the edge of the field like he'd been scared by the employees who were paid to dress up like zombies and roam the cornstalks at night. Only it wasn't zombies that chased him but a large green tractor with an old man smiling behind the wheel.

Following them both was a short, curvy redhead wearing glasses and layers of clothing. Her laughter rang out even louder than the rumble of the tractor. "Pete!" she yelled. She continued laughing as she ran. "Pete, that's not your tractor."

Tandy couldn't help cracking a smile at the woman's infectious laughter. The lady had to be Yvette. She wasn't hiding from the law. She was chasing down a rogue resident. Had the activities' director just offed one of her employees with a shovel, it wasn't likely she'd be this jolly. Unless, of course, she was excited about the prospect of the resident running over the sheriff who was investigating.

"Pete." Connor stood, took a few long strides, and leaped onto the steps that led to the cab of the John Deere. He climbed inside and cut the engine.

Griffin bent over, panting, hands on his knees.

The redhead bounced their way, giggling infectiously.

Griffin stood tall and glared. "This isn't funny."

The woman wiped a hand across her smile. "I'm sorry. I'm so sorry," she said, though she continued to peel with glee between each apology. "I giggle when I'm nervous." She turned toward the cab where Connor ushered the lanky, gray-haired driver out of the cab first. "I'm so glad you were able to stop the tractor, Connor."

So Connor knew Yvette?

Connor shrugged. "You know this isn't the first time I've had to chase Pete down."

Tradition? The property for The Farmstead *was* located right next to Grace Springs Manor.

"I know." Yvette's tone sobered. She placed a hand on Pete's back and guided him toward the parking lot.

Pete walked like a scarecrow, all knees and elbows. A big grin remained on his face as if he'd just gotten off a rollercoaster, not a tractor.

"I planned to watch him. Except I was sidetracked with Hubert's accident." She giggled again, though Tandy could now pinpoint the nervousness in the sound. It wasn't like she was happy about Hubert's death.

Yvette didn't act like a criminal. With her soft middle and joyous demeanor, she could easily be a favorite patron of Tandy's coffee shop. She definitely didn't look like she would have committed a crime of passion the way Birdie suggested. Though Tandy knew appearances could be deceiving.

"You've had an intense day," Tandy sympathized. "Let me help you get your residents back to Grace Springs Manor while the sheriff finishes up here."

"Oh, would you?" Yvette's shoulders sagged in relief. "Hubert drove us here, and I'm licensed to drive the bus back, but I could really use someone to sit with the residents. Especially since I don't know how they are going to react to the news of his passing."

"Hubert died?" Pete's grin faded. "Boy howdy. Let's not say anything to Birdie. She liked Hubert and is probably going to be sad he's gone."

So Birdie was the one with the crush on Hubert, not Yvette. Tandy bit her lip. She'd wanted to go to the retirement center to do some snooping, but now she felt compassion for her only suspect and wanted to help the woman out.

Marissa watched Tandy go. She'd thought her friend was going to stick by her side as maid of honor, but at least she'd offered to call Greg. And they'd see each other again that night at their shop, Caffeine Conundrum.

The new manager of their coffee shop and tea house, Zam, used to own a bar before he came to work for the women, and he'd asked if he could continue his old Halloween tradition of "Skary-oke" at their location. Basically, it was karaoke in costume, though she wasn't sure which was supposed to be scarier, the costumes or the singing. Zam would probably enjoy the event more than she would since he was deaf and wouldn't have to suffer through the terrible vocals. At least it would help keep Marissa's relatives entertained during their stay in Grace Springs.

"Connor," Griffin barked. "I told you not to move from the picnic bench."

Seriously? Marissa pinched her eyes shut and wished the whole nightmare to go away. Unfortunately, when she opened her eyes, she only found Connor standing his ground.

"I just saved you from getting run over by an old man on a tractor. I think a 'thank you' is in order."

Griffin hooked his thumbs in his belt loops. The tractor incident seemed only to have made the cop angrier. "How is it that he has access to your tractor? What kind of operation are you running here?"

Connor threw his arms in the air. "I sent Vince to help you in the maze, which is the only reason the keys were left in it."

"I told you I didn't want your help."

"Griffin," Marissa interrupted, saying the sheriff's last name in the same tone she used to call him Little Lukey when she babysat. "Operations are not running as normal because a man died here today. The activities' director got distracted as did the tractor driver. Let's not lose sight of our focus."

Connor's shoulders relaxed. He turned his back on Griffin to stroll toward the picnic table and put his arm around her. "I'm sorry, hon. I can't believe this is happening. I feel sick inside." He turned his head to sneeze away from her.

"And sick on the outside." She rubbed his arm.

Why had she thought a fall wedding was a good idea? She'd known he had allergies.

He hugged her and rested his chin on her head. "This is a big week. I need to be here for you."

Griffin huffed. "Connor, I've known you too long to believe you're a killer. Yeah, you made a threat you shouldn't have. Yeah, some people thought they saw you shove Hubert off the bridge. Yeah, you dripped blood all over him. But unless we get back evidence that his blood is on the shovel as well as your fingerprints, I'm going to trust that he accidentally fell."

Connor squeezed Marissa even tighter, his sigh warm on her scalp. "Thank you."

Griffin waved him off. "It pays to be a good citizen. I don't always like you, but I always respect you."

Connor chuckled. "I'll take it."

It had been a crazy day, but now Marissa could return to planning her wedding and worrying about her insane relatives.

Griffin nodded in approval. "I guess I'll be on my way then. Though you'll need to keep the Zombie Corn Maze closed tonight in case we have to come back and look at anything."

"Agreed," Connor held out a hand to shake. "I'll go call all my employees right now."

"Great." Griffin lifted his hand to shake, but his phone rang the tune to *Bad Boys*. He swiped his thumb across the screen and held the device to his ear instead. "This is Sheriff Griffin."

Marissa looked out across the cornfield. She'd had her first kiss with Connor in that field two years ago. That's why she'd wanted to get married here. Good memories. Though at that time, she never would have imagined Connor could possibly be accused of murder in the very same place. She still couldn't imagine it. Thankfully, neither could anyone else.

"You're sure?" Griffin said to whoever had called him.

She was sure. Sure she'd picked an amazing man to spend the rest of her life with. She snuggled deeper into his warm chest and counted down the days until they said, "I do." Only five left.

"Thanks for letting me know," Griffin said.

When you know, you know. And though she'd had doubts about Connor before, they'd worked through them. Well, she'd worked through her stuff. He'd patiently waited for her.

"All right. I'll arrest him now."

Connor had arrested her heart. In fact, she could hear her heart thumping. No, that was Connor's heart. With her ear against his chest, she listened to its tempo surge.

Wait. What had Griffin said again?

The sheriff hung up and pulled out his handcuffs. "Connor." His tone sank with dread.

Connor's chest rose and fell against her. "It was Hubert's blood?"

No. It couldn't be.

"Yes. I wasn't expecting results back so soon, but I'm guessing the analyst is friends with your family and hoping to prove you innocent." Sheriff motioned for him to turn around and read him his rights.

Connor let her go, and Griffin cuffed him.

"He didn't do it." Marissa fought back tears. It wasn't about her wedding anymore. It was about Connor's life. "Griffin," she pleaded. "We weren't the only ones here when Hubert was allegedly hit with a shovel."

"You're right. There are buses from the elementary school and retirement center here, as well. I've already questioned those folks, and they all appear innocent." Griffin led Connor toward the cop car. "But if you find out a kindergartner or geriatric guest hit Hubert in the head, let me know, and I'll put them behind bars instead."

Chapter Four

"EVERYBODY IN THE WHOLE CELL BLOCK was dancing to the jailhouse rock," Winifred sang as the bus rolled down the road.

The rest of the passengers joined into the Elvis song. Except for Archibald who took turns glaring at each of them like he suspected they should all go to jail.

Obviously, the residents weren't missing Hubert too much. Not even Birdie, whom Pete had been worried about. She'd forgotten some of the lyrics, but she clapped along to the beat. As for Winifred, she twisted like Chubby Checker while belting out the second verse.

Speaking of jailhouses, this would be a good time to call Greg and see if he could help Connor. Greg picked up on the second ring. It was hard to hear him answer over the '50s tune. The seniors sounded surprisingly good.

"Tandy?" Greg questioned in confusion.

"Yeah. I'm on a bus with a bunch of residents from Grace Springs Manor."

Pause. "Why?"

"I'll explain later." She didn't want to give all the grisly details in front of the old folks. "I'm calling because one of their employees died at The Farmstead today, and Connor might be getting arrested. If he is, can you get him out of jail in time for his wedding?"

"Is this a trick? Because I'd much rather have the treat."

"No, it's real."

Greg sighed. "You're dating me for the free legal advice, huh?"

"Yes, though you're pretty cute too." The bus pulled up to the huge brick establishment with white shutters and a steep roof. "I've got to run. Call Marissa for more details."

"You're okay?" he asked before hanging up.

"I'm fine." She smiled before hanging up. He was sweet, and she'd been worse.

"Tandy?" Yvette looked back from the driver's seat. "Will you help everyone else out while I unhook Winifred's wheelchair?"

"Sure." That's why she'd come.

Tandy exited first and stood in the parking lot, holding residents' hands to help steady them as they descended the steps. When it was Birdie's turn, she appeared holding a small carton of donuts. Tandy didn't remember her having those when she'd walked the woman to the bus, though she had sniffed their cinnamon scent on the ride over.

She motioned Birdie forward. "Come on."

Birdie clutched her carton tighter and didn't move.

"Uh..." Tandy spoke louder so Yvette could hear her. "She's not taking my hands because she's holding donuts."

Yvette's laughter practically rocked the bus. "Birdie, where did you get those donuts?"

"I'll take them," Archibald offered from behind the little old lady.

Birdie turned away from the man. Tandy didn't blame her.

"For cryin' out loud, woman." Archibald gave a little growl then scowled at Tandy like it was her fault Birdie wouldn't give him the donuts. He reached for the box. "Just because you used to be a spy, doesn't mean you have to be suspicious of everyone."

Tandy blinked. A for-real spy? Like she stole government secrets from Russia in the cold war? If so, was that supposed to explain the donut situation? It seemed like it would also explain Birdie's statement concerning Yvette. What secrets did she know about Grace Springs Manor?

Yvette laughed again from her spot behind the wheelchair. "Birdie's experience certainly made her good at sneaking cookies and probably those donuts. She's got quite the sweet tooth."

Tandy's lips quirked. "The donut shop at The Farmstead locked up when the sheriff arrived. Not sure when Birdie would have gotten these."

Archibald grunted. "She can pick locks."

Tandy's eyebrows skyrocketed. An elderly resident who could pick locks sounded dangerous. Even if she were just picking locks to get donuts, she still could have burned herself on hot oil or something.

"Hobble-dee-gobble-dee." Winifred motioned from her wheelchair. "Let Archie hold your donuts, sugar. He won't eat them."

Birdie eyed Archibald. "Where's Hubert? I want Hubert to hold my donuts."

Tandy had told Birdie that Hubert had an accident. Did the woman not realize Tandy meant he'd died?

Archibald's anger melted ever so subtly. Like coconut milk in the steamer. He ignored Birdie's question but gave the woman his full attention. "I'll hold the donuts and give them back once you reach the ground."

"Okay." Birdie's voice wobbled, but she passed over the donuts and reached for Tandy's hand.

Tandy gripped the woman's fragile bones and skin worn as smooth as suede. The touch made her miss her own grandmother who had died a few years back. Grandma had been her closest relative since Mom and Dad split up in elementary school. Now she just had Marissa.

Birdie found her footing on the asphalt and turned for her donuts. Tandy reached a hand up to help steady Archibald, but he knocked it away and climbed down without even holding the handrail.

"Fantastic." Yvette adjusted the wheelchair lift for their last passenger. "I'll be down in a minute to take Birdie to the memory care wing."

Memory care. So the cute little old spy was suffering dementia. That made sense, but it also made her accusation of Yvette less relevant. Tandy would talk to the activities' director anyway.

Winifred waved and smiled like she was walking down a red carpet when the wheelchair lift lowered her to the ground. She clasped Tandy's hand even though she didn't need to in the same way the other passengers had. "Thank you for your help today, Tammy."

Tandy could correct the woman on her name, but it wasn't like they'd be seeing each other again. Instead, she marveled at Winifred's firm grip. Though she looked soft, she wasn't weak. "And thank you. Your singing made for a wonderful distraction."

"I love music. Music moves my soul." The woman practically sang the words.

Tandy smiled. That's how she felt about coffee. "I wish you could come to our Skary-oke night at my coffee shop tonight. Then you could sing on a stage."

"I would love to sing karaoke." Winifred looked over her shoulder at Yvette. "Can you take us tonight?"

Yvette laughed like the request was a hilarious joke, though she always seemed to laugh like that. "I wish, but I'm not sure Mr. Cross would want me driving you all by myself. We'll put it on the calendar for next year."

Winifred sighed. "I guess I can't complain, since you did talk Mr. Cross into letting you take us to Costa Rica for a vacation next month."

"One of my best ideas yet." Yvette giggled. "I've heard it's like heaven on earth, and I'm thrilled I get to go too."

Tandy arched an eyebrow. "Yeah, that beats a trip to the coffee shop." She'd known the retirement home was more of a resort, but she didn't realize the residents got to take lavish vacations. Based on what Connor and Marissa were paying to go there for their honeymoon, it was lavish. Though she would pay that price just to drink fresh Costa Rican coffee. "You could tour a coffee plantation while you're there."

Yvette grinned. "Oh, I'll need lots of coffee to keep up with these folks."

Another employee arrived to push Winifred's wheelchair away. She blew kisses as she disappeared inside.

"Tomfoolery." Archibald snorted but continued the parade.

"Quite the characters," Tandy commented.

Yvette laughed her infectious laugh. "They keep me entertained."

Tandy fell into step as the woman walked Birdie through sliding glass doors into the grand entryway of the ritzy retirement home with its soaring ceiling, marble tile, and Grecian columns. Not a bad place to work. "Is that how Hubert felt about them too?"

Birdie piped up. "Hubert is sweet on me."

Tandy simply nodded. Now that she knew Birdie had dementia, she wasn't sure how to respond. Or what to believe.

Yvette patted Birdie's hand and led her down a side hall like the place was a hotel, except this hallway had a door that required a keycode. Inside the door was a picture of Pete and a warning not to let the man out by himself.

"Hubert isn't the only one sweet on you," Yvette said to Birdie. "I think Archibald is sweet on you too."

Tandy had suspected as much. Though she would consider the cranky old man to be more bittersweet than sweet. Like her new espresso blend.

"Archibald is old," Birdie argued.

Tandy pressed her lips together to smother a smile. How young did Birdie think she was?

Yvette cackled. "Lady, you've got so much spunk, you make *me* feel old."

She stopped in front of a door and pulled out a keychain. Ironic that the employee needed to unlock Birdie's door for her when the woman could break into food trucks and steal donuts on her own.

"Is it dinner time?" Birdie asked.

Yvette pointed to the box in her hand. "It's donut time."

Birdie's faded blue eyes lit up like a jack-o-lantern. "Ohh…"

"Then you can take a little nap before dinner."

"Okay." Birdie wobbled to a tiny table and sat down.

"I'll send someone to come get you when it's time." Yvette closed the door, smiled at Tandy, and gave a big sigh. "I love her to pieces, and it's hard to watch her lose her memory like this. She thinks Hubert has a crush on her because he was always going into her room to steal prescription drugs."

Tandy's lips pursed in surprise. That was a piece of information she wasn't expecting. If he'd been stealing from Grace Springs Manor the way he'd stolen from The Farmstead, then how did he still have a job here? "He didn't get fired?"

Yvette clicked her tongue and headed back toward the main lobby. "I hadn't proven it yet. Mr. Cross, the owner, fired someone else a while back and wanted to make sure the missing pills were from a new thief. I'd caught Hubert again this morning, but he claimed he was giving Birdie her pills even though that wasn't his job."

Perhaps the dead man had more enemies than Connor. And Yvette could still be one, but not for the reasons Birdie suggested.

Though, if she'd killed him, then why would she have so freely shared this information? The explanation actually gave a reason for Birdie's off-base suspicions. "Birdie saw you two arguing this morning?"

"Yes. It upset her." Yvette sighed. "I guess one benefit of Alzheimer's is that she's forgotten about it already."

Except she hadn't. At least her mistaken accusation led to Tandy's latest discovery of the drugs. "I'm glad Birdie isn't taking it too hard."

How crazy that the one man the old woman trusted was the one who'd been taking advantage of her. Tandy had to talk to Sheriff Griffin right away. Hopefully, this information would help keep Connor from going to prison.

Marissa's phone flashed with the word "Mom" again. She knew she needed to answer and iron out their wedding plans for the week, but she'd prefer to do it when her groom wasn't in jail. She paced the old brick police station, waiting for Griffin to return from taking Connor's mugshots and fingerprints.

Kristen, the receptionist who'd always had a crush on Connor, watched from behind her desk. "Are you still going to marry him?"

"Yes," Marissa didn't even pause before answering. Just because her fiancé was behind bars, that didn't make him a criminal. "I'll have the judge do our ceremony during the bail hearing if I have to."

She pictured herself standing in her wedding dress next to Connor in an orange jumpsuit. And she'd thought black bridesmaids' dresses were bad. Would Tandy even be there to catch the bouquet, or would a court reporter have that honor?

Greg, Tandy's boyfriend, strode in the front door with all the authority of the superhero he resembled. No, he wasn't wearing red boots and a cape, but his shiny black hair and perceptive blue eyes made him look like Superman in disguise. Marissa had never been happier that her best friend had fallen for an attorney.

"Greg." She scrambled toward him and his leather briefcase. "Please tell me you can get Connor out. I don't want a justice of the peace to preside over my wedding ceremony."

Greg tilted his head, eyebrows drawn together. "I don't know what's going on yet, but I'll talk to Connor and see what needs to be done." He nodded at Kristin. "Please let Griffin know I'm here to meet with my client."

Kristin jumped up and headed down a hallway.

Greg set his briefcase on a chair and crossed his arms. "Griffin knows Connor's character, so there's got to be some pretty airtight proof against him for him to have been arrested."

"Hardly." Marissa waved her arms as if to demonstrate the way the sheriff had pulled evidence out of thin air. "Only some witnesses who heard him make a threat."

Greg's eyebrows arched. "I've never heard Connor make a threat before."

"Well," Marissa wrinkled her nose. "He's been taking allergy pills because he gets nose bleeds this time of year."

The corners of Greg's lips turned up. "Is he allergic to losing in fantasy football?"

"What? No." Marissa huffed. *Men.* "He's allergic to ragweed, and his medication makes him moody. It's also how he got his blood on the body."

Greg lifted his chin. "So Connor threatened the deceased and then got his blood on the body? If that's all—"

Marissa winced.

Greg huffed. "What else?"

"There was a shovel."

Greg ran both hands through his hair. "Please tell me the shovel doesn't have the victim's DNA and Connor's prints on it."

"Uhh…"

Griffin strode down the hallway. "Yes, the shovel has Hubert's blood on it. I took Connor's fingerprints, so we'll be able to verify that part soon enough."

Heat rose to Marissa's face and she stomped her foot. "That doesn't even seem fair, Griffin. Of course it's going to have Connor's fingerprints on it. It's his shovel, like he told you."

Greg shook his head slowly. "Marissa, you might want to postpone your wedding."

"What?" She splayed her hands wide. Greg was supposed to do his superhero stuff. "My relatives arrive today. If they know my fiancé is in jail, they aren't going to come back for a rescheduled wedding." Not that she really wanted them there, but she didn't want to have to deal with their judgments either.

Greg grabbed his briefcase. "I'll do what I can, but unless there's something the police missed…"

The front door swung wide. Tandy blew in with a cool breeze.

Marissa shivered.

Tandy's dark eyes glistened, and she rubbed her hands together. Either she was cold too or she'd found a clue. "Hubert was stealing drugs from the retirement center."

A clue. Marissa turned expectantly to see how the news hit Griffin and Greg. Neither of their expressions changed. They just stared.

She turned back to Tandy. "What does that mean?"

Tandy held out her palms like she was handing over evidence on an invisible platter. "You suspect Connor because he had a motive of being angry at Hubert for stealing. Well, obviously Connor isn't the only person he stole from. So there should be other suspects."

Griffin narrowed his eyes. "Who did he steal drugs from?"

Tandy shrugged. "All I know of is a little old lady named Birdie."

"I'll question Birdie."

Marissa nodded. That sounded like a good idea. Another suspect.

"No, no, no." Wrinkles lined Tandy's forehead.

"No?" Marissa tried to follow.

"Birdie thinks Hubert had a crush on her. She has dementia."

"Hmm." Greg stroked his chin. "That would be a good defense for murder."

Marissa perked up once again. "Yeah."

Tandy rolled eyes. "You guys. I don't think Birdie did it. She's not strong enough to lift a shovel. I'm just saying Grace Springs Manor is worth looking into rather than assuming you already have the criminal in jail."

"Thanks, Tandy." Greg sounded professional as he headed toward the hallway, but Marissa caught him winking at his girlfriend. "I will keep that information in mind as I talk to my client."

Marissa would keep it in mind too. Because if someone really had hit Hubert with a shovel, it would be someone other than Connor. "Griffin?" she prompted to see how the sheriff would respond.

He looped his thumbs in his belt loops. "I'll continue to look into Hubert's background, but I can't let Connor out on such a flimsy argument. He'll be staying here tonight."

The sheriff might as well have hit *her* with a shovel. Her vision went into a pinwheel of darkness, and she took little sips of air. Tandy's grip held her steady until a folding chair scraped close enough to catch her when she sank down.

"I can't… I can't…"

"You're okay," Tandy cooed. "You can breathe."

She knew she could breathe. Even if her lungs had to pant for breath. "I can't let my relatives know."

Would Connor's arrest be in the newspaper? Or online? She'd never live it down. It could tarnish her parents' good name, as well. And she'd just started repairing the relationship with her mom.

Griffin's gaze lost its sharp edge. "We don't have to release the name of our suspect yet."

Marissa nodded her thanks and forced her breathing to slow. Griffin was giving her time. "After I see Connor, I am going to keep preparing for the wedding like everything is normal. Because it's going to be."

Tandy lifted one dark eyebrow in a way that always made Marissa feel like her sanity was being questioned. "What do you mean by normal? You mean you're still going to Skary-oke tonight? You can't even breathe normally. One look at your face, and everyone will know…"

Marissa held her hands to her warm cheeks. Tandy was right. If only she had a costume that came with a mask. Or a full-face helmet. "Let me wear your costume."

Tandy's lips parted, speechless. Probably because if she let Marissa wear her biker costume, that would leave Tandy with Marissa's Marilyn Monroe costume. "No way."

Marissa grabbed both Tandy's hands. This was the only way she could make it through the event. And she had to make it through. So they could buy time for Connor.

They'd investigate tomorrow, and Greg would work his magic. Then Connor would be released, get his haircut, and say, "I do," in five days. Nobody would ever have to know how close he'd been to going to prison instead of having her be his ball and chain.

"Please, Tandy. You'd make a great Marilyn Monroe."

Tandy's eyes bulged in disbelief. "I hate dresses. I hate heels. And besides, you didn't get a wig, did you? I don't have your blonde hair."

"I do," Kristin's voice cut in.

Marissa turned to stare. Kristin wanted to be Marilyn?

Kristin shrugged. "I was going to wear Griffin's old police uniform. You could wear that."

Chapter Five

TANDY ROLLED UP THE BROWN SLEEVES of Griffin's old uniform and adjusted the flat-brimmed hat with a dent on either side of the badge. He must have put on weight since his deputy days because the old uniform fit her comfortably. While this wouldn't have been Tandy's first choice of costume, it sure beat trying to keep Marilyn Monroe's white skirt from flying up.

Her fluffy, brown Pomeranian yapped when she stepped out of her bedroom. She scooped him into her arms.

"It's just me, Cocoa." His warm, wet tongue licked her cheek before she could stop him. "I think it looks ridiculous too, but I'm glad you still like me."

Her cell phone vibrated on the laminate kitchen counter. Marissa's name flashed on the screen. Once Marissa and Connor returned from their honeymoon, Tandy would have to hire him to build her a house with a huge kitchen where she could experiment with new coffee drinks. That was *if* they could keep him out of prison. Maybe his bride was calling with good news.

Tandy swiped the screen to answer. "Hey, Marissa."

"Where are you?" Marissa huffed breathlessly.

Tandy snapped up straight. Cocoa growled. "Why? Are you okay? Did the killer strike again? Did he capture you, and you're being held prisoner?"

"Worse."

Tandy released her pup and grabbed her keys. She'd chase down murderers to save her friend. "What happened?"

"My cousins arrived early, and we're out of gingersnap crumbs to top our gingerbread lattes."

Tandy blew out her breath and rolled her eyes. "I suppose you don't have time to bake more."

"Are you kidding?" Marissa screeched. "Zam's Skary-oke idea seems to have brought in the whole town. Oh my goodness. There's even a bus outside from Grace Springs Manor. They're lowering a woman in a wheelchair to the ground."

Tandy smiled. Winifred was going to get to sing for her audience after all. "Does she have spiky brown hair?"

"No. It's red and chin length."

"Huh." Maybe Winifred had a gang of friends in wheelchairs. She could sing *Leader of the Pack*. "Okay, I'll stop at Grace Springs Pharmacy and pick up some of those gingersnaps we snacked on when in line for your painkillers last summer."

"Yes." Something clattered on the other end of the line. Hopefully, Marissa hadn't broken her ankle again. "Hurry. It's crazy here. The only good thing I have going for me is that your helmet hides my face. Unfortunately, it makes it harder for me to see, and I keep tripping over things."

Tandy shook her head. She should have known that was coming. "I'll be right there."

She hung up and bent over to let Cocoa lick her goodbye. "I'd bring you, buddy, but there are going to be a lot of people in masks, which I know you hate. And I wouldn't want you to get your tail run over by the wheelchair gang." They'd faced enough danger for one day.

Grabbing a pair of aviator sunglasses to complete her look, Tandy headed out the door into dusk. A huge orange moon hung low in the sky, reminding her why she liked this time of year so much. That and pumpkin spice lattes. The new gingerbread lattes with its sweet molasses and spicy kick ran a close second.

Grace Springs Pharmacy was only a couple blocks down Main Street from their shop. With all the cars parked along the curb, Tandy couldn't have gotten any closer anyway. She pulled her black Beetle in front of the pharmacy's green awning and strode inside the old building with its checkerboard flooring. Rows of practical personal care items stood behind rotating stands displaying keychains and postcards for tourists.

"Hey," she greeted the clerk by the door.

The middle-aged woman just stared at her with big, round eyes.

"Cookies on aisle three?"

The woman motioned toward one of the aisles with her head. Okay then.

Tandy had met the woman before but couldn't remember her name. Maybe the checker was having the same problem with remembering Tandy's name, which is why she didn't respond. Tandy was an unusual name. Hence Winifred calling her Tammy.

Tandy passed a display shelf for sunglasses and caught her reflection in a tiny mirror at the top. Oh, yeah. She was in costume. The woman at the counter probably didn't even recognize her and was wondering why their town had another new deputy.

Tandy smiled to herself. Maybe she'd enjoy the costume more than she'd expected.

She made her way down aisle three. Her stomach growled. With all that had happened at the farm, she'd skipped dinner. She grabbed the crinkly bag of cookies and continued farther down to get herself a meal replacement bar. She'd need fuel to help sustain her energy for the evening.

A blue neon light at the back of the building advertised the pharmacy. Someone dressed in black stood at the window. Tandy would have expected the pharmacy to be closed by now. The pharmacist was probably helping a final customer past closing time the way small towns were known to do. Congeniality was still something she was getting used to, having come from Cincinnati.

She nodded then turned to read the label on the box of protein bars. She didn't want something too sweet. She preferred to drink her dessert in the form of mochas.

The sound of pills clattered to the floor, reminding Tandy of when she'd helped Marissa pick up her prescription. She glanced over her shoulder to see if anybody else needed help.

The customer in black looked her way. He must have been headed to Scary-oke, because he also wore a Halloween costume. His looked like a white hockey mask.

She did a double take to find him shoving bottles of pills in his jacket pocket with one hand. His other hand held something that would have better gone with *her* costume.

Sure enough, he had a gun. And it was trained on her.

What was taking Tandy so long? Marissa checked her sparkly diamond watch again as she climbed the stairs to tell her cousins their lattes would take a little longer. The timepiece didn't really match her leather leggings, riding gloves, and full-face motorcycle helmet, but without it, all her customers might have assumed she was Tandy.

Of course, the way she'd tripped up the last stair to the tearoom in the loft of their shop would have given away her identity, as well. She blamed her misstep on the fact that Zam had dimmed their chandelier and brought in blacklights for the evening's event. It made for a fun ambiance, especially with the old lady in the wheelchair singing *Monster Mash* under a spotlight, but it wasn't conducive to serving tea.

Ashlee and Amber watched in amusement. The sisters were Marissa's least favorite cousins, and the fact they were twins made them twice the trouble.

"Where have I seen that move before?" Ashlee referred to Marissa's trip. She flipped her long golden waves over a shoulder. Her hair was what Marissa always wished for. While Marissa also had wavy blonde hair, Ashlee's was longer, lighter, and shinier. "Oh, yeah. When you fell off the stage of the Miss Ohio pageant."

Marissa's cheeks burned inside her mask. The glass hiding her face fogged up.

Amber picked at a manicured fingernail that seemed to glow pink in the dark. Marissa now kept her nails trimmed to better serve tea, but Amber's nails were longer and pinker than Marissa's had ever been. "I would have died of embarrassment if I'd fallen off the stage. You're so brave to show your face again after that. Oh, wait. You're not."

Marissa ground her teeth. Of all the times for her to trip on a stair and not have a hot drink in her hand to dump all over her customers. If Tandy were here, she'd tell them off. Marissa, however, had been raised better.

"I'm in costume for the event," she defended, never mind the fact that she was purposely hiding her face.

"Yeah?" Ashlee looked her up and down. "Nice pleather, babe."

Marissa balled her fists like a real biker. "I guess you don't have to wear costumes when you're already witches." Oops. She wanted to be better than that. Better than she used to be.

Amber cackled, obviously unaware she was proving Marissa's point.

Ashlee clicked her tongue. "Does your fiancé know you talk to family like this? Where is he anyway?"

Seeing Connor in jail had been surreal. A nightmare. A punch to the gut that could very easily become a total knock out. And she was supposed to be the one helping him to stand back up and keep fighting.

At least her helmet hid the pain on her face. If the twins were still making fun of her for falling off the stage at the Miss Ohio pageant years ago, then they'd put on a whole standup comedy routine should they find out her groom had been arrested for murder.

"He got detained by some things that happened at the farm today." It was the truth at least. But she needed to ask a question in return if she was to avoid answering any more of theirs. "Where's your brother? Didn't you order a drink for him too?"

Austin wasn't quite as bad as his sisters. At least, he never said cruel things. But she could tell he was thinking them by the way he looked at her from underneath his thick eyebrows. Of course, Marissa probably deserved every one of those thoughts since she'd been mean to him when they were kids. She'd always felt bad at the time, but she'd wanted to fit in with his sisters.

"He's coming." Ashlee flipped her hair again and surveyed what she could see of their shop in the dark. Apparently, she'd already grown bored with judging Marissa and needed something else to rip apart. "Austin has been having stomach issues and had to run down the street for some Tums. Maybe because we made him wear a clown costume."

Amber chuckled. "I don't care about Austin. I just want to know more about your barista. What's his name?"

"Zam." Marissa gave her sweetest smile before remembering nobody could see it. She let her face relax.

Though she wasn't going to tell them about Zam's past or his disability. He was actually a pretty tough looking dude with tattoos and a receding hairline, but that was all hidden in his Lone Ranger costume, making him look attractive to her cousins. She'd stay out of that as best she could. "I should have your drinks ready before Austin gets back."

She grabbed the stair rail to keep herself steady on her way down to the coffee part of the shop. Zam filled Italian sodas with plastic ice cubes lit with neon-colored LED lights, and he juggled syrups as he poured drinks. He was good at keeping the guests entertained, but she needed someone to distract her from her problems. At the moment, she was ready to stress eat a whole tin of caramel corn. If Tandy didn't arrive soon, Marissa would kill her.

Too bad Tandy's costume hadn't come with a weapon. Not that she wanted to shoot anyone, she just wanted a way to defend herself. As it was, all she could do was dive behind a huge bin of teddy bears wearing Halloween costumes.

A gunshot shattered the stillness. The metal bin in front of her jerked, and stuffing fluffed into the air. Footsteps pounded, a back door squeaked open, and a chilly breeze swept some of the teddy bear stuffing onto the floor.

Once the door banged shut, Tandy checked her numb body for blood. No liquids wet her hands or dripped on the floor.

Was she safe now? Her thumping heart needed to know.

As her pulse eased back into its normal pace, the buzzing of overhead lights grew louder. Strange she'd never noticed that sound before. Were the employees quiet with stunned silence, or had they been wounded?

She jumped to her feet and checked the pharmacist first. The young man's pasty face stared at her through the window as if he'd frozen in place.

"He wanted hydrocodone and oxycodone."

Opioids. The pharmacist must have handed them over with all the pill bottles she'd seen the gunman juggle. At least the employee hadn't been shot.

"I'm not in trouble, am I? Please don't arrest me."

Arrest him?

The clerk at the front counter ran down the aisle. "I was trying to point out the robbery when you entered."

The woman's weird nod now made sense. Too bad Tandy wasn't better at Charades. She was still trying to learn sign language to communicate with Zam.

"Why aren't you chasing him down? Why didn't you shoot back?"

Oh, the costume. They thought she was the police. The thief must have thought so too. Being a cop was a dangerous job.

Tandy pulled off her glasses in hopes they'd recognize her as the coffee shop owner. "I'm wearing a costume. But I'll call Sheriff Griffin." It couldn't be a coincidence she'd learned about drugs being stolen twice that day.

Chapter Six

TANDY PAID FOR HER COOKIES WHILE they waited for Griffin to arrive. So bizarre to make such a normal transaction after she'd been shot at, but she knew that if she didn't get the gingersnaps back to Marissa soon, she'd still get killed. Only her business partner would be the one to end her life.

She didn't buy the protein bar because she'd lost her appetite. But she did buy latex gloves so she could poke around without contaminating evidence.

She pulled them on and strode to the back of the store where the perp had made his hasty escape into the alley. She slowly pressed the crash bar to peek out.

"What are you doing?" The pharmacist's tone lowered with condescension.

Tandy peered through the crack into semi-darkness. A lamppost from the street shone off a blue dumpster and white truck. "I want to see if he dropped anything."

"You're not a real cop."

She listened for footsteps or movement, though the perp was probably long gone. "You think just anyone can borrow the sheriff's old uniform for Halloween? I've helped him solve a few murders in the past year."

"Murders?" The guy yelled then repeated in a whisper, "Murders?"

"Yeah," she whispered back, straining to hear a clomping sound grow louder.

An electronic bell chimed at the front of the store. The clerk screamed. Heavy footsteps headed Tandy's way. Had the robber returned?

She dove for cover behind the bin of stuffed animals once again. The motion brought her nose to toes with her very own biker boots. Straining her neck to look up, Tandy found her partner wearing her helmet.

"You would not believe what I've been going through at our shop." Marissa popped the face shield up, brown eyes wide in bewilderment and desperation. She really could have made a good Marilyn Monroe. "What's going on here?"

"There was a guy in a mask."

Marissa tugged the cookies out of Tandy's hands and ripped the package open. "You mean my cousin? He's at our shop now, and I was supposed to have his drink all ready and waiting for him. But I don't."

Marissa's cousin? Could the crime be that easy to solve?

"Do you know why I don't have his drink ready?" Marissa pulled a cookie from the bag and bit into it. "Because you've been rolling around on the floor of the pharmacy with the cookies I needed. What were you doing? Trying to crush them? I can do that with a rolling pin."

Tandy jumped to her feet and brushed off the ugly brown pants. "Is your cousin wearing a hockey mask?"

"No." A wrinkle appeared between Marissa's eyebrows. "He wasn't playing hockey. He was coming to Scary-oke. He's in a clown mask."

Tandy sighed.

"Oh yeah," the clerk called to them. "I sold a guy in a clown mask some antacids before either of you arrived. It didn't scare me as much as the biker costume."

The biker costume wasn't scary, the clerk was just jumpy. Which explained her scream.

As for Marissa's cousin, he could have worn the clown mask to case the pharmacy then changed masks and returned to steal drugs. "Was the clown wearing all black?" she asked the clerk.

Marissa shoved the rest of the cookie in her mouth and answered with the food stuffed in her cheek. "Clowns don't wear black. You're thinking of mimes."

Tandy opened her mouth to explain but wasn't sure where to start or if Marissa could even handle more stress at the moment. She didn't normally eat like a hamster.

Marissa licked the rich, spiced cookie from her teeth. Now that she had what she'd come for, she should get back to her shop, but she wanted Tandy by her side like a bodyguard. Her friend's cop costume could come in handy. The way her cousins treated her should be illegal.

"You ready?" she asked. She held up her bag. "Did you already pay for these? If not, we should get two bags. I might finish this one before we walk back."

"I paid for them, but I need to do something before we go." Tandy pursed her lips. "Come this way." She headed toward a back door and switched her phone to flashlight mode for some reason.

Marissa followed with the cookies since they'd already been purchased. She'd have to slow down so she didn't eat them all, but one more wouldn't hurt. Except for the way the helmet pushed against the side of her face and made her bite her cheek when she chewed. She swallowed. "This helmet is giving me a headache. Is my head really that much bigger than yours?"

"You just have a lot of hair." Tandy led the way with her beam of light on the black asphalt in the smelly alley. Why did she want to go this way?

Marissa stepped past her and paused in awe of the bright orange moon hung above the buildings and perfectly framed by the brick alley walls. Gorgeous. She waited for Tandy to catch up. She should be hurrying her along, but maybe if they took their time, Ashlee and Amber would leave. "I don't have as much hair as my cousins."

"The clown?"

The clown? Oh yeah. Austin. She still hadn't filled Tandy in on her horrible night. "No. The clown has twin sisters. I wasn't very nice to them at the shop, but they were meaner."

"Do any of them have drug addictions?" Tandy asked, her voice more muffled than before.

"Probably." Marissa had heard that addictions made people treat others poorly in their effort to feed their cravings. That could explain why the twins didn't seem to care about her feelings. Though they'd been like that as kids too. "We were friends when we were little, but something changed when we graduated high school. I'd like to think I grew up."

Marissa waited for confirmation. Tandy always knew how to make her feel better. Well, she usually knew how to make her feel better. At this moment, she was remaining unnervingly quiet.

It probably wouldn't help Marissa's case to whine like a teenager.

She looked over her shoulder to find Tandy crouched low enough to peer underneath the stinky dumpster. "What are you looking for?"

"Pills."

Marissa's eyes bulged. What was with Tandy's new obsession. Maybe Marissa should share the cookies. "Is there something you haven't told me?"

Tandy stood, holding a hand to her head to keep the sheriff's hat on. "Yeah, I'm a druggie."

Marissa stepped back. "What?" Was she in the twilight zone? Tandy had as much a chance of being a druggie as Connor did of being a murderer.

Tandy rolled her eyes. "Why would I need pills? I survive on coffee and sarcasm."

Marissa exhaled. "Well, you *are* acting strange."

"What you don't know is that right before you came in, someone robbed the pharmacy and shot at me because they thought I was a cop."

Marissa jolted, dropping her bag of cookies in a puddle. While she'd been stress eating over a squabble with her cousins, Tandy had been dodging bullets. "Someone shot at you?"

Tandy held a finger to her lips and looked over Marissa's shoulder like she suspected the shooter might come back.

Marissa hadn't meant to yell. She lowered her voice and looked around. "We need to call Griffin."

"I already have."

Marissa was just about to sigh in relief when movement caught her eye. Two silhouettes headed her direction, backlit by moonlight. Her heart sputtered, but then she remembered how intimidating she and Tandy looked. She spun toward them, lifting fists. "You don't want to mess with us. I'm a biker, and my friend is a cop."

"No, you're not," said a grouchy old man in a hunting hat. He looked familiar. "You're in costume like everyone else at Caffeine Conundrum, though it sounds like you're in more of a conundrum over here. Someone shot at you? Let me see the bullet hole. You can tell a lot about a man by the casings he leaves behind."

That's right. The military vet from the corn maze. He just kept showing up when she was in trouble. "What are you doing here?" she demanded.

He motioned to the little old lady next to him. "Yvette brought us to Skary-oke, but it was too loud for Birdie, so I was taking her on a walk when I heard you yell that someone shot at you. I thought you'd need my help."

Birdie nodded, stretching her wrinkly neck skin every time she lifted her chin. These were definitely not people to be afraid of.

Tandy joined them. "The sheriff is on his way over. He'll look at the bullet hole."

Birdie lifted a shaky finger. "But did he see the perp running away? I can I.D. him."

"Oh…" Marissa clapped. "A witness."

Tandy slid her gaze sideways to frown at Marissa out of the corner of her eye as if to remind her of their conversation about Birdie at the police station earlier.

Oh… A witness with dementia.

The door to the pharmacy slammed open. Sheriff Griffin stood with one hand on his holster. "What are you doing out here?" he barked. "Were you all in the store during the robbery?"

Tandy lifted a hand. "Just me. I was looking to see if the robber dropped anything on his way out."

Griffin looked at the bag of cookies in the puddle.

Marissa scooped them up. Water dripped off the bottom. "Those are mine. Sorry." She should head back to the shop, but with her gingersnaps ruined, she still couldn't serve her cousins their lattes the way they were designed to be served.

Griffin finished scanning the ground and looked back at Tandy. "You didn't find anything?"

"They found me," the old guy answered for her.

Griffin tilted his head. "Are you turning yourself in? Did you rob the store?"

The man snorted. "No, but Birdie saw the guy who did when I was getting her jacket out of the bus. She used to be a spy and knows how to identify a criminal."

Birdie's mouth opened in wonder. "My lands. I used to be a spy?"

Griffin rubbed his face.

"He had spiky brown hair." Birdie paused thoughtfully. "It was like Winifred's, but he didn't have a wheelchair like her."

Griffin held the door wide and motioned them all inside. "I'll take your statement, but the shop also has security cameras, so I'm not sure you can tell me anything the recorded footage won't."

Tandy held Marissa back and let the old folks go first.

"Is that a Glock nine-millimeter?" the old man asked Griffin as he passed.

"Yes," the sheriff answered shortly.

The old man patted the side of his khaki canvas jacket. "I carry a Colt forty-five caliber."

Griffin's eyes followed the man inside. "Thank you for letting me know."

Marissa bit her lip. Kinda convenient the old guy had a gun on him at the same time Tandy had been shot at.

Tandy leaned in and whispered. "Hubert was caught stealing drugs today, then he died. I was shot at when someone else was stealing drugs. I think if we solve this crime, we'll solve Hubert's murder and get Connor out of jail."

Marissa sucked in a deep breath. She hadn't made the connection, but now she needed to be sure Griffin made it. She gripped Tandy's hand like a lifeline. "Was it the old guy? Did the old guy do it?"

"Archibald?" Tandy gave a surprised shake of her head. "Is he wearing black underneath that jacket?"

"I don't know yet, but I'm going to find out." She rushed past Tandy into the store.

Archibald stood at the big bin of teddy bears. He looked from the pharmacy window to the spot where Marissa had found Tandy on the floor. He rolled the metal bin back a foot and pointed to a hole in the floor. "Thirty-eight special."

Marissa tilted her head. What were they talking about? The bullet hole? The weapon that fired it? "Is that a gun?" It certainly wasn't the kind of gun Archibald said he was carrying.

The old man scowled. "Exactly like I suspected. Drug thieves have no class."

Griffin narrowed his eyes to study Archibald in either suspicion or jealousy. If the old man could guess guns and figure out ammo like that, he had more skills than the sheriff. He certainly had half a century of experience on him. But he wasn't wearing all black. The pants were black, but he wore it with a red plaid flannel shirt.

Marissa held up a hand to muffle her voice as she asked Tandy, "Did the robber move like a ninety-year-old?"

The clerk waved from the front of the store. "Sheriff, I pulled up the recording from our security camera."

Archibald and Birdie followed Griffin toward the checkout counter. Marissa hung back for a moment so she and Tandy could watch the old guy walk.

Tandy frowned in concentration. "I don't think so. They were probably about the same size, but Archibald walks stiffer. Like his bones are brittle."

Drat. Because she could spin a great narrative about how he hadn't actually been getting Birdie's jacket from the bus when Birdie saw the gunman leave the store.

"The suspect had spiky brown hair like Winifred," Birdie said again, as she wobbled to the front counter. "He was skinny. Too skinny. I wanted to share my donuts with him to fatten him up."

Tandy rolled her eyes. "What does Birdie have with wanting to share her donuts with bad guys?"

Marissa tossed her own sweets in a nearby trashcan. She needed to text Zam to make sure he was doing okay. "You don't really believe the perp was skinny with spiky brown hair like Birdie says?"

"I don't think she's reliable. She could be remembering a perp from her career days." Tandy headed toward the front of the store to join Griffin and gang. She spoke over her shoulder so only Marissa could hear. "We'll get more accurate info from the video footage than we will from her."

Marissa pulled her phone out of her jacket pocket and tapped on Zam's name. She typed, *Tandy witnessed a crime at the pharmacy. I'm keeping her company as she gives the sheriff her statement. Are you doing okay without us?*

Birdie continued describing a criminal she'd once witnessed, possibly Tandy's shooter. "He had dark hands. With a lighter circle where his wedding ring should be. I always look at a man's ring finger in case he decides to act sweet on me."

Well, that was specific. Did Marissa know anybody who had recently gone through a divorce?

They crowded around the computer monitor to get a better look at the grainy video. On screen, a skinny guy in black held a gun to the pharmacist with his right hand. He wore a hockey mask and had spiky brown hair as Birdie had told them.

"Can you zoom in on his left hand?" Tandy asked.

The clerk paused the screen and clicked on a button to enlarge the image. The guy's left hand hovered above a jacket pocket, frozen with a clear view of the white strip in place of a wedding band.

"Huh." Maybe the old lady was more trustworthy than Tandy realized. Marissa glanced her way to gauge her reaction.

Tandy squinted at the monitor. "Does he look like your cousin at all, Marissa?"

Marissa studied the image once again. The guy on screen appeared to be a little shorter than she thought of Austin. "I can see my cousin assuming he's above the law, but he's never been married, so I don't think that's his hand."

She glanced at Archibald's hand to find a plain gold band above his weathered knuckles. She didn't really think he was the perp, but she bet he wouldn't mind Birdie sharing her donuts with him.

Griffin huffed. "Which cousin, Marissa?"

He knew most everyone in her family from growing up in the same small town. "Austin."

"Nah, he wouldn't have shot at Tandy."

Tandy held out her arms. "Does she have other cousins you think would have?"

Marissa patted Tandy's innocent face. "You haven't met the twins yet."

Her phone vibrated in her pocket. She reached for it again.

Zam: *Hope she's okay. Speaking of crime, there's some lady dressed like Marilyn Monroe hogging the microphone.*

Marissa pouted. If her day had gone as planned, she'd be wearing the white halter dress and Connor would have met her cousins in a white t-shirt with his hair slicked back like James Dean—the only reason she'd been okay for him waiting so long to go to the barber.

Instead, she was dressed like a biker. But maybe that would make her appear tough enough to be the bouncer back at her shop. Working could take her mind off the fear of Connor not being released in time to marry her.

She gripped Tandy's arm. "You take it from here. I've got to get back to the shop."

Tandy placed a hand over hers. "We're gonna get Connor out."

Marissa wanted to believe her, but the faux sheriff also thought Birdie was an unreliable witness.

Chapter Seven

MARISSA PEEKED THROUGH THE WINDOW INTO Caffeine Conundrum. It looked more like a night club than a coffee shop with the black lights glowing purple and the music blaring as Kristin sang *I Wanna Be Loved by You*. The only good thing about having Connor in jail was that the woman wearing Marissa's Marilyn Monroe costume couldn't sing to him.

Marissa took her eyes off Kristin in the spotlight to scan the crowd. Was anyone wearing all black? Besides her, of course.

Something tapped her shoulder.

She jumped and screamed. Spinning around, she found a man in black and screamed again.

Austin held up his hands. "Calm down, Cuz." He'd taken off his clown costume, so she had full view of his mocking expression.

Taking a deep breath to stabilize her emotions, she studied him head to toe. His hair was more messy than spiky and also more blonde than brown. Maybe the video footage at the pharmacy just made his hair appear darker.

Should she be relieved that the guy who tapped her on the shoulder was her cousin, or should she be concerned that her cousin might be a killer?

"Why did you take off your costume?" she asked. Surely if he were trying to hide from the law, he would have left the yellow and red polka dot pantsuit over his incriminating clothing instead of carrying it wadded up in a ball.

"I'm no clown. I'm a businessman. I own my own real estate company." He tilted his head toward the tea loft inside. "For some reason I trusted my sisters to pick out my costume this year. I should have known they'd give people a reason to laugh at me."

Marissa's pounding heart slowed and softened. "Well, thank you for dressing up." Perhaps Austin had become a jerk because he had to deal with the twins all the time. It had certainly been enough to make her act like a jerk to him when they were younger. She probably owed him. "You sure you don't want to try our gingerbread latte before you go?"

"Nah. I've already got heartburn." He lifted a shoulder. "Probably stress related. Do you know how stressful it is to listen to the twins make fun of your costume?"

"Yeah." Marissa clicked her tongue. "Well, drop by later on this week, okay? I'll whip up some chocolate chip pumpkin muffins just for you."

One corner of Austin's mouth curved up. "If you're alive that long."

Marissa's eyes bulged. Was that a threat?

He shot a thumb toward the window. "Go back in there, and I worry about your safety."

His words made sense in the way that his sisters were treacherous, but could he be the real danger? She nodded numbly.

He turned to head down the street.

"Hey, Austin," she called. She already had enough to worry about when it came to dealing with her family. She didn't want to have to suspect her cousin of being a killer too. So, she'd ask a quick question to invalidate her fears. "When did you guys get to town?"

He narrowed his eyes to study her up and down. If he was innocent, he wouldn't know about the shooting down the street. He wouldn't know Connor was in jail. Her question would seem innocent.

Austin stuffed his hands in his pockets so she couldn't see his ring finger. "We arrived around noon. It's been about seven hours."

Seven hours would have given him enough time to get to The Farmstead and kill Hubert. But why would he do that?

"Why do you ask?"

She shrugged. "Just wondering what you did all day."

"I took a nap."

"Oh." So he had no alibi.

"You would've too if you'd been forced to drive across the state with the twins."

"True." She waved. "See ya." They'd both had rough days. Sadly, only one of them got to go home.

Marissa had to get back to work. With a sigh, she pulled the door open.

The twang of country music greeted her ears. Good ol' Pete from Grace Springs Manor stood in the spotlight now, singing *She Thinks My Tractor's Sexy* in his suspenders and John Deere cap. No costume needed for that character.

Even though the old farmer had taken a joyride in Connor's tractor earlier, his giant, toothy smile warmed a place in her heart. She hated to imagine what cruel things her cousins had to say about him. She glanced up to the loft and the twin trouble she was going to have to face. Except the women weren't there.

A high-pitched giggle drew Marissa's gaze to the counter where Ashlee and Amber watched Zam juggle mugs in his Lone Ranger costume. Maybe he could keep them distracted so she wouldn't have to deal with them anymore. Almost as nice, was the fact that no line formed behind her cousins. It seemed everyone had their beverages already and were simply enjoying the entertainment.

"Have a seat," called the large redhead in the wheelchair. She scooted a metal chair Marissa's way.

Marissa could use a break, and it didn't look like she was needed elsewhere. She sank down opposite the woman swaying back and forth to Pete's performance, but she continued to check on Zam and company over her shoulder.

"It's the look of love," the redhead said, and Marissa turned to find her also watching the barista and twins.

"I don't think that's love," she argued. The looks on her cousins' faces were probably similar to that of a black widow before devouring its mate.

"Maybe a love triangle?" suggested the redhead.

"More like the Bermuda Triangle." Definitely an area she would stay away from.

The redhead rocked with laughter.

Who was this lady? Marissa held out her hand to introduce herself. "Hi, I'm Marissa Alexander."

The woman took her hand and peered closer. "The Marissa who fell off the stage at the Miss Ohio pageant a few years back?"

Not exactly what she wanted to be famous for. "The Marissa who owns this shop and has way too much family in town because she's getting married this weekend." She flipped up her visor with a free hand to give her new friend a look at her face.

"Nice to meet you, Marissa." Rather than letting go of her hand, the woman squeezed tighter. "I'm Winifred, and I'm so excited for you. Weddings are magical. Is your fiancé here?"

"I'll have to introduce you to him another time." Marissa pulled her hand away to fan her cheeks. And not only because the room was full of people and she was wearing leather. She needed to change the subject quickly before she spilled the coffee beans about Connor's arrest. "Are *you* married, Winifred?"

"Hobble-dee-gobble-dee." Winfred gazed lovingly at Farmer Pete. Her husband? "I had a beau propose to me once, but Broadway was my first love."

Marissa leaned back in her seat. She'd never met a star of the stage before. Well, besides Farmer Pete. "You performed on Broadway?"

"Back in the day." Winifred wasn't looking at Pete dreamily. She was looking at the small stage they'd built for live music. "Dancing was hard on my body though. Because of that, I'm stuck in a wheelchair and have no children or grandchildren to spend my days with."

Marissa's chest tightened. She'd missed her own grandmother so much that she'd opened this shop in memory of their tea parties. Winifred would have made a lovely grandmother. "I'm sorry."

"It was a choice I made." Winifred waved Marissa's concern away. "And now, since I don't have a relationship of my own, I choose to meddle in the relationships of others."

The woman not only took responsibility for her choices, but she was honest about it. Marissa admired that. Maybe she could put the woman's meddling to good use.

She glanced over her shoulder at the coffee bar to find Zam standing behind Ashlee, teaching her how to juggle. The guy had been through enough in his life already. He didn't deserve to have Marissa's cousins ruin the rest of it. "Can you meddle by breaking up Zam's little love triangle?"

Winifred's eyes sparkled in a flash from a strobe light. "Like a cue ball to a billiards rack."

Marissa glanced over her shoulder to gauge the angle she should take that would bust them all apart.

Amber had a hand on one hip as she watched her sister get all Zam's attention. She turned her head and caught Marissa's eye. Her plump lips pursed disdainfully.

Warning sirens went off in Marissa's head. What did it say that she was more terrified of the twins than she was of their brother who could possibly be a killer?

She slammed her face shield shut and jumped to her feet to hide behind Winifred's wheelchair. "Winnie, what do you say we get you into the spotlight right now? You can sing a slow song so the twins start fighting over who gets to dance with Zam." Then they would be too busy waging war on each other to come after her about her missing fiancé.

Tandy marched into her shop in time to see Marissa whiz by with a woman in a wheelchair. The woman looked like Winifred, but she had a bright red chin-length bob rather than the spiky brown hair Tandy remembered. Her costume for Skary-oke perhaps?

Though it wasn't Winifred's hair Tandy was curious about. She wanted to check out Marissa's cousin Austin to see if he had hair like the man in the surveillance video. She scanned the crowd and didn't find anyone resembling either the perp's description or a clown. She followed Marissa toward the stage, which was a good thing because it took both of them to push Winifred up the ramp.

The woman's sequin top glittered like a disco ball under the spotlight, but her smile flashed even brighter.

Sultry saxophone filled the air. Piano keys and bass strings joined in. The shift in music seemed to send the room into a trance.

"Hey, all you lovebirds out there," Winifred's seductive voice spoke over the beginning of the song. "There's room up here for a dance floor if you dance real close. Gentlemen, grab your favorite dame and show her your love is here to stay."

Like a radio DJ, she smoothly transitioned from talking to singing. A few couples actually rose to rock together.

Maybe Tandy could dance with Austin to get a close up of his ring finger. Greg wouldn't mind since it would be in the name of finding evidence to release his client from jail.

She leaned toward Marissa to be heard over the speakers. "Where's your cousin?"

Marissa pointed past her. "They're fighting over Zam the way I'd hoped."

Tandy craned her neck toward the coffee bar. Two blondes seemed to be having a hair tossing contest in front of a cowboy wearing a mask. And she'd thought Marissa had been bad when they'd met.

"Not them. I mean your cousin in the clown costume."

"He went home." Marissa flicked her visor up. Probably to be heard better. The full-face helmet muffled sounds. "I tried to get a look at his ring finger, but he had his hand in his pocket."

Of course he did. Tandy's head fell back in disappointment. "If he hadn't left, I could have danced with him."

A strong hand slid around her waist. Greg gave her a teasing smile. "Who'd you want to dance with?"

He didn't seem to be intimidated by her talk of dancing with another man. But that could be because he was dressed like Superman and filled out the costume nicely.

She couldn't help but smile. "A suspect."

He circled in front of her and slid his hand from her back to her fingers, pulling her after him between tables to the area in front of the stage. He spun her once so that she ended up in his arms. Tandy had never considered herself much of a dancer, but he made it feel easy. She snuggled closer and inhaled his fresh, soapy smell.

He tilted his head down to look at her, and a black curl slid perfectly over his forehead. "I would have dressed up like an inmate if I'd known you were going to be a cop."

"That might have hit a little close to home." Tandy glanced over her shoulder to check on Marissa who was hiding behind the helmet face shield once again. "This was a last-minute change."

"Yeah." Greg rocked her side to side. "I'm glad I noticed Marissa's watch, or I might have pulled her onto the dance floor thinking she was you."

"I wish she had Connor here to dance with." Tandy twisted her lips before updating him on the latest suspect. He wasn't going to like it, but it could help his case out. "Someone robbed the pharmacy and shot at me."

Greg stilled. "Oh, babe." He looked her up and down. "You're okay?"

She tugged her hand from his to drape both around his neck and reassure him. "Yeah. I think he must have thought I was a cop for real, which would mean he's probably new to town. I suspect Marissa's cousin."

"And that's the guy you wanted to dance with?" Greg lifted his chin and looked around the room. "Where is he? I'll 'dance' with him."

Tandy pulled his face back toward hers and gave him an indulgent smile. "Just because you're dressed like Superman doesn't mean bullets will bounce off your chest."

"I do have some new martial arts moves I could try." He hugged her closer. "Though neither of us need any extra trouble. You should stay away from him and let Griffin investigate, okay?"

Tandy kissed him rather than make promises she didn't intend to keep. Her job as maid of honor required her to be there for the bride. She glanced toward Marissa once more and found Zam swinging her around in a Lindy Hop kind of way while her cousins glowered. Then another couple caught her eye.

"That wasn't an answer, Tandy."

"Look." She nudged Greg and nodded toward Archibald rocking with Birdie. For once the cranky old man wasn't complaining, and the confused old lady gazed at him with clarity. Was he Birdie's husband even though she couldn't remember him?

A corner of Greg's lips turned up. "Is that us in fifty years?"

"I hope not." Though if Tandy lost her memory of him, Greg would certainly have a reason to be cranky. "She's the dementia patient Hubert was stealing from."

"Hmm…" Greg continued to watch the old couple as if the two of them could somehow save Marissa's wedding.

Tandy looked around for the activities' director. She'd said she wasn't going to bring the residents from Grace Springs Manor, but here they were.

A redheaded Mary Poppins waved from the balcony. Yvette. She held her hands to her heart, obviously watching Archibald and Birdie too.

The music faded along with Winifred's last note. "Our love is here to stay…"

Tandy let go of Greg to clap politely, though the rest of the crowd went wild. Skary-oke was a hit.

"She's got talent," Greg shouted above the din.

Zam and Marissa rolled Winifred down the ramp backward, so Marissa wouldn't trip and accidentally dump the singing superstar.

Birdie wandered past. "Are there cookies here?"

Archibald harrumphed and went the other way, perhaps to guard the door so the old woman didn't escape after she found her snack. Or perhaps to go rob another pharmacy. Tandy wasn't really sure yet, but his devotion to Birdie made her want to believe the best about him.

Winifred bowed repeatedly as much as the wheelchair and her belly would allow. Marissa rolled her to a stop in front of them. Zam locked her wheels in place.

"That was beautiful, Winifred." Tandy raved.

"Wasn't it?" Winifred tilted her head and smiled dreamily. "I knew that song would bring Birdie back. Even if only for a moment."

Tandy swallowed down her emotion. While she'd been talking about Winifred's voice, the woman had been thinking of the elderly couple's dance. "Birdie is married to Archibald, isn't she?"

"Yes. Her dementia has been hard on both of them." Winifred clasped hands with a few people walking by as they thanked her for sharing her gift. "That's how I talked Yvette into bringing us tonight. I thought it would be good for Birdie. Romance seems to remind her of how much she'd once been in love."

Zam nodded at them and took off for the coffee bar, oblivious to the depth of their conversation. He must not have been reading lips but watching for customers who needed drinks, which was what they paid him to do.

Winifred pointed after him. "Looks like we broke up his love triangle, but if your fiancé showed up, young lady, he might have been in another one."

Marissa shook her head. She could have said something in response, but with the noise around and her face shield down it was hard for Tandy to tell.

Tandy would answer for her. "Connor couldn't make it tonight because—"

A biker boot smashed down on her toes.

"Ow!" She pushed Marissa off.

"Sorry, sorry." Marissa's voice came out muffled as she regained her balance.

Tandy grimaced. Even with as accident prone as Marissa was, that was no accident. Apparently, they were still supposed to pretend Connor hadn't been arrested earlier that day.

"Well." Winifred clapped her hands. "I can't wait to meet your young man. You should introduce him to Birdie too. Maybe seeing how twitterpated you two are will be another reminder of her wedding to Archie."

Marissa's helmet nodded, but her face shield stayed down, and Tandy felt bad for her in spite of the toe stomp.

Yvette's laughter reached them before she did. She arrived alone, so Tandy couldn't be sure what she'd been laughing about this time.

"What a wonderful event." Yvette waved her Mary Poppins umbrella around dangerously.

Tandy ducked in time to avoid getting hit by the handle. Marissa didn't duck in time, but she had a helmet on, so she was okay. She should wear helmets more often.

"I'm so glad you talked me into bringing you all, Winifred."

Winifred grabbed the wild end of the umbrella. "There's something else I want to talk you into."

Yvette took off her flat hat with the flower and fanned herself. "What's that?"

"We need to have a wedding shower for this young lady. After all she and her friends have done for us with helping us home from the corn maze and inviting us here tonight, it's the least we can do."

Yvette laughed in delight. "And it could bring Archibald and Birdie back together for another moment."

"Exactly."

Tandy blinked at their enthusiasm.

Marissa flipped up her face shield and shot Tandy a look of pure panic.

It was a nice offer and a nice goal, but how could her friend say yes to a shower for a wedding she didn't even know was still going to happen?

Chapter Eight

TANDY ROLLED UP HER JEANS AND eyed the massage chair with its foot spa. She'd walked past The Spa at Grace Springs almost every day on her way to her coffee shop, but she'd never been inside. "If we're wearing cowboy boots during the wedding, why do I need to get my toenails done?"

Marissa kicked off her high heels and slid onto the massage chair. She didn't have to worry about pant legs since she'd come prepared in a sweater dress. Her cherry red toenails already looked manicured. "We want to have pretty fingers for photos, and it would just be wrong not to have our hands match our feet."

Tandy grunted but complied. The hot water made her feet itch. "Nobody is ever going to see my pedicure." She didn't even wear sandals in the summer.

"Well, then enjoy the massage chair. That's really what I need today." Marissa reached over and pressed buttons on a remote attached to Tandy's chair.

The chair came to life, pummeling Tandy's lower back and working its way up her spine to her head. "Is this supposed to be relaxing?" Her voice vibrated with the seat.

Marissa closed her eyes. "Turn on the heat and imagine you're lying on a beach."

"Like you will be next week?" Tandy didn't close her eyes. She watched the nail tech suspiciously. The woman's rolling cart held metal tools that looked like they belonged in an operating room at a hospital.

"I hope so." Marissa sighed. "If Connor isn't released from jail, do you want to go to Costa Rica with me?"

"Not if I have to wear flip flops."

The pedicurist patted a small white towel on the far edge of the spa bowl. Tandy lifted a foot from the water and cautiously placed it within the woman's reach.

Marissa turned her head to face Tandy. She opened her eyes, though the sadness reflected there reminded Tandy of spilled coffee. "What am I going to do?"

Tandy shifted uncomfortably, and not only because a cuticle clipper dug at her big toe. She'd try to lighten the mood with humor. "Don't worry. You won't be alone. It sounds like the residents at the retirement center are going on a trip to Costa Rica too."

"Oh good. I can zipline with Winifred and cliff jump with Birdie." Marissa gave her a mock glare. It had as much impact as decaf.

Tandy could almost imagine Birdie cliff jumping. She'd probably been a daredevil back in her spy days. Tandy pictured her hang gliding off the Kremlin in the dead of night. As for Marissa... "As accident prone as you are, you shouldn't do those things anyway."

Marissa groaned. "The honeymoon isn't my biggest problem right now. What am I going to do about the wedding? About Connor?"

Tandy sighed. "You know how large cities have crime hotlines?"

Marissa's espresso eyes simmered. "Yeah. But we're not a big city. We're a little town with a gossip line—which I'm currently trying to keep Connor's name off of."

The nail tech pulled out a rough looking pumice stone. Tandy curled her toes in dread. "You might want to reconsider that tactic. Because if the town knows Connor has been accused of murder, they'll come out in droves to defend him. And they might unknowingly have information that could help set him free. It would be even better than a crime hotline."

The rough stone grated Tandy's heel. She instinctively jerked her foot back into the tub. The pedicurist stared in shock.

"Sorry." Tandy replaced her foot where it was supposed to be, while the pedicurist wiped water droplets off her face then went back to work.

Marissa kept staring. "But my relatives from out of town don't know him. They would only know I'm engaged to a man arrested for murder. Imagine what would happen at my wedding then when the minister says, 'Speak now or forever hold your peace.' They'd all have objections."

Tandy might have argued if she hadn't seen Marissa's cousins in action the night before. She gritted her teeth and forced her foot to relax. "Not if the town helps us find the real killer."

Marissa scrunched her nose. She didn't even seem to notice her pedicurist was rubbing grainy goop up and down her calf. Was Tandy going to get that done too? "You think Hubert's killer is the same guy you saw last night?" Marissa asked.

"I do." Clippers dug underneath Tandy's pinky toenail. She was pretty sure she'd heard of this kind of treatment as a method of torture. If not, it should be. She gripped the armrests until her knuckles turned white. "Griffin is tracking down leads from the bullets and casings, thanks to Archibald."

Marissa gazed past her out the picture windows onto Main Street. "And the perp's image is caught on camera. I hope Griffin is looking into the sale of hockey masks at the costume shop, as well."

The pedicurist motioned for Tandy to switch feet, and she took a breather. If she survived one foot being assaulted, she could survive the other. "Unfortunately, it's Halloween. There are probably a lot of hockey masks sold this time of year."

"You think?" Marissa sat up straighter. "Because there's one now."

Tandy jolted upright, splashing water all over again. She looked out the window to find a man in black turning into the alley across the street. She leapt barefoot from the chair and charged out the front door. She'd be sure to tip her nail tech well when she returned, but right now she had to stop the perp from hurting anyone else.

Cold pavement stung Tandy's feet after the warmth of the water inside. Pebbles poked at her soles as well, but it wasn't nearly as painful as her attempted pedicure had been.

"Stop!" she yelled. She didn't really expect the guy to stop, but maybe others would hear and join in her pursuit.

The guy looked back. Sure enough, he wore a white mask over his face. And he had the same spiky hair as the guy from the night before. He turned and disappeared into the alley.

Marissa skidded out the door after Tandy and smashed into Tandy's Volkswagen parked at the curb. The woman couldn't even run in running shoes, and here she was trying to race with goop smeared over her bare feet.

Tandy looked both ways before darting into the road. Greg's gold Mercedes slowed to let her cross. His head swiveled to gape after her. Good timing. Maybe he could help.

She pointed toward the alley and shouted, "The drug thief from last night."

Wind chilled her skin and lifted her hair as she leaped onto the sidewalk and picked up speed. Behind her, tires rolled forward then squealed to a stop once again.

Something thudded. Marissa yelled, "I'm okay. I'm okay."

Tandy glanced back to make sure Marissa wasn't bleeding in the street. Her friend continued following Tandy, though she bumped into another car as if she didn't realize her objective was to avoid them. She'd apparently never played Frogger as a child, but she somehow made it safely to the sidewalk.

Tandy focused forward in time to see the man in black dart behind garbage cans at the end of the block and out of sight. She wouldn't be able to catch him barefoot, but Greg could chase him down in his car. She turned back to jump in his passenger seat. The warm interior welcomed her.

Marissa was still in the alley, and they couldn't take time to wait for her.

Tandy grabbed for the seatbelt. "Go, go, go."

Greg stepped on the gas, rocking her deeper against his leather interior. "Where are we going, and why aren't we taking your shoes?"

Tandy leaned forward, scanning the people on the street around and pointing for Greg to turn at the next corner. "I was getting my toenails done with Marissa when we saw the guy in the hockey mask head for the alley."

Greg slowed enough to turn. "Call Sheriff Griffin."

"I will, but right now—"

A female voice with a British accent interrupted. "Calling Sheriff Griffin."

Oh yeah. Tandy had forgotten he'd had the car's speaker phone set up after their last high-speed chase. The phone rang.

She scanned the distance for anyone in black.

There.

She jolted straighter.

Nope. Only a nun.

Griffin's phone rang again.

There.

No, that was Cat Woman.

Cat Woman? She frowned at the supervillain as Greg drove past. The woman was clearly in costume, as she had a little Batman with her. Maybe the nun had been in costume too. Tandy had never actually seen a nun in real life. If there was some costume event going on, that would have made it easy for the guy in the hockey mask to blend right in. If he hadn't run away from her, she might think he could be innocent.

"This is Sheriff Griffin."

Greg slowed for a woman carrying her toddler across the street toward the library. The woman wore a bright yellow ball gown, and her son wore something furry. They had to be Beauty and the Beast. "Oh, it's story time."

"What?" Griffin barked over the speaker.

Greg cleared his throat as he stepped on the accelerator. "Tandy saw the man in the hockey mask again. We're looking for him by the library, but there's a lot of people in costume right now for Spooky Story Time."

Tandy left the explanation to Greg as she continued to scan. If there was a gunman loose around children, the situation was extra dangerous.

A black sweatshirt caught her eye. "There." The guy didn't have a mask on anymore, but he had messy hair. It was lighter than she remembered, but that could be the way the morning sunshine lit it.

"Don't attempt to confront him," the Sheriff ordered. "Just keep your eyes on him, and I'll be right there."

Tandy grabbed the door handle.

Marissa slid after the perp like she was wearing ice skates. The grains from her sugar scrub rubbed her soles raw, but she'd be okay if it also gave her extra smooth skin for her honeymoon.

And if her pursuit helped her catch the real criminal so Connor could take her on said honeymoon.

Greg had picked up Tandy to pursue the bad guy around the block, so the perp might see them and back track, in which case she'd…she'd what? If only she still had on Tandy's biker costume. Then she could head butt the guy with her helmet.

She slowed her steps to catch her breath and prepare for his return. Something sharp poked her right foot. She shifted her weight to lift her leg and wipe the debris away.

Her weight continued to shift. Gravity pulled. She really should have grabbed onto something for balance before attempting to stand on one foot. Waving her arms, she reached for anything solid.

A metal garbage can filled the space between her body and the pavement beneath her. She exhaled in relief and leaned against it.

The lid slipped off the side, clanging onto the ground, and she followed. Twisting to catch herself with her hands, she knocked into the can itself and sent it rolling. She closed her eyes and braced for impact.

Something slick and squishy cushioned her fall. She lay there with her belly on the mound for a moment, listening for the clanking of trash cans, ignoring the smell of rotten eggs, and taking mental inventory of her pain. She really didn't want to have to wear a walking boot again or worse. How would Connor put a ring on her finger if her hand was in a cast?

But nothing throbbed or pulsed. The worst pain was her big toe, and that was from the pedicure.

She opened her eyes to find herself on top of a few, full black garbage bags. Gross. But preferable to losing a tooth or getting a black eye.

She laughed and looked up toward heaven to thank the good Lord. Instead, she saw a cranky old man squatting in front of her in an Elmer Fudd hat. Archibald. Did the old man really hang out in alleys that much, or could he be the perp?

"What are you doing here?" she demanded.

He eyed her position on top of the garbage bags. "I could ask you the same thing, but I'm not sure you'd be able to come up with a logical explanation."

She scurried back into a seated position. Better for defending herself against this man if he had any ill intent. After all, she knew he carried a gun. At the moment, he only held something furry. A rat?

She crab-walked backwards. "What is that?" Her voice squeaked.

Archibald lifted the little animal. "I'm pretty sure it's Winifred's wig."

Marissa shuddered. That was still pretty bad. "Why would you take it out of the garbage? She was wise to get rid of it."

Archibald scowled. "Winifred didn't throw it away. A man in black did."

Marissa gasped. "You saw him?"

Or maybe Archibald *was* him. He wore black pants, but his shirt was gray. Could he have stuffed a black jacket in the garbage can, as well?

"Yeah, I saw him." Archibald harrumphed. "I was staking out this location because I noticed those shoes last night." He pointed overhead to where a pair of high-top sneakers dangled.

Marissa glanced up quickly, afraid to look away. The old man could be trying to distract her in order to run or attack. But the only thing that moved was his eyes as he rolled them.

She shrugged in confusion. "What about the shoes?"

"That's the sign for where to buy drugs."

Marissa's lips parted. Was he making this up as a cover? She looked at his feet to see if he'd thrown his own shoes up there and was barefoot like her. Nope.

He continued. "Birdie's been having her medications stolen, so I thought I'd watch to see if the yahoo who's been stealing from her is selling her meds here."

"Huh." The story actually made sense. "Did you see who it was?"

He grunted. "I would have if you girls hadn't caused such a ruckus."

Marissa bit her lip. They'd been so close. "Maybe Tandy caught him," she hoped.

"I caught *this* guy," Tandy announced, marching around the corner with Austin. "He claims he was headed to the coffee shop for pumpkin muffins, but he's the only man I saw in black."

Marissa groaned and dropped her head back. "No…" Even worse than the possibility of her cousin being a drug-dealer was the possibility that he was going to find out why they were chasing him in the first place and learn her fiancé was suspected of murder.

Austin smirked when he saw her sitting on the ground barefoot. "Marissa?" He looked at the Converse sneakers hanging directly above. "Why did you throw your shoes up there?"

Marissa huffed, stood, and brushed herself off. "I have better taste than to wear high tops with a sweater dress."

Tandy crossed her arms and glanced at the shoes. "I think it would look cute together."

Marissa didn't have time to deal with Tandy's fashion faux pas. "You guys, this is my cousin."

Archibald scowled at them all as he righted the garbage cans Marissa had knocked over.

The police siren whooped, announcing Griffin's arrival. He parked at the entrance to the alley and climbed out. "Hey, Austin."

"Hey, Lukey."

"Good to see you again," the sheriff reached to shake his hand.

"Griffin." Tandy clamped a hand on Austin's shoulder, holding him back from accepting Griffin's greeting. "I think he's the guy who robbed the pharmacy."

Austin shoved his hands in his pockets. "Because I'm wearing black," he said like it was the punchline to a joke.

Griffin chuckled.

Greg pulled up behind the cop car and climbed out of the Mercedes in his suit. "Tandy, you were supposed to let the sheriff confront him."

Tandy crossed her arms. "Like that's gonna happen. Apparently, they are buddies."

Austin's grin grew. "Lukey knows me so he knows I wouldn't rob a pharmacy." Austin nodded toward Greg. "Why don't you suspect *him*? He's wearing black." He lifted his thick eyebrows. "Is it because *you're* buddies?"

Greg held his hands wide and looked down at his suit as if offended anyone would dare besmirch such a classy ensemble. Marissa could relate. That's how she felt about the shoe suggestion.

Archibald certainly didn't have as much care for appearances since he was currently rifling through the garbage cans.

"Griffin," Tandy motioned at Austin like he'd already pled guilty. "He's got the spiky hair, and he's the only one on the street wearing black besides a nun and Cat Woman."

Austin held up a finger. "I bet the nun did it."

"Also, he was in the area last night when the pharmacy was robbed."

Austin tilted his head to include Marissa in their conversation. "Is that why you were asking me so many questions at Scary-oke, Cuz? You think I'm a criminal, as well?"

Marissa didn't know what to think. She simply wanted Austin to leave before they started discussing Connor. Though if he'd been the one to rob the pharmacy, Tandy assumed he was the one to hit Hubert with the shovel at The Farmstead. In which case, he probably already knew about Connor's arrest.

She peered at his ring finger to see if there was a white line where a band should be. Instead there was a ring. She squinted and looked closer. She'd expected a ring even less than she'd expected a tan line from one. "When did you get married?"

"What?" His face went blank for a moment. Like being married was more shocking then being accused of robbery. "Oh." He glanced down at his hand. "I wear this for my work in real estate. It helps put female buyers at ease."

Well, that wasn't creepy at all.

The alley grew quiet as they all stared at him. In their silence, Archibald's banging around in the garbage can grew louder.

Griffin rubbed a hand over his face. "What is he doing here?"

Archibald set the garbage can down to scowl at the cop. "I'll tell you what I'm doing here. I'm doing your job once again."

Griffin pressed his lips together as if keeping himself from exploding. Finally, he gave a nod. "How so?"

Archibald peered up at the shoes. "I was staking out the shoes to watch for drug deals, and I saw the same guy from the pharmacy last night. Same mask, black clothes, and spiky hair.

He was about to lift his mask up and reveal his identity, when these girls started chasing him." He glared back at Marissa. "I couldn't see which way he ran from my hiding spot behind these garbage cans, but he did throw a wig in it. I was looking to see if he got rid of anything else."

"Ha." Austin guffawed. "A wig? So it doesn't matter that I have spiky hair at all."

Greg narrowed his eyes. "How do we know the wig belonged to the perp?"

Archibald circled the garbage cans, holding up a wig in one hand and a hockey mask in the other. "Any more questions?"

Marissa relaxed at the possibility Austin was innocent. She didn't want her cousin to be guilty of anything worse than wearing a wedding ring when he wasn't married. And not just because they could let him go and continue the search for Hubert's killer without her family ever finding out why she cared.

"I've got a question," Griffin responded. "Why are you getting your fingerprints all over the evidence? That's what got Connor arrested for murder yesterday."

Austin's head slowly turned Marissa's way, and his mouth fell open. His wide eyes were almost gleeful. "Your fiancé, Connor?"

Yeah, he definitely hadn't known her fiancé was in jail. But he did now.

Chapter Nine

MARISSA'S HEART SANK. SO MUCH FOR avoiding family drama.

Tandy gave Austin one more suspicious glance before wrapping a comforting arm around Marissa's shoulders. "At least now that your family knows about Connor, we can question the townsfolk and see if they have any information that will help him."

"Wait." Austin held up his hands. "Nobody in our family knows your fiancé is in jail?"

Marissa caught her breath. Was there a chance Austin wouldn't tell? With the pranks she'd pulled on him as children, he'd probably want to be the one to break the news. "*You* know," she pointed out.

Austin lifted a shoulder. "I also know our family. Believe me, I wouldn't want my sisters to have ammunition like this on me."

Marissa studied him. She'd felt a pang of sympathy the night before. Maybe he did understand. "It would mean a lot if you keep this to yourself. Connor's innocent, and we're going to prove it before the rehearsal dinner Friday."

"I'll keep your secret."

Marissa exhaled with relief.

Tandy jutted her chin forward. "We might have more trouble proving Connor's innocence if we can't put the word out to the community that he's in jail. Why don't you want us to put the word out, Austin?"

Austin shot her one of his condescending glances. "Hey, it doesn't affect me either way. I just understand why Marissa would want to keep this a secret. She still hasn't lived down the whole Miss Ohio thing yet."

Archibald handed over his finds to Griffin and glanced at Marissa. "You're that yahoo who fell off the stage in a beauty contest a few years back? I thought you looked familiar."

Marissa held out her hands. "How?" The old man should have been hunting wascally wabbits when she was competing.

"My granddaughter beat you. Maybe you've heard of her. Lavella Moon?"

Marissa ground her teeth. Lavella would have gotten along well with the twins.

Archibald nodded toward the garbage cans. "You can keep looking for a black jacket, Sheriff. If he got rid of his disguise, that might be why this young lady didn't see anyone else wearing black."

Tandy nodded thoughtfully. "That would explain it."

Griffin snapped latex gloves on his hands as if to make a statement about doing his job. "I will."

"Griffin," Marissa added like he wanted more advice. "If that wig belongs to Winifred, then it's even more likely that the perp has a connection to the nursing home and could be involved in Hubert's death. You should go out to Grace Springs Manor to talk to her."

Griffin motioned to the garbage can. "Did you want to dig through the trash for me so I can head over there now, or are you going to let me do one thing at a time?"

Austin covered his mouth to hide a smile, though Marissa saw it. Griffin was supposed to be his buddy, but her cousin wasn't above mocking anyone. Would he really keep her secret?

Tandy stepped in. "I'll head to the nursing home. Winifred knows me."

Marissa looked at her friend's bare feet. Tandy hadn't even gotten to the sugar scrub yet. That must have been why she didn't have as much trouble running. "What about our pedicures?"

Tandy grinned. "This is a great excuse to get out of it."

Austin straightened his collar. "I'll go with you to the spa, Marissa. Then you can catch me up on this murder your betrothed allegedly committed."

Marissa looked to Tandy for help. How did she get out of this one? If she wanted Austin to keep her secret, she'd apparently have to pay for it. Was it worth sitting through a mani-pedi session with him? And why would he want to do that? She knew some guys got their nails done professionally, but none that she'd met before.

Tandy arched an eyebrow at him. "You really like getting your feet tortured, or are you wanting to find out how the investigation is going because you're guilty of the crime?"

Austin shrugged off her insinuation. "The only thing I'm guilty of is hating callouses."

Greg reached for Tandy's hand. "Come on, babe. I'll take you to Grace Springs Manor so I can ask some questions too. Let's get your shoes. Marissa can handle her cousin."

Marissa waved and took a few steps backward. She didn't know that she could handle Austin, but she knew she needed to get her toes back in the warm water before they turned any bluer.

Tandy laced her boots up over her jeans as Greg drove to Grace Springs Manor. "Is the fact that we just interrupted a drug deal going to help you defend Connor?"

"Defend him, yes. In a few months." Greg drove along the river and past The Farmstead where the whole debacle had started and where Marissa's wedding was supposed to be held in four days. "But what we need right now is another suspect with both means and a motive."

Tandy pointed back toward town. "We have another suspect."

Greg grimaced. "What you have is an alleged drug deal. You're suspicious that the man in the hockey mask was going to sell drugs, but you have no evidence."

Tandy twisted her lips in frustration. "We have a mask."

Greg slowed to turn into the parking lot for the fancy retirement community. "Which could very well be a Halloween mask. You, yourself, pointed out that a man in a hockey mask would fit right in with all the costumes being worn downtown."

Tandy sniffed. "Well, we have a wig that Archibald says belonged to Winifred." She hadn't even realized the spiky brown hair was a wig. She'd thought Winifred's brown hair was real, and the woman only put a red wig on as part of her costume. "I know Winifred was a Broadway performer, but why would she need so many wigs?"

Greg shrugged. "Disguises?"

Tandy chewed on the idea. Winifred was bigger and in a wheelchair. That would be hard to disguise. Unless the wheelchair was part of her disguise too. "She *is* an actress."

"Well, even if she can walk, we know she wasn't the one running down the alley." Greg pulled into a parking space close to the overhang covering the front door. "Where was she when Hubert died?"

Tandy tried to picture the joyous older woman swinging a shovel to hit Hubert in the head. The image didn't fit. "We can ask her."

Greg led the way, stopping at the front desk to get Winifred's room number. That didn't seem to help them with the way many of the door numbers along the hallway had been covered up by autumn decorations for the contest the receptionist told them about.

A door on their right was almost completely wrapped in toilet paper to look like a mummy. Two giant eyes made out of paper plates peered at them as they passed.

The door across from it had been decorated with giant books on a shelf. The fake spines read *Frankenstein*, *The Legend of Sleepy Hollow*, and *Dracula*. Tandy bet the resident who lived there was a big reader.

"Where's the door decorated for the Cincinnati Bengals?" Greg questioned as seriously as he would question a witness. "A football theme should win a decorating contest this time of year."

"Why?" Tandy challenged. "Because their chances of making the playoffs are scary?"

Greg gave her a playful snarl.

"Hey." Tandy pointed to a door with no decorations. "I bet that's where Archibald lives."

"Probably." Greg glanced past it. "Yvette said to find a room with sunflowers on the door. What does that say about Winifred?"

"It doesn't scream druggie or killer." Tandy wasn't sure whether she should be relieved or disappointed. She wanted another suspect, but she really didn't want it to be Winifred.

The woman's door was covered in burlap with a white picket fence attached at the bottom half. Silk sunflowers appeared to grow up behind it and a straw hat hung on the top in place of a sun. Cute and clever.

"Marissa would like this," Tandy surmised. "Though I kinda want the mummy to win."

Greg knocked.

"Come in," sang a strong voice from the other side. "It's unlocked."

Greg opened the door and let Tandy enter first. The room looked like a small apartment with kitchen appliances along the left wall, a two-person table on the right and a living room area behind that. A door in the back must have led to a bedroom.

Winifred sat in a chair at the table, putting together a jigsaw puzzle. She looked different with her gray hair pulled back in a bun. She looked like a normal grandma, which she most definitely was not. So that could explain the wigs. But where was her wheelchair?

"Oh, Tammy." Winifred clapped. "Are you here to help me plan Marissa's wedding shower?"

Greg turned to grin at Tandy. "I didn't know you were planning a wedding shower, *Tammy*."

Tandy scratched her head. Should she correct Winifred or let the name go? She didn't want to get distracted from their mission, and she certainly didn't want to have to plan a shower for a wedding that might or might not happen. Also, Greg seemed to be enjoying the name. "Actually, I wanted to talk to you about your visit to the corn maze yesterday."

"Oh, yes. It was such a beautiful day. Apart from poor Hubert's demise, of course."

"Of course." Tandy widened her eyes at Greg. Nobody really seemed to miss the deceased orderly.

"But I got to meet you. And I got to sing at your lovely establishment." Winifred motioned toward an antique looking teal loveseat that had legs like a chair. "Come sit down."

Tandy respectfully made her way to the stiff love seat along with Greg, though the position wouldn't be conducive to facing Winifred during their conversation. The elderly woman solved that problem by reaching for a walker and hobbling into the sitting area with them to claim her place in a recliner.

So she *could* walk. But not well. And it wasn't like she was trying to hide that fact. They needed to know more about the wig. "Winifred, I'm wondering if you still have that wig you wore yesterday when I met you. The brown, spiky one."

"Oh, yes. I call that one Sheena after Sheena Easton."

Tandy nodded, pretending to understand. The name sounded vaguely familiar.

"She's a singer from the 80s," Winifred explained, obviously reading through Tandy's act. "I name all my wigs after singers. Last night's is named Reba after—"

"Reba McEntire," Tandy finished for her. That singer she'd heard of.

"Bingo." Winifred beamed. "You should see me as Beyoncé."

Tandy envisioned her singing *Single Ladies* with Yvette and Kristin, Griffin's receptionist, Kristin, dancing behind her. Birdie would try to join them, but Archibald would distract her with a cookie.

Greg leaned forward, resting his forearms on his thighs. "Could we see Sheena?"

Winifred's drawn on eyebrow dipped for a moment, but then her expression bloomed like one of the silk flowers on her door. "Nobody has ever asked to see a certain wig before, but I do have quite the collection. Come on in." She leaned forward and grabbed her walker to stand then motioned them ahead of her through the door into her bedroom.

Greg waited for Tandy to go first. She would have let Winifred lead, but they didn't have all day to wait for her to walk from the chair to the door.

The bedroom was warm and inviting with striped wallpaper and a floral quilt on a bed with a carved antique headboard. But what stood out the most was a bright pink wig stand in the corner. It resembled a coatrack but held three levels of hooks in the shape of human heads.

"Wow," was all Tandy could think to say.

Greg topped her with, "Impressive."

"Hobble-dee-gobble-dee." Winifred shuffled in behind them. "You can try them on if you like."

"Um..." Tandy was still getting used to all the hats worn by townsfolk of Grace Springs. She wasn't ready for wigs.

"Try on the Sheena," Greg suggested. He was good at keeping her on track.

"You would look adorable in the Sheena." Winifred scooted past. "Let me..."

She circled the wig tree and reached toward the bottom. Her hand froze above a bald black head hook. "Sheena's gone."

Marissa bit into another chocolate chip pumpkin muffin. She was stress eating again, but man did she do a good job with using cinnamon as a secret ingredient.

Austin seemed to be enjoying the muffins, as well, and he was washing it down with orange spice tea. Being that he preferred tea to coffee, he couldn't be all bad.

In fact, at the spa he'd helped her go through the events chronologically to look for clues she might have missed. Now he kept her company as she baked. And ate.

At this rate, even if they got Connor out of jail by the end of the week, she wouldn't fit into her wedding dress. At least she had one cousin who would understand.

He perched on the stool across the stainless-steel kitchen island from her. "Is Connor as well-loved by the community as your friend seems to think?"

Marissa pictured Connor's square shoulders sculpted from hard work and shrugging in his laid-back way. He was both strong and supportive, and everyone knew it. "He's loved even more than Tandy expressed." She was one lucky girl—or she would be if they made it down the aisle.

"So…" Austin spooned batter from her large mixing bowl into the mini muffin pan. "Do you also think that if they knew he was in jail, they'd have some information or evidence that could help him?"

Marissa grabbed a rag to wipe flour off the counter and sighed. "Maybe. Maybe someone saw the perp take off his hockey mask and recognized him, or maybe someone knows who else might have issues with Hubert."

"Huh." Austin scraped the bowl clean. "Too bad you don't own a shop where locals come through every day and talk with you. Because if you did, you could ask them questions without them even knowing your fiancé is in jail."

Marissa stood up straighter. She looked out toward the coffee bar where Zam was somehow spinning in circles and pouring coffee back and forth between stainless steel pitchers like it was a liquid ribbon. He might have all the skills in the area of a circus performer, but he was deaf and wouldn't be able to talk with customers while he made their drinks. She should get out there and ask questions as she served. "That's a really good idea."

Austin nodded toward her new oven. "I'll take care of baking these. Thirteen minutes?"

Marissa nodded absently as she craned her neck to see their latest customers. Billie, the owner of the antique store across the street and her beau. Joseph Cross owned Grace

Springs Manor among other businesses. If she was going to talk to anybody, she should talk to him.

She shook her hair loose from the hair net and attempted to breeze out of the kitchen like her future wasn't currently locked behind bars. She hit her head on the aluminum coffee sign that hung out over the place where the rolling coffee cart usually stood. She'd forgotten they'd moved it to be a prop table for Skary-oke the night before.

She rubbed the throbbing spot on her scalp and made her voice as cheerful as possible. "Billie."

The tiny, older Asian woman with a salt and pepper pixie looked up from her caramel apple cider. "Hello, Marissa. Are you ready for your big day?"

Apart from the lack of a groom... "Sure." She forced a smile the way she'd learned to in her pageant days. "I sure am. Though there's been some trouble at my wedding venue." She tilted her head to smile at the attractive older gentleman in a sports coat. He could have played 007 in his younger years. Maybe that's where Birdie had met him and why she moved into Grace Springs Manor. "I heard about your former employee dying in the corn maze at The Farmstead. What was his name? Hubert?" She held her breath, hoping she came across as sweet and sincere.

Billie patted Mr. Cross's hand to comfort him, though she was the emotional one. He was all business.

His lips turned down, surrounded by his trim silver beard. "Yes. Hubert. Sheriff Griffin said there's an ongoing investigation. He had a few enemies."

Marissa's heart leaped up to follow this new trail. "Is that right?" She blinked in hopes of appearing innocent. "Who were his enemies? Do you know?"

Mr. Cross rolled his eyes toward the ceiling. "A few people at Grace Springs Manor wanted him fired for stealing medications, but I couldn't be sure it was him. I mean, I have one resident who used to be a spy and steals stuff all the time. Not to mention, many of them are forgetful. They might have even swallowed the drugs themselves and not remembered. I was looking into it before he died."

Marissa pouted. This wasn't anything new. "Would anyone have wanted Hubert fired enough to kill him?"

Cross gave a derisive laugh. "I think the bigger question is who would be capable of murder? And we all know who that is."

Marissa narrowed her eyes to try to make out who the man was referring to. He hadn't met the twins yet as far as she knew. "We do?"

The front door banged open and Sheriff Griffin marched through. He scanned the room and caught Marissa's attention. "Have you seen Archibald Clack?"

"No." Not since she'd knocked over the garbage cans he'd been hiding behind.

Mr. Cross glanced at the sheriff then back at Marissa. "Like I said, we all know who is capable of killing."

Chapter Ten

TANDY STARED AT THE SPOT WHERE the dark brown spiky wig should have hung. What did it mean that it was gone? They'd already guessed as much, but Winifred hadn't seemed to know it was missing. Did this mean that she was involved or only that someone with access to the retirement center could have stolen it?

"Who could have taken it?" Tandy asked.

Winifred scooted backwards toward her bed and sat down with a squeak of box springs. "Any of the staff, but why would they do something like this? And how did you know it's missing?"

Greg squatted for a closer look at the wig tree as if the culprit would have left behind a thread of clothing like they did in the movies.

Tandy left him to sit next to the older woman. "The wig is related to a robbery at the pharmacy downtown. We didn't realize it was a wig until the perp left it behind today. Sheriff Griffin has it."

Winifred looked back and forth between her and Greg as if trying to verify the truth. Her wide brown eyes reflected vulnerability. "When would someone have stolen it? While I slept? I don't feel safe here anymore."

Tandy chewed on her bottom lip. She didn't want to cause panic with the residents, but she also wanted the crime to be taken seriously. "The robbery was committed while you were at Skary-oke. I'm guessing whoever took your wig came in while you were gone."

Winifred held a hand to her heart. "I can't believe I didn't notice. I wonder if anything else is gone." She pushed up to hobble to her ornately carved dresser and lifted the lid on a jewelry box. "My nephew told me to get a safe, but I thought he was paranoid."

Tandy glanced at Greg to read his take on the situation.

He tilted his head in compassion. "Is anything else missing?"

"I…" Winifred rifled through earrings, necklaces, and brooches. Her voice broke. "I don't think so. My old engagement ring is here, and if someone were going to steal something, I think they would have taken that."

Tandy didn't believe Winifred could be connected anymore. She personally wished she could take the woman home and let her sleep in the guest bedroom until Grace Springs Manor was safe again, but she lived on the second floor of an apartment complex. "What can I do to help?"

Winifred looked up, eyes dazed. "Why are you here taking care of me? Why are you the one tracking down the owner of the wig? Shouldn't the sheriff be doing that?"

Tandy looked down at the Berber carpet. Marissa didn't want the news about Connor's arrest to become public, but it wasn't like Winifred was going to tell Marissa's family. Plus, the woman knew Hubert and might know more than she realized. "I think the robbery is related to Hubert's death. My friend Marissa's fiancé was accused of killing him, and we want to prove him innocent in time to get out of jail for their wedding."

Winifred remained still. Finally, she said quietly, "I met Marissa last night, and she didn't tell me that part."

"Yeah." Tandy quirked her lips. "She doesn't want her cousins to know."

"I met them too, and I don't blame her for keeping this a secret. Though…" Winifred narrowed her eyes. "Is Marissa's fiancé tall with short hair and sideburns?"

Tandy glanced at Greg who was listening and looking around like he was a detective rather than a lawyer. She didn't know what he was hoping to find, but this is what she'd been hoping for when suggesting they make Connor's arrest public. Winifred knew something. "Yes. How'd you know?"

"Well." Winifred grabbed her walker and hobbled out the bedroom door. If she was in fact involved with the crime and trying to get away, she'd made a huge mistake in thinking she could outrun them. Tandy would pretty much have to slow her normal strides in order to catch up.

Greg rubbed his jaw and gave the room one more scan before motioning for Tandy to precede him back into the living area. They found Winifred sitting at her table, except this time she was holding her phone, and it was a smart phone too. Not the old flip phone like Tandy's grandma had refused to give up.

Winifred scrolled through some photos. She clicked on one of the pictures, starting a video. Tandy heard Connor's voice threatening Hubert before she saw the stalks of corn. The clip had been taken right before Hubert's death.

This is not what Tandy had hoped for. She needed proof that would help set Connor free, not secure his prison sentence.

Winifred held up her phone so Tandy and Greg could get a better view. The video continued, first scanning the beauty of the farm as Winifred's clear voice sang "Jimmy Crack Corn," but then Connor's voice interrupted her song with his "Hey!" The shot zoomed in to frame Connor and Hubert on top of the bridge in the maze. Connor lunged, his back blocking the view of what happened between the two of them, but it gave a clear shot of Hubert toppling to his death.

Greg ran a hand down his face. "Not good."

No matter how innocent Connor was, this evidence made him look guilty.

Marissa followed Griffin out the front door of her shop. "Why are you looking for Archibald?" It couldn't be a coincidence that the owner of Grace Springs Manor listed him as his first murder suspect.

Griffin hooked his thumbs in his belt and surveyed the street. "We found a black jacket, and it's his."

Marissa shook her head in surprise and leaned away. She'd suspected him at one point, but the man she'd seen running away in the mask seemed to have the agility of a younger man. Plus, Archibald's devotion to Birdie appeared genuine. Maybe he'd gone overboard in trying to protect her. "How do you know the jacket is his?" DNA? But when would they have gotten his DNA to test?

"His name is written inside on the tag."

Marissa shivered and crossed her arms to chase away the chill. "Anybody could have written that there."

Griffin lifted his chin. "Who would have known they could frame him? Who would have known to write his name inside?"

Marissa scrunched her forehead. "Someone from the retirement community." She'd already suspected they were involved. "If he was the man in the mask, why would he have helped you find the mask in the garbage can?"

"Because you bumped into him hiding behind the garbage cans. He needed an excuse to be there."

Marissa played back the morning's events. "He'd already said he was staking out the spot for a drug deal." She studied the sheriff's baby face. Could he be jealous that Archibald knew more about stakeouts than he did? Or maybe the old man knew so much because he'd been the one to wear the mask, shoot the gun, and hit Hubert with a shovel. He'd been in the vicinity during all three events. If he were guilty, Connor would be set free. But the accusation just wasn't adding up to her. "Why would he tell you to keep looking for the jacket if it belonged to him?"

Griffin glowered. "There was no jacket in the trash can. We found it because the security camera from the bank across the street caught him tossing his jacket in the bed of a pickup before we arrived."

Marissa closed her mouth. She couldn't argue with that.

The guy's wife had dementia and a crush on her orderly. The orderly was suspected of stealing his wife's drugs. The orderly was hit in the head with a shovel in the corn maze. Archibald was there when he died. He fingered Connor at The Farmstead, then robbed the drugs to set up his own sting in the alley where he planned to catch whoever it was that was buying from Hubert. He'd been in all three locations on all three occasions.

He had the motivation, and as a military veteran who knew his guns, he had the means. Mr. Cross was right about him being capable of killing.

It still didn't sit right that he'd been trying to help out the sheriff, though that could have been part of his cover. But that wasn't her biggest concern. "Are you going to let Connor out?"

Griffin studied her. "Let me track down Archibald first. If we can take his fingerprints and match them to prints on the shovel, then yes. Connor will be a free man."

Tandy's fingers itched to erase the video on Winifred's phone. She knew when they verified with Griffin that the wig had belonged to a resident, he'd have to come down and investigate further. And when he did, she'd show him the recording.

Was it wrong to erase a video that would oppose justice? Is this how criminals defended their actions? Could doing so get Greg disbarred? She peeked at him.

He shook his head like he could read her thoughts. He followed the letter of the law, which was one of the things she most admired about him.

Her phone vibrated in her pocket. Probably Marissa sending an SOS message about her cousins. Tandy didn't have the time to talk about the twins, and she especially didn't want to tell Marissa about the video. She pulled her phone out anyway. If it was Marissa, she could avoid talking to her by sending a "What's up?" text.

The screen displayed a photo of Marissa holding a silver teapot.

"Is that your friend?" Winifred asked.

Tandy nodded glumly.

"Are you her maid of honor?"

Perceptive old woman. Definitely more so than Birdie anyway. "Yeah."

"You'd better answer that."

Winifred was right. Tandy had maid of honor duties to uphold. She swiped her finger across the image of a green old-fashioned phone icon as she headed toward the door to talk in private. "Excuse me." She stepped into the hallway with its festive doors and scent of sandalwood air fresheners. "Hey, Marissa."

"Archibald did it."

Marissa's words rocketed through Tandy's veins. She jerked upright and scanned the hallway to make sure nobody was eavesdropping. Specifically from behind the boring door she suspected to belong to the old man. Though if Griffin thought he was the perp, he was probably in custody.

"He confessed?" Good news for Connor, bad news for Birdie. Though maybe this was why God allowed Birdie to have dementia in the first place. She'd never miss her husband.

But she also wouldn't have anyone there for her who loved her as much as Archibald seemed to. Grief warred with joy.

"No." Marissa explained the whole jacket thing as best she could, though Tandy was going to have to ponder a little longer to put all of it together. "Griffin is looking for Archibald. I just thought since you're at Grace Springs Manor, you could keep an eye on him until the police get there."

Tandy swallowed. The man may be old, but if he could kill Hubert with a shovel, she wouldn't consider herself safe around him. "I think I'm outside his door," she whispered. "I'll keep my eye on it."

Winifred's door swung open.

Tandy jumped.

Greg stood in the frame and cocked his head. "What are you whispering about?"

Tandy took a deep breath to help her heart rate settle back down. She leaned toward Greg to not be overheard. "Griffin is on his way down here to arrest Archibald." She looked past him to the gray-haired woman at her puzzle table and raised her voice. "Does Archibald live in the room next to you?"

Winifred's mouth hung open between her jowls. "Hobble-dee-gobble-dee. You think he stole my wig?"

Tandy wasn't sure how to answer. Marissa had been there when Archibald recognized the wig as Winifred's. Was that because he'd taken it himself, and if so, then why did he tell Griffin? "Maybe."

A familiar nervous giggle drew Tandy's attention. Yvette's short round frame bowled down the hallway. "Hello, you two," she greeted. "That's very kind of you to visit Winifred."

Tandy looked over her shoulder at the older woman. She seemed frailer than when Tandy had met her, but she wasn't a charity case. She was a beautiful human who had a lot to offer through her music and her heart. If she was alone, it wasn't she who was missing out.

Tandy would advocate for her well-being. She stepped into the hallway. "Yvette, it looks like someone stole one of Winifred's wigs."

Yvette jerked to a stop. One last chuckle bubbled up. "Are you sure she didn't misplace it?"

Tandy shook her head. Winifred took good care of those wigs. Gave them names and everything. "Sheena is gone."

Yvette rocked with laughter. "I'm sorry. I'm sorry. It's just that if someone was to put in the effort to steal one of her wigs, I would have expected them to go for Dolly."

Greg joined them and closed the door behind them. Probably because Winifred might take Yvette's jokes the wrong way. "Well, we think it was Archibald who stole it. A Dolly Parton wig might have brought him more attention than he wanted."

Yvette threw her head back, squealing with laughter. "That image. Archibald in long platinum curls." She wiped tears from her eyes. "Okay. Okay. I gotta…" She caught her breath. "Does the sheriff know about this? Because he called to ask me to check on Archibald and see if he's here."

Tandy lifted her gaze to look at Greg. Archibald was probably nothing to be worried about, but it was better to be prepared.

He kept his expression even, but said, "We'll go with you."

Yvette smiled. "We don't have to go far. Here's his room." She stepped to the undecorated door and knocked.

Tandy listened. No footsteps. No voice. Not even a television set.

"Welp." Yvette drew out her key ring. "I'll have security look for him on the monitors to see if he's in the dining room or pool area, but I need to check for him inside too. I want to make sure he's not sick or injured."

Tandy's heart hitched. "Have you found residents in the past who have..." What word should she use in place of "died"? "...fallen down?"

"I have." The subject subdued Yvette's laughter.

Greg grabbed Tandy's hand. She murmured a prayer.

Yvette swung the door open. No sign of the man's body.

Tandy exhaled. Greg squeezed her hand.

"Archibald?" Yvette called the man's name.

Nothing.

She glanced back at Tandy and Greg. "One second while I check his bedroom and bathroom."

"Okay," Greg agreed.

Tandy scanned the hallway in case the man returned while they were snooping around his room.

Yvette gasped.

Chapter Eleven

TANDY RAN INTO THE BATHROOM AFTER Greg, expecting the worst. She saw nothing but shiny gray subway tiles and lots of extra safety railings attached to the walls to help residents keep their balance. If Archibald needed that much help balancing, could he really be capable of running down alleyways?

Greg had his fists up in guard position like he was ready to punch someone. He'd grown protective as of late. But there was nothing for him to protect her from.

There was no body. Tandy looked around for blood, but the room was spotless. "What's wrong?" She demanded to know why Yvette had gasped.

Yvette held a hand over her mouth and pointed to an empty shelf.

Tandy looked at Greg then back at the shelf. He seemed to be as perplexed as she.

Yvette lowered her hand. "Archibald took his go-bag."

A go-bag was for emergencies. Something you packed ahead of time and hoped you never had to use. Like if you were expecting a hurricane. There were no hurricanes in Ohio, so what was Archibald trying to escape?

Padded footsteps brought murmuring residents to the door of Archibald's room before Yvette could explain.

"His go-bag?" repeated one resident with crazy eyebrows and a gruff voice. "I always thought Archibald was making up government conspiracies, but apparently he believed them."

"If he left," a frail female voice chimed in, "what will happen to Birdie?"

Yvette's hand slipped from her mouth. "That's what I'm worried about. I have to call security." She reached for her phone and giggled nervously. Her fingers trembled.

Tandy remembered how to get to Birdie's room. She could probably get there faster than Yvette could make the call. She placed a hand on Yvette's shoulder. "What's the door code for the memory ward?"

Yvette looked into Tandy's eyes, judging whether she could be trusted. She must have decided Tandy could help because she gave the number without her normal mirth.

Tandy pushed through the crowd to get to the hallway. Greg followed.

"You think he's on the run?" she asked as they jogged toward the lobby.

"From something," Greg answered in his vague way that could help him get into politics someday.

Whether Archibald was guilty or not, this made their situation that much more complicated. But at least they hadn't found him dead in his room. Would he really have been able to leave Birdie behind?

Tandy slowed at the door to memory care and tried to peek through the window in the door while punching the security code. The door buzzed, signifying that it had been unlocked. She grabbed the handle and pulled.

She barely registered Pete's appearance before he was trying to squeeze past with a lift of his trucker hat and a, "Thanks, sweetheart."

"Wait." She caught his wrist and blocked him with her body. "Where are you going, Pete?"

He pointed to the front doors with his free hand. "It's harvest season."

Greg frowned in confusion until his gaze landed on the sign warning visitors not to let Pete out. He pointed at the picture of the old farmer. "Is this you, Pete?"

"Nope." Pete shook his head, but his unmistakable grin stayed in place. "Boy howdy. That's some other bloke."

"Are you sure? Because you're wearing the same hat." Greg filled the doorway with his body and crossed his arms, nodding for Tandy to continue her mission. He would make sure Pete didn't escape.

She smiled her thanks and patted Pete's calloused hand once before jogging down the hallway. How sad for Pete that he had no more fields to plow. Though he was staying in the swankiest retirement community she'd ever seen, he was a prisoner like Connor. Hopefully, Birdie was still confined as well.

She focused on the door at the end of the hallway on her right. Crime scene tape crisscrossed it.

Her heart lurched. How had she not heard about a crime? Had Griffin beaten her here? Did he have an old-fashioned shoot-out with Archibald? Was Birdie okay?

She banged a fist on the door and offered a prayer for the woman's protection. Could prayers be retroactive?

The door swung open. Birdie's wrinkles creased deeper when she saw Tandy. Her faded blue eyes sparkled behind her clear plastic glasses. Everything appeared to be normal, but maybe something bad had happened and the woman had already forgotten.

Tandy motioned to the door. "There was a crime? What happened?"

"Crime?" Birdie echoed feebly. "Oh, you mean my door decoration?"

Decoration? Tandy's shoulders relaxed. Of course. Just because Birdie's husband didn't have a creative bone in his body, that didn't mean Birdie didn't. Though the woman couldn't have reached the top of the doorframe by herself. "You did this?"

"Not me. Some sweet kids from the high school student council came by this morning and helped us all decorate for Halloween." Birdie admired the door. "I told them they should add blood splatters like it was a real crime scene, but their teacher didn't think that was appropriate."

"Huh." And the woman seemed so sweet. "I'm just glad you're okay." Tandy peered past Birdie for the first time to see into the room. Archibald wouldn't hide out here, would he? "Are you by yourself?"

"Yes. Come in." Birdie turned around and led the way across an oriental rug to a plush couch under a wall of paintings hung in ornate frames. "I was hoping Hubert would stop by, but I haven't seen him for a while. Your name is Tammy, right?"

Tandy rolled her eyes to the ceiling. The one thing this little old lady remembered had to be Winifred's misunderstanding of her name. "Close. Have you seen Archibald?"

"Archibald," Birdie repeated like the name sounded familiar. "Oh, yes. I think my door decorations scared him too."

Crime scene tape was probably not the best décor to hang the day after an employee died, but it wasn't like Birdie remembered the man's death. At least it gave credit to her memory of Archibald stopping by. "How long ago did he leave?"

"Who?" Birdie asked.

Well. It was fun while it lasted.

"Oh, you mean Archibald. Strange old man. When I answered the door, he just kissed me on the cheek and ran off."

Tandy's heart squeezed tight. Had Archibald been kissing his wife goodbye for good? It seemed like everything he'd done, he'd done for her.

Maybe he hadn't even meant to kill Hubert with the shovel. He could have been provoked, or he might have even thought he was protecting people. Of course, then he shouldn't have tried to pin the crime on someone else.

Griffin barged in, hand on the gun in his holster. "Why is there crime scene tape on the door?"

Birdie held her hand to her heart. "My lands. Has there been a crime?"

Tandy closed her eyes at the realization she'd lost Birdie again. "No. Not here."

Greg ran in. "What happened? Is everything okay?"

"Who are you?" Birdie looked from face to face. "Are we having a party? Are there cookies?"

Tandy took Birdie's hand. She couldn't bring Archibald back, but she could offer cookies. "I have cookies at my coffee shop and tea house, and I can give you some if Yvette brings you by."

"Do you serve high tea? I have a fancy hat for high tea."

"My business partner would love to serve you high tea." Maybe that would cheer Marissa up in the midst of her wedding mess.

Griffin grimaced. "Tandy, have you seen Archibald?"

Tandy smiled sadly. "Birdie said he stopped by and kissed her on the cheek. Sounds to me like he's on the run."

Griffin stomped his foot in frustration then looked Birdie over. "How reliable is that information?"

Tandy shrugged. "Birdie said the door decorations scared Archibald too, so it sounds accurate to me."

Greg stepped forward. "Sheriff, if you have another suspect, will you be releasing my client?"

Griffin rubbed the back of his neck. "I thought if I could find Archibald Clack's fingerprints on the shovel, Connor would be free to go, but after seeing the video from The Farmstead that another resident recorded..."

"Winifred." Tandy groaned.

"Yes, Winifred." Griffin shook his head. "If Connor pushed Hubert down the stairs, he could still be guilty of manslaughter. We're going to have to wait for the autopsy report."

Marissa held out her arms, dancing the waltz with an invisible partner on her way to the shop window. Golden sunshine kissed her skin as she flipped the sign from Open to Closed. Tandy's VW Bug pulled up at the curb outside. Perfect timing. They could go together to pick up their dresses from the bridal boutique. Marissa was finally free to focus on her wedding now that Archibald was being arrested and Connor was about to be released.

She grabbed the door handle and yanked the door open for her friend. The smoky scent of logs burning in fireplaces filled the air and ruby leaves skittered across the sidewalk. "Isn't it a glorious day?"

Tandy climbed out of her car with a groan. She probably hadn't wanted to see Archibald go to jail either, but even if he'd had his heart in the right place, he'd broken the law.

"Was it hard watching Archibald be handcuffed?" Marissa sympathized. "At least he's the cranky one. It would have been even worse if someone sweet like Winifred got arrested."

Tandy trudged past and swung her little black backpack off a shoulder and onto the counter with a thud. "He wasn't arrested. He's on the run."

"Oh, no." Marissa stayed in the doorway, unsure if they were still going to the wedding shop. "But that in itself should prove his guilt. Griffin should still let Connor out."

Tandy sank down into a metal chair and kicked her boots up onto the one across from her. "Except Winifred gave him a video from her phone that makes it look like Connor pushed Hubert down the stairs."

"That hag!" Marissa jerked the chair out from under Tandy's feet and plopped into it. "Why would she do that? I bet she's really the one who hit Hubert with the shovel. She's probably just trying to frame my fiancé."

Tandy's feet thudded to the floor, forcing her upright out of her slouch. "You realize you're talking about the woman who offered to throw you a wedding shower, right?"

Marissa ran her fingers through her hair. "Only because she wants to keep her eye on me so she knows how close I get to figuring out her secrets."

"Well." Tandy leaned forward against the table, propping her chin up with a fist. "She claimed the shower was to help bring Archibald and Birdie back together, which isn't even an option right now, so I wouldn't worry about it."

"I can't believe I let her play me like this." Marissa tapped her perfectly manicured fingernails on the table. If only the video had been taken from a different angle, it would show Connor never connected with Hubert. That was it. She slammed her palm against the cool, smooth tabletop. "Does the video show how close Winifred was to Connor and Hubert? Maybe it could be used to put her in the vicinity of the shovel."

Tandy arched an eyebrow. "The woman is strong, but you have to remember, she's also big. She wasn't the person we saw running down the alley this morning."

Marissa dropped her forehead to the cool table. Her life was like the corn maze. She was blocked at every turn. Archibald had helped her get to Connor through the maze like he'd known where he and Hubert had gone, but he couldn't help her with this. "What now?"

Tandy brushed Marissa's hair to one side. The soft strands tickled her cheek. "We don't give up. We look for Archibald."

The shop phone rang from behind the counter. Normally, Marissa would let it go to voicemail after hours, but she'd given out the store phone number to all her wedding vendors, and she needed to make sure there wasn't any trouble with the photographer or catering.

When it rang again, she stood and trudged across the barnwood floor. Actual barnwood from Connor's old barn. He'd remodeled the shop for them. It was part of their love story. And now that story was going to end if she couldn't find Archibald.

"The man has a military background. He's a hunter. He knows how to hide. Finding him is going to be impossible."

The phone rang a third time, and she picked it up before it could finish. She lightened her tone to fit her cheery spiel. "Caffeine Conundrum. This is Marissa, the resident tea-lover. How can I serve you today?"

"Marissa," a rough voice addressed her. "This is Archibald."

Tingles shot through Marissa's body. The answer to all her prayers was on the other end of the line. If she said the right things, she might be able to get Connor out of jail. But what was the right thing to say? She covered the mouthpiece so she could stage whisper to Tandy, "It's Archibald."

Tandy's eyes bugged.

"What do I do?"

Tandy motioned back to the phone. "Ask him what he needs. We want him to think you're on his side."

Oh, that was good. Marissa lowered her hand to talk to the killer on the run. "What can I do for you, sir?"

Archibald coughed. "It's what I can do for you. I'm going to help you find the yahoo who wore the hockey mask so you can free your betrothed."

Marissa leaned forward to hear more clearly. She should have known better than to expect a confession, but she never expected the killer to play the hero. "The sheriff found your jacket. He thinks *you're* the yahoo."

Tandy stood and crossed the room to listen in.

Archibald grunted. "I'm not the yahoo, but he wore my jacket."

Oh, she'd never thought of that.

"I moved the jacket from the garbage can so the sheriff wouldn't assume it was me, but I wanted him to know he was looking for a man who wasn't wearing black any longer, so I told him to look for it. Then I figured I'd better disappear in case I'd become a suspect."

Did Archibald really expect her to believe that? "How did the masked man get your jacket?"

Tandy leaned across the counter to listen in.

Archibald coughed again. "For cryin' out loud. Same way he got Winifred's wig."

Tandy's eyes narrowed. She yelled loud enough for him to hear. "And I suppose the hockey mask was stolen from Pete?"

No answer.

Marissa sucked in a breath. Did the man hang up when he realized he was basically talking on a party line?

Tandy slapped a hand over her mouth.

"Hello, Tammy," the old man finally greeted.

Tammy? Marissa wanted to laugh at the name and in relief that Archibald was still there, but she needed to keep quiet to hear his response.

"I don't know where the mask came from, but I do know Hubert was involved in stealing drugs and selling them. He would have had access to our rooms." That was true. "I think he must have had a partner, and the partner must have been chompin' at the bit to take over. Maybe someone better at business."

Marissa looked into Tandy's sapphire eyes. Was the other woman buying this, and if so, where would they go from here?

Tandy met her gaze. "Someone better at business," she repeated.

Marissa's heart sunk. Because the only other guy that they knew of who'd been in the area at the time of the robbery and alleged drug deal was Austin. And he prided himself on his business skills. "Austin."

Chapter Twelve

MARISSA EYED AUSTIN AS HE SLID into the rounded booth next to her at Mama's Kitchen. After Archibald's call last night, she'd been both dreading and awaiting breakfast with her extended family. She wanted to interrogate him, but she had to play it cool. If she provoked him, he would definitely reveal to the rest of her relatives that her groom was behind bars.

She wasn't even sure if she wanted Austin to be guilty or not. He was family, so she should hope him innocent, but someone needed to go to jail, and Archibald was on the run.

"Good morning," he greeted, glancing toward the door as if to make sure his family was still far enough away that he could whisper without being overheard. "Any news on the masked man?"

She studied his smirk. Was he entertained by her pain because he'd caused it or because he was a jerk? And to think she'd started to like him.

She cupped a hand around her mouth to keep her family from listening in as they converged on the table, though with as loud as they were talking, they wouldn't be able to hear anything else. "Sheriff Griffin went to the retirement center to arrest Archibald, but he'd taken off already."

"Whoa-ho." Austin's eyebrows arched, and he leaned away in surprise. Though his smirk remained in place. "At least Connor will be able to attend the wedding now."

If only it were that easy.

Ashlee scooted into the seat next to Austin. "Why wouldn't Connor be at his own wedding?"

Marissa admired her belted plaid wrap coat before comprehending the woman's words. Then she kicked Austin in the shin with the heel of her tall gray suede boots to keep him quiet. She'd update him later on the fact that Connor wasn't released, and that Archibald suspected a businessman to see how her cousin would respond. For now, she had to figure out a way to answer Ashlee's question.

"Uh…" She was not off to a good start.

"Marissa," Austin and Ashlee's mother cooed. She slid in on Marissa's other side and pulled her into a hug. "I'm so happy you're getting married."

Marissa leaned her head on the fluffy fur trim of Aunt Linda's long sheepskin coat. The woman was happy, encouraging, and nothing like her girls. The only thing the twins seemed to inherit from her was her great taste in outerwear.

Amber seated herself on the other side of Ashlee. "Where's your groom, Marissa? And what did I hear about him not coming to the wedding? Are you going to keep wearing your ring even if you get jilted at the altar the way Austin does?"

Marissa blinked wide. Austin said he wore the ring to keep professional distance when working with women.

He avoided her gaze. Maybe this was why he was willing to keep her secret.

"What?" Aunt Linda pulled away to cup Marissa's cheek and look Marissa in the eye. "The wedding isn't called off, is it?"

Marissa's heart tripped over the possibility.

"Of course not," Austin answered for her. "She was just telling me that Connor wasn't going to be able to make breakfast this morning because of an incident at his farm, and I was joking that it was fine as long as he made it to the wedding ceremony."

Marissa exhaled, hoping his words came true.

"Don't scare me like that, honey." Aunt Linda's eyes flicked toward Austin for a moment.

Uncle Matt slid in on Aunt Linda's other side, completely penning Marissa in. "Maybe we can all take a trip out to The Farmstead later today to meet Connor."

Marissa grabbed her glass of water to help her choke down her fears. And to keep from having to respond with a lie. Austin was much better at those.

Mom and Dad pulled up chairs at the flat end of their rounded booth, so they faced her. They both beamed with pride. How would their expressions change if they knew the truth?

Marissa focused out the window at Caffeine Conundrum across the street where she wished she were working with Tandy. How long could she carry on like this?

Tandy dipped a pretzel rod in dark chocolate then rolled it in orange and yellow leaf-shaped sprinkles. Normally Marissa would be baking pumpkin cheesecake crepes, blueberry glazed cardamom donut holes, and maple-pear tarts for the display case, but she was at breakfast with her family. Tandy was in charge of the day's goodies, which was a trial run for when Marissa went on her honeymoon. She'd felt overwhelmed at first since the last time she'd tried to bake she'd set the shop on fire, but Zam had come up with this fun and fool-proof creation.

He dipped his pretzel rod in white chocolate and rolled it in bat-shaped sprinkles. "We could also make caramel apples."

"Good idea." Delicious and not too dangerous. She turned her face toward Zam so he could read her lips. "What else can we dip?"

Zam lined his latest pretzel on a piece of wax paper next to the ones she'd made. "I don't know about dipping, but my mom used to mix candy corn with peanuts. That's the only way I like candy corn."

Tandy wasn't a fan of candy corn at all but appreciated any idea that didn't involve the oven. "We could fill up those small mason jars left over from the sweet tea lemonades. Then we'll tie a bow around the jars with twine."

Zam pointed to their new business cards designed to look like a chalk art. "We could tie those on them. People will buy them as gifts, and we'll get paid to advertise."

"Brilliant." He was definitely good at the business end of things. Gave her more confidence in her creative abilities. What else could she serve for breakfast while Marissa was gone? Preferably something warm and hearty to eat as the weather turned colder. "You think I could handle oatmeal?"

Zam grinned indulgently. "How have you not starved to death yet?"

She lifted her chin. "I run on coffee and combat boots."

"Oh, yeah." Zam wiped down the counter. "Don't worry. I'll get my mom's crockpot recipe for brown sugar oatmeal. I think that's pretty hard to mess up."

See? They were fine. And hopefully Marissa was doing okay too, being that she was out to eat with the guy who very well could have killed Hubert. Depending on what Austin had to say about Archibald's claim, they'd update Sheriff Griffin.

Tandy looked out the window toward Mama's Kitchen. Despite her friend's beauty queen smile, Marissa wasn't known for being cool under pressure. Or ever.

A familiar black bus pulled to the curb, blocking Tandy's view.

"Heads up," she warned Zam. They were about to get inundated with old folks who were as hilarious as they were hazardous. But whether or not they were wearing wigs and stealing donuts, they had much life experience to offer and deserved all Tandy's attention.

He grinned at the sight of Winifred waving while being mechanically lowered to the ground in her wheelchair. "The Broadway star."

Today she wore a long, blonde, curly wig. Tandy guessed its name was Dolly, and she hoped it was a sign the woman was doing better emotionally.

Zam trotted to open the door for the group to enter. Yvette waved everyone forward in front of her before following with Winifred's wheelchair.

Pete led the charge, not because he moved fast but probably because everybody knew to stay behind his bony knees and elbows that stuck out when he walked. He grinned across the counter like he shared a secret with Tandy. She hoped it wasn't that he was going to try to escape again. "I'll take a black coffee, young lady," he ordered without looking at the menu.

"Yes, sir." Tandy grabbed the pot to pour him a mug. If everyone ordered the old-fashioned stuff, she'd have to make another pot. She looked for Yvette to ask about what kind of orders to expect.

The activities' director was already standing next to Pete at the counter. Usually her merriment entered a room before she did, but today the woman wasn't smiling. Her round face looked older without its lines being creased in laughter.

"You okay, Yvette?"

"No, I'm not." Yvette took the mug from Tandy and set it on the closest table for Pete.

Pete cackled with glee. "Heap of thanks to you," he said to Tandy before following Yvette, his torso leaning backwards as if it couldn't keep up with his legs.

Yvette returned before Pete reached his seat. "Is Marissa here? I need to talk to her."

Tandy glanced at her watch. It would probably be another hour or so before Marissa returned. "No, she's across the street at breakfast with her family. Can I help you with something?"

Yvette stood to her full height, which really wasn't very high, and looked around at her residents. Birdie and a few of the other ladies in big hats gingerly made their way up to the tea loft, and some of the men surrounded the table with a chess board painted on it. Those remaining waited in line.

"Yes." Yvette pulled a credit card out of her pocket. "Serve drinks and keep an eye on these guys for me. I have to go tell Marissa that she needs to stop encouraging Archibald with phone calls about how he might be able to pin his crimes on her cousin."

She took off toward the door, the sides of her cranberry duster flying behind her like a cape.

"Wait." Tandy stepped around the counter to stop her. Yvette couldn't confront Marissa about suspecting her cousin *in front of* her cousin. Not to mention the fact that such a confrontation would reveal to Marissa's family that Connor had been arrested for murder.

"Ma'am, could I get some coffee?" the gentleman with the crazy eyebrows called after Tandy.

She pointed Zam the man's way and made a grinding motion with both her hands in the sign for coffee. "Yvette, wait. What happened? How do you know about Marissa's cousin?"

Yvette pushed open the door and paused to look back. "Archibald called me this morning, asking to speak to Birdie. Afterwards, my cell phone went missing."

Tandy held her hands wide. She got the Archibald connection but how was Marissa to blame for Yvette's missing phone?

"Hey," Zam's thick voice carried over the hiss of steaming milk. "What happened to our pretzel sticks?"

Tandy looked up at the tea loft toward the former spy. Oh, that was impressive. "You think Birdie…?"

"Yes. Though I wasn't able to find my phone on her." The front door swung closed with a thunk. Yvette was on the other side, marching across the street.

Tandy's stomach flipped. She had to stop the train wreck. "Zam, I'm going to—"

"Block the back door," Winifred finished for her in song. "Pete just took off around the corner to the bathrooms and back exit."

Tandy closed her eyes. She wouldn't let the old guy leave on his own. It was already bad enough that Archibald had disappeared. They couldn't lose Pete too. Though, wasn't that Yvette's job? Instead the woman was going to drop a figurative bomb in the middle of Marissa's breakfast.

"You're getting your hair colored, aren't you, Marissa?"

"Yeah, your roots are showing."

And Marissa's mom wondered why Marissa didn't want to invite the twins to be bridesmaids. There was no way to win with them no matter what she said, so she'd go with the truth. "I actually just had my hair done."

Mom leaned forward, her bleached white teeth gleaming. She didn't used to be any better than the twins, but lately she'd been trying. "You're wrong, girls. Marissa's hair is the latest style. It gives her that effortless look, don't you think?"

Marissa swallowed her bite of smoky salmon omelet and smiled her thanks. She'd bet on the bull against the wolves.

"Wow," Ashlee said in a sticky sweet tone. "You're right."

"I never would have thought of that." Amber tucked a platinum strand behind an ear as if to better display her lack of dark roots. "By effortless, do you mean lazy?"

Mom leveled Amber with a challenging stare. "I mean natural."

Austin chuckled. "Do you two even know your natural hair color anymore?"

Ashlee tossed her locks like she hadn't heard while Amber scowled.

Aunt Linda gave a breathy laugh. "I think you're glowing, Marissa. Love looks good on you."

Marissa smiled at the compliment and at the memory of how Connor had helped her overcome her desire to please people like this. "Thank you." Maybe she'd see if Aunt Linda wanted to visit the tea loft by herself later.

Uncle Matt reached for the bill like he always did. "Your groom must be one great guy."

Austin arched his eyebrows but kept his mouth shut. Apparently, Marissa hadn't had as much to worry about with him as she'd thought.

The front door whooshed opened, and a breeze cooled Marissa's sweaty skin. She could finally relax. Except angry footsteps announced the arrival of someone new.

Yvette's rosy round cheeks matched the sweater she wore, and for some reason she wasn't laughing.

Dad held up a hand to stop the woman. "Excuse me, ma'am. This is a family breakfast."

"Oh, yeah?" She planted her hands on her curvy hips and laughed wildly. "Then where is Marissa's fiancé?"

Marissa's heart plummeted. All heads turned to watch her face heat up. Of all the people she'd thought would tell her secret, she never imagined it would be Yvette. "He couldn't...he couldn't be here," she stammered and considered crawling underneath the table to escape.

"You're right he couldn't be here." Yvette nodded once, her double chin jiggling. "Because he's in jail for manslaughter."

Mom gasped.

Aunt Linda gripped Marissa's arm.

Uncle Matt leaned forward, likely pulled by his drooping jaw.

Ashlee's eyes lit up.

Amber's lips twitched.

Austin leaned back to watch.

All the while, Marissa held a hand to her chest to keep her heart from pumping right out.

Dad stood to defend her. "That's not true."

"It *is* true. My coworker died in the corn maze Monday." Yvette narrowed her eyes. "Not only did Marissa's fiancé get arrested, but she suspects her cousin here might actually be a killer, thief, and drug dealer."

Marissa watched for Austin's reaction, heart in her throat. But it was the twins who put on a show.

Ashlee's mouth dropped wide. "What?"

Amber turned to glare at Marissa. "You think I'm a murderer?"

Austin shrugged a shoulder in response to his sister. "If looks could kill..."

Yvette waved a hand to dismiss the twins. "Not them." She pointed at Austin. "You."

Austin sat upright and turned on Marissa as if she'd betrayed him. "After I kept your secret?" he demanded.

"I..." How did one properly explain to her family why she suspected her cousin of the crime her fiancé had been arrested for?

Mom's hands pressed against her cheeks in a gesture that Marissa often made. "You knew?" she demanded of Austin.

"Hey." Uncle Matt held up a hand. "Austin didn't do anything. He may have let his fiancée take advantage of him, but he certainly isn't engaged to a criminal and lying about it."

Aunt Linda's light green eyes darkened in condemnation. "Marissa," she scolded.

Dad stared down in disbelief. He motioned toward Yvette. "Is this true?"

Marissa gaped at the man who was supposed to walk her down the aisle and give her away. Looked like she might have to elope now. "No," she blurted the half-truth.

Yvette crossed her arms.

Why was *she* so upset? And why was she even here?

"Well, Connor is in jail. But only because he tried to resuscitate a man who was hit with a shovel on his farm." Her belly churned. She really shouldn't have ordered fish for breakfast. "Since he's in jail, we know he didn't rob the pharmacy or try to sell the drugs. Someone else is out there, and he is probably the same person who killed Hubert. I just have to prove it before my wedding day."

"So you're blaming my son for it?" Uncle Matt retrieved his credit card from the tiny leather folder that held the check before he got charged. "After all we've done for you, Marissa."

Marissa reached a hand toward him. Not because buying breakfast absolved his children from criminality, but because she didn't want to seem ungrateful. "I'm not blaming him, but he was the only man dressed in black at the scene of a crime."

Yvette chuckled crazily. Even for Yvette. "You're forgetting Archibald who tried to hide his black coat from the police."

Marissa wrinkled her nose. There was that.

Aunt Linda watched the argument like a ping-pong match, her eyes reflecting the uncertainty of which team to cheer for. "Who is Archibald?"

Yvette folded her arms. "He's a resident of the retirement community where I work. He's on the run but left his wife behind because she has Alzheimer's. He called me to check on her this morning. When I tried to talk him into turning himself in, he said he was going to help Marissa find the real criminal, and that she suspected her cousin."

No wonder Yvette was angry. But now everyone else would be angry at her too.

"The cloak and dagger needs to stop, Marissa." Yvette leaned forward. "I overheard Connor say he's taking a drug that makes him moody. So you might as well accept the possibility that your fiancé is a killer because he's mixed up with drugs himself."

Marissa sunk into the seat cushion, not sure from whose view she most wanted to hide.

Chapter Thirteen

TANDY CLIMBED THE STAIRS WITH THE silver tea set. She might not have been able to help Marissa by stopping Yvette in time to keep from destroying her breakfast, but she could serve high tea in Marissa's tearoom.

Birdie and her buddies had all put on big floppy hats for the occasion. And sure enough, under Birdie's colorful brim, a trace of dark chocolate proved she had indeed swiped Tandy's pretzels. Should Tandy add the purchase to Yvette's bill or consider it on the house to help appease the angry activities' director?

"Thank you, Tammy." Birdie lifted her wrinkled chin to be able to see Tandy from underneath her turquoise hat with the peacock plumes. "Do you like my hat?"

It wasn't a hat Tandy would normally admire, but on Birdie, it added to her charm. "Yes," she said, though she couldn't help wondering if the old woman had purchased it or simply swiped it off a mannequin.

Birdie looked her up and down. "I see you dressed for Halloween."

Tandy set the tea tray down and dished out Marissa's teacups with the Jack-o-lantern faces before looking down at her leggings and bulky black sweater. This was how she normally dressed.

"You need a headband with cat ears," another of the ladies added in a warbly voice. "I used to have some from an old costume, and I'd let you borrow them, but I didn't see them when I was getting out my hat earlier."

Tandy poured the steaming rosemary tea. Marissa had taught her that rosemary was supposed to help with memory, and she'd figured Birdie could use it. "That's okay. I don't need your cat ears. I wouldn't want to give anybody bad luck by crossing their path."

The women tittered.

The one with the warbly voice joked, "Either I'm getting more forgetful or there's a thief at Grace Springs Manor."

Tandy smiled at the cat burglar in the group before turning to go. She'd have to ask Marissa if there was a tea that helped former spies not steal things.

"My lands. That reminds me." Birdie held up a fragile hand to stop her. "I wanted to give you something."

Tandy lowered the empty tray to her side so she could take whatever Birdie had brought her. She couldn't imagine what it might be.

The old woman reached into an inside pocket of her trench coat and retrieved a smart phone with a sparkly case.

Tandy sighed. Should she be disappointed that Birdie had swiped Yvette's phone or glad she could give it back?

Birdie held it out. "In case you don't believe Yvette had her eye on Hubert. Look."

Tandy took the device, running her thumb over the screen to confirm it belonged to Yvette. With what she knew Birdie was capable of, it could belong to Joseph Cross, and the woman could have used it to hack into his computer network and be holding all his digital files for ransom. It wouldn't be the first time that happened to him.

But no. The photo used as wallpaper on the phone showed an image of Yvette laughing with Hubert. Tandy tilted her head as she studied the image. It was no surprise that Yvette was laughing in the pic, but why had she saved a photo of Hubert when she'd wanted him fired? Could Birdie be right, and Yvette was trying to hide their relationship for some reason?

Tandy watched the old woman return to sipping her tea and chatting with her friends like she hadn't just committed petty theft. Was she as innocent as she seemed, or could she be as good at playing forgetful as she was at swiping electronics?

Tandy couldn't rule out the fact that Archibald was a suspect too. Perhaps he'd prompted Birdie to swipe the phone from Yvette since the activities' director wanted him to turn himself in—or because he wanted to be able to get ahold of Birdie more easily.

Would it be snooping if Tandy tried to crack the code on Yvette's phone? Not that there was anything wrong with snooping. It solved crimes.

Marissa clung to the vinyl booth seat as if it were her life preserver. After Yvette rocked the boat, she sailed. Uncle Matt and Aunt Linda stormed out as well, followed by Mom and Dad, who seemed more concerned with smoothing things over on the surface than helping Marissa deal with the deep issues.

Ashlee reapplied her lipstick in a compact mirror and popped her lips. "Awkward..."

Amber gave a pout like she was the one wearing fresh lipstick. "I guess there are worse things than falling off the stage at a beauty pageant."

They both stood and flipped their hair in unison before strutting away.

Marissa closed her eyes and waited for Austin to leave. Once she was alone, she'd be able to breathe again.

"I'll get the bill," he offered.

She peeked one eye open. Was Austin kidding? After he'd found out she suspected him of murder?

He gave a half smile though his hooded eyes expressed more amusement than sympathy. "If I'm selling drugs, I should have plenty of cash."

Marissa rolled her eyes to heaven. She wasn't sure if she should be angry or apologetic, and God was the only One who would have any solutions for the mess that was her life.

"I'm kidding, though I will pay for breakfast." Austin sniffed. "It was kinda nice to see my dad defend me for once. Thanks for that."

Marissa bit her lip. She never would have expected Austin to be the one to stick around after the rest of her family deserted her. Especially after she accused him of murder. Did she really think he could be guilty?

He pulled his credit card from his wallet. "You don't really care who did it, do you? You just want your fiancé out of jail, even if he's the guilty one."

The idea that Connor could have committed murder never crossed Marissa's mind, nor the possibility he stole or sold drugs. Yeah, some people had secret lives, and addicts were often desperate enough to do things they never would normally do, but Connor wasn't either secretive or codependent. She'd been the one to make mistakes, and he'd stuck by her. She would do the same for him.

Marissa lifted her left hand and looked at her antique engagement ring. She knew Connor well enough to know he hadn't committed any crimes, but she wondered about killers who lied to their wives, and their wives had no idea what they'd done. How did they feel afterwards? Did they leave them? Did they still love them?

She would. And truth would only help her love better.

She sighed. "I want the truth. Whether it's Connor or whether it's you, I'll still love you."

Austin waved the leather folder for the waitress to pick up. "I like that idea. Maybe that's what I like about you now. You've changed."

Marissa studied him. He'd changed too. Not necessarily for the better but like he wanted better. And she wanted it for him.

Tandy's pulse raced her footsteps down the stairs from the tea loft. She scanned her shop for Yvette, even though it was likely she'd probably hear the woman laughing before she saw her. No sign of her inside.

Tandy peered out the window to the street. The view should have been bright and cheery with blue sky above storefronts and bright leaves on the small trees that lined the sidewalks. But there was also a small group of people who seemed to be pointing and yelling at each other. With all the blondes, that had to be Marissa's family.

Tandy grimaced. She didn't see Marissa in the mess, but she spotted Yvette's curvy frame and cranberry duster, which gave Tandy a little time to check out the woman's phone.

She continued on to the kitchen and out of sight. Safely hidden behind the curtain that divided the dining area, she pulled out the cool, slick phone she'd tucked up her sleeve. She took a deep breath and swiped a finger over the screen again.

The photo of Yvette and Hubert popped up once again. The man looked to be around Yvette's same age with wire-rimmed glasses, a mustache, and dark brown hair long enough to part down the middle. And Tandy had thought only high school kids took seasonal jobs at pumpkin patches.

If he had been stealing drugs, it was weird that Yvette had made it her wallpaper. Now Tandy needed to figure out how to crack the security code so she could check out texts between the two of them and see what kind of relationship they really had.

With as jumpy as she felt just looking at a phone that belonged to a possible killer, she would make a horrible spy. But if Birdie could do it, so could she, especially with what Marissa was probably going through across the street.

Tandy started by swiping across the top dots and diagonally down to the left corner as if drawing the number seven. Because seven should be lucky. But nope. The screen wiggled as if shaking its head at her.

She peeked around the curtain before continuing. She hadn't heard the door open or close, and her senses were on high alert, but she wanted to be sure. Safe for the moment.

She studied the phone again and tried swiping a shark fin. Denied.

A box? Nada.

If she tried too many times, she could get herself locked out. In which case Yvette would know she'd tried to crack her code.

The curtain parted.

Tandy's heart misfired, shooting tingles through her body. She screamed, almost dropping Yvette's phone in the process. She juggled it a few times then clutched it to her stomach before it clattered to the floor.

Zam stood in front of her, holding up another kitchen creation. "It's not a real spider. Calm down."

Tandy's chest heaved with every breath she gulped to regain her composure. Yvette hadn't caught her, and Zam didn't even know what she was doing.

He looked from her to the creepy peanut butter ball in his hand. "I added cocoa powder to turn it black, then I used licorice for the legs and edible googly eyes."

They'd hired Zam for the drink mixing skills he'd learned as a bartender, but his talent with baked goods rivaled that of any preschool mom. He looked up proudly, waiting for her to respond.

She had to say something so he didn't get suspicious. "Edible googly eyes make the world a better place."

He grinned mischievously. "They'll make my world a better place because if Marissa's snooty cousins get too close to me again, I'm going to try to freak them out with one of these. Hopefully, they react the same way you did."

"Uh... yeah."

The door to the shop swung open behind him. Yvette breezed in with a few crisp leaves. So much for cracking the password on the woman's phone before she returned. But maybe Tandy could ask questions instead.

Yvette laughed and waved, back to her normal self as she bounced Tandy's way. "Oh, I feel much better now that I got all that off my chest. Did you realize that Marissa hadn't even told her family that Connor was in jail? It's like, 'What's she hiding?'"

Somebody was hiding something, but it wasn't Marissa anymore. And it wasn't Tandy.

"Hey!" Yvette pointed to the phone Tandy didn't put back up her sleeve fast enough. "You got my cell from Birdie. I checked her pockets. Where did you find it?"

Tandy's fingers itched to hold onto the device, but she handed it over, making sure to hit the side button to light it up as she did. The wallpaper photo flashed before them.

Tandy nodded at the image. "Was that Hubert?" she asked like it wasn't weird for it to be displayed there.

"Yeah," Yvette looked down with a giggle. "He wasn't my favorite person, but I'm sad he's gone. I decided to post his pic here in memoriam until after his funeral."

Tandy nodded her understanding. She might do the same for someone she worked with even if they frustrated her. Like Sheriff Griffin.

Hey, perhaps Griffin had Hubert's phone at the police station. They could check Yvette's texts from that end.

Chapter Fourteen

MARISSA JUST WANTED TO SEE CONNOR. It wasn't like he could make anything better, but she could be there for him.

She waited until her family dispersed from the little spectacle they'd put on in the street and Yvette left their shop to climb back on her bus before she trudged across the street to her shop. The place had cleared out after their morning rush, and only a few remaining residents straggled toward their ride home to Grace Springs Manor. Marissa sank onto a metal barstool and rested her forehead against the cool counter. If Tandy and Zam could do without her for a while longer, she'd head over to the jail.

"I'm not sure whether to cancel my wedding cake or ask Bunny to bake a file into it."

"What did she say?" Zam asked Tandy since he couldn't read her lips from her facedown position.

"She's trying to decide between canceling her wedding cake order or baking a file into it and delivering it to Connor in jail."

"The file sounds exciting." Zam chose for her. "Do that."

"Goodbye," a couple of ladies called as they passed on their way out the front door.

"'Bye," Zam and Tandy called back.

Something bright and fluffy waved off to the side of Marissa's eye. She turned her head to lie on her cheek and get a better view of the women in crazy hats. "Is Birdie wearing feathers?" Maybe that's where the woman got her name.

"Yep," Tandy answered proudly. "I served them high tea."

So not fair. Marissa had to serve her cousins at Skary-oke while Tandy got to serve a bunch of cute little old ladies in fancy hats. She lifted her face so she could communicate with her manager as well as her co-owner. "Even if the file in the cake worked, which I don't know if it ever has in the history of the world—"

"Actually," Zam held up a finger. "You'd probably have better luck drugging a cake to put the sheriff to sleep. That's worked in history."

Tandy tilted her head at him. "I'm disturbed you know this."

Marissa tried to remember what kind of cake Griffin liked best, but then shook the idea out of her head for reasons including, but not limited to... "Even if I got Connor out, my family wouldn't want to come to my wedding now that they think he's a criminal. We'd have to elope."

"Vegas?" Zam guessed.

"Costa Rica," Tandy corrected.

Marissa stared at the crazies, jaw slacked. "Not helping." She reburied her face against the counter.

Tandy rubbed her back. "Rough breakfast?"

"Here." Zam set a spider down on the counter in front of her face.

Marissa shrieked and jumped backward before realizing the blob was just a chocolate peanut butter ball. Her pulse settled into its normal pace. A fake spider wasn't the worst of her problems.

"Zam!" she admonished.

"Sorry." His crooked smile belied his apology. "I thought you'd like to see what I'm selling in place of your pecan pie cookies."

"Yeah?" She reached into her blush-colored double-breasted dress coat pocket. "I'll leave you to sell those while I go see Connor."

Tandy grabbed a denim jacket and buffalo checked scarf then followed her toward the door. "I need to ask Sheriff Griffin some questions too."

Tandy filled Marissa in on her suspicions of Yvette during the short drive to the police station. She wanted her friend to have some hope that neither her fiancé nor her cousin would end up in jail, and she was probably not Yvette's biggest fan after the way the woman had confronted her at a family breakfast.

Marissa parked at the curb by the tall, skinny brick building that looked more quaint and charming than any jail should. She pulled her keys from the ignition and turned to face Tandy. "As much as I want to believe Yvette is a cute little giggly perp, it doesn't fit. She's too curvy to be the person who robbed the pharmacy or ran from us down the alley. So that would mean the drug dealing is unrelated. Which could be, but that leaves Yvette hitting her boyfriend with a shovel in the cornfield for no reason. We know there wasn't a love triangle with a resident of Grace Springs Manor. Not only that, if she did kill him, why would she both try to hide the relationship and keep his photo on her phone?"

Tandy twisted her lips to one side. "Maybe they'd just broken up. And she was afraid it would make her a suspect, but she still wanted to look at his face."

Marissa gave a sad smile before tugging her door handle and climbing out. "Did a little Birdie tell you that?"

"Pretty much." Tandy followed suit with a huff. "Though I'm going to see if Griffin has Hubert's phone. Then he can look at their texts and find out if there is any credence to it."

"Okay." Marissa headed toward the door. "I have to go break the news to Connor that his future in-laws think he's a drug-dealing murderer."

"I don't envy you." Tandy strode into the warm room, glad Greg wasn't the one behind bars, and glad he'd given her a chance to prove herself innocent when she had been. "But you know what?" She paused and waited for Marissa to enter and close the door behind them, thus chasing her chill away. "Now that Connor's arrest is public, we can start asking townsfolk for help."

Marissa signed in at the front desk under Kristin's watchful eye. "I'll let you do that if you want, Tandy. I'm tired of having people scrutinize my life, waiting for me to mess up again."

Kristin looked away. "I'll get Griffin for you." She headed down a hallway to where Tandy had once been locked up.

Tandy looked out the window at the seemingly benign streets. She'd spread the word about Connor's arrest around town. Even if nobody had clues from what had already happened, they would keep their eyes open to help Connor.

The sheriff stepped into the hallway and waved Marissa toward him. "Come on down, Marissa. I'll bring out Connor to see you."

Marissa bit her lip before striding past Tandy with the clip-clop of her high heeled boots.

Tandy lifted her hand to get the sheriff's attention. "I wanted to talk to you too, Griffin."

The man nodded, his wide-brimmed hat bobbing. "Kristin," he looked back into the room from where he'd come. "Have Romero get Connor so I can help Tandy."

130

Tandy looked around the small front office as she waited. An orange bottle of prescription drugs on Kristin's desk caught Tandy's eye. She should ask if Hubert had drugs on him too.

The sheriff took a seat at his desk by the back wall and motioned Tandy to sit across from him. "If Greg hasn't answered your questions due to client-attorney privilege, I won't be able to either," he warned.

Tandy slowly lowered into a plastic chair, surveying his desk to see if there was anything that would answer questions for her. Just a bunch of paperwork and folders that seemed to be about strategizing security for the upcoming holiday parade. "What if my questions are about the drugstore robbery?"

Griffin leaned forward, forearms on his desk. "Are they?"

"Yes." Kinda. "Did Hubert have drugs on him when he died?"

Griffin narrowed his eyes. "That seems to be directly related to Connor."

"It's related to drugs," she insisted. "If Hubert had drugs on him, the same person who stole from the pharmacy might have killed him."

Griffin cleared his throat. "If there were drugs on him, I wouldn't be able to answer this question, but the fact is that there were not."

Tandy ground her teeth. There went that theory. Unless... "Perhaps he was killed as part of a theft."

Griffin sighed. "When we catch Archibald, we will take his fingerprints and compare them to those on the shovel. If they match, we can ask about drugs."

If Archibald had killed Hubert, it was probably to stop him from taking drugs. Which made her wonder... "Were there drugs in his system?"

"Now that I cannot answer."

"Yes!" That was all the answer she needed.

The sheriff stood. "I've said more than I should." He headed past her toward the hallway.

"Wait." Tandy jumped to her feet to follow. She hadn't yet found out what she came for. "Griffin, I came to ask about Hubert's phone." She scurried after him. "I have reason to believe Hubert was in a relationship with Yvette. Have you checked his phone for texts between the two of them? That could give you more leads."

He reached the door to the room with a window revealing Marissa inside. He grabbed the handle like he was about to go in, and Tandy guessed she wouldn't be allowed.

He stopped and stared at her. "Hubert only had a burner phone on him. No contacts were saved, and all correspondence deleted."

Tandy's mouth fell open. "Doesn't that prove he's the criminal you should be investigating, and not Connor?"

"Killing a criminal is still a crime."

True. But where did that leave them?

The door swung open and Connor stepped into the visitor's room, wearing dark blue scrubs, golden stubble on his chin, and gray shadows under his eyes like an overworked doctor. He trudged in, and his muted movements lacked their usual energy. But his gaze was electric as he focused on Marissa. Even with his current condition and unknown future, he seemed to be more concerned for her wellbeing.

Tears blurred her vision, and she blinked away the weakness. She had to be strong for him.

Marissa shoved to her feet, the metal chair legs scraping across the floor. Then she was in his arms, aware all over again of how much she missed his sawdust scent and solid frame. He was her home.

She closed her eyes as if she were lying down on her couch at the end of a long day. His shoulder pillowed her cheek. His heartbeat ticked down their time together. His lips brushed the top of her head.

"Oh, honey," he choked out.

Her throat clogged, and she clung tighter to let him know what she was thinking before she was able to speak. She could tell him about her breakfast. About chasing the perp in the alley. About Archibald's phone call and angry Yvette. But none of that mattered as much as him knowing she was here for him. Nothing mattered as much as this embrace.

"How are you doing?" he finally asked. "Are you safe?"

No. Her home was currently built on shifting sand. But he needed to know they would withstand this storm together. "Yes."

He chuckled, his chest rumbling against hers. "You say that like you don't have a history of being thrown from steamboats, chased down by cars, and trapped in burning buildings."

"This is worse." Those experiences had been scary, but not as scary as this. Because in each of those situations, he'd been there for her. But she didn't have it as bad as he did. "How are *you* doing?"

He gave his half smile. "Griffin let me listen to Monday night football on the radio, so that was nice."

She sighed. "I'm going to get you out of here so that next Monday we can listen from Costa Rica."

Connor backed up far enough to run his eyes over her face. As if wanting to commit her appearance to memory in case he never saw her again. "You can't promise that, Marissa. What if

I am tried and convicted? What if it's years before I get released from prison?"

Marissa reached to cover his hand with both of hers. She looked at their entwined fingers for a moment, waiting for the dampness in her eyes to dry so he wouldn't know how scared she was. She took a deep breath, squeezed, and met his gaze. "You're innocent. They'll let you out."

He didn't squeeze back. "If I'm proven guilty in a court of law, I'll be punished. And I don't want you to be punished with me."

Marissa's heart constricted. She couldn't accept such a possibility. "I'll marry you in jail."

He gave his crooked smile. "You didn't even want to marry me with shaggy hair."

She shrugged. "There probably wouldn't be a photographer at a prison wedding, so I'll let it slide."

He lifted her hands between them. "You thought being known as the beauty queen who fell off the stage was bad. This would be a million times worse."

She gave her bravest smile. "You've been there for me, so I'm going to be there for you. Love never fails."

Connor kissed her hand. "Our love fails all the time. It's only God's love that doesn't fail. That's the reason we include Him in our wedding vows. The reason that no matter what happens in this investigation, we will both be okay."

Marissa didn't want to be okay. She didn't want her groom to have to sing worship songs in jail like the apostle Paul. She wanted happily-ever-after. And she wanted it now.

Chapter Fifteen

MARISSA SLID SUNGLASSES UP HER NOSE even though the afternoon was dark and rainy outside Caffeine Conundrum. She'd spent the night wrestling with God over whether the idea of His love never failing meant that Connor would have justice on earth or only once he got to heaven. Her insomnia hadn't left her with any answers, and it had contributed to her sleeping through her morning alarm. This left her with less time to track down Hubert's killer, but more determination...along with the dark circles under her eyes. Though that wasn't the only reason she was currently hiding behind her shades. She also didn't want Austin to see she was watching him.

She concealed herself behind the curtain to the kitchen as her cousin sipped his Frappuccino and scrolled through his phone. Why was he drinking coffee? He'd had tea when they'd made muffins together. So suspicious.

Zam stepped in front of her with a plateful of pretzels dipped in orange chocolate, most likely to resemble pumpkins since green M&Ms had been stuck to the top of each twist, presumably in the place of a stem. "What do you think?" he asked.

Marissa scooped up a handful of the pumpkin pretzels and popped one in her mouth. She needed something to nibble on to calm her nerves. The sweet white chocolate mixed with the salty pretzel satiated her cravings. "Perfect."

"It's hard to read your lips when you talk with food in your mouth."

Tandy joined them, swiping a pretzel for herself. "Marissa said perfect. Though I think dipping rice crispy treats in green chocolate and adding edible googly eyes to make them look like Frankenstein heads would have been more perfect."

Even though Marissa wanted to keep focused on her cousin, she couldn't help imagining the treat Tandy described. She frowned. "Rice crispy treats are for elementary schoolers."

Zam nodded. "That's what I said."

Marissa looked down at the pretzel pumpkins with new understanding. "You two can't bake, so you're just dipping things in chocolate."

Zam grinned proudly.

Tandy reached for a mini mason jar on the shelf. "Well, we mixed peanuts with candy corn too."

Marissa closed her eyes. She needed to prove Connor innocent and go on their honeymoon so she could return in time to bake her sugar cookie truffles, candy cane cheesecake, and meringue Christmas trees.

"I think she's stunned by our brilliance," Zam stated.

"No, I'm pretty sure she's mourning for our customers."

"How can you tell? She's wearing sunglasses."

"Why are you wearing sunglasses inside, Marissa?"

Marissa held a finger to her lips then pointed past them to where Austin stood. He waved their direction before heading toward the door.

Marissa ducked. "Did he see me?"

Tandy and Zam waved goodbye. Hopefully, their bodies hid hers.

Zam chuckled. "I understand wanting to hide from your other cousins, but not him. What's up?"

Marissa scooted Zam out of the way so she could rush to the door in a crouched position. "I'm going to follow him." She peeked out the window to see Austin climbing inside a silver SUV.

Tandy followed to the window, not even bothering to hide out of sight. She crossed her arms and watched Austin pull on his seatbelt. "If you'd wanted to blend in, you shouldn't have worn red boots."

Marissa looked down at her rainboots in surprise. At least they weren't yellow. "I wore rubber boots because they are the quietest when I walk."

"You've never heard of running shoes?"

Was she going to have to run? Marissa twisted her hair and tucked it up underneath a wide-brimmed hat.

An engine revved outside. The SUV. Well, now she'd have to run. She grabbed the door handle. "Gotta go."

Tandy tugged Marissa's free hand to hold her in place. "Wait." She dug in her pocket. Keys jingled. "He knows your Jeep. I'll drive."

Marissa didn't have time to lose. She checked on Zam over her shoulder. "You good?"

He shot them a thumbs up then continued juggling miniature pumpkins for their customers.

Tandy pulled up the hood to her camo sweatshirt before leading the charge into the drizzle. Marissa chased after her, shivering in her taupe knit poncho. It wasn't exactly as rainproof as her boots, but the hat helped shield her a little. As for the sunglasses, they blurred with the drops of liquid.

Tandy clicked her remote and unlocked the doors to her little bug. Marissa dove into the backseat to stay covert.

Tandy stopped and stared at her. "You know this makes you even more conspicuous, right?"

Only because Tandy was standing there like a scarecrow. Marissa waved her forward. "Hop in. He's getting away."

Tandy slipped behind the wheel, started the engine, and eased onto the street.

Marissa tugged off her glasses and slid to the floor to peer between the front seats without being seen from anyone outside the vehicle. The SUV disappeared around the corner at the end of the block. "He turned left." If Austin had been heading back to her parents' house, he would have turned right.

"I see him, Dick Tracy."

Tandy turned, and Marissa gripped the top of the seatbacks to keep from falling over. "Do you think he knows we're following him?"

"He hasn't sped up or anything."

As the neighborhoods gave way to rolling hills, a giant stenciled sign for The Farmstead directed visitors to take the next right. Marissa sucked in a breath. "Is he returning to the scene of the crime?"

The SUV continued by the entrance to the pumpkin patch.

Tandy's head swiveled to look at it as they passed. "Apparently not, but we should. Griffin said Hubert didn't have a regular phone on him. Maybe it fell out of his pocket when he got hit with the shovel. We should go look tonight."

"Good idea." Marissa glanced down at her boots. They would serve her well for traipsing through mud as well as sneaking up on potential murderers. And the red color wouldn't stand out nearly as much as Dick Tracy's trench coat would have. "Isn't it weird that Dick Tracy wore yellow? I'd think *that* would have been very conspicuous."

"He had an image to uphold," Tandy reasoned.

"As do I." Marissa gave a curt nod. She could understand the importance of looking the part.

"I'm sorry I gave you a bad time about the red boots. They're not the worst thing you've ever worn."

"Thank you," Marissa said before realizing the compliment was backhanded. "Hey!" She scrunched her eyebrows together to help think of a comeback. Something about Tandy dressing like G.I. Jane might work.

"He's turning into Grace Springs Manor."

Marissa's spine jerked straight, and she forgot about her wardrobe. "No..." She leaned forward to get a better view. "We don't have any family here."

"Maybe he has a crush on Birdie too."

"That's dangerous," Marissa whispered. "Everyone who supposedly likes Birdie either gets killed or disappears."

Tandy pulled into the lot and parked between a pickup and compact car. Austin climbed out of his SUV and pulled a beanie over his spiky blonde hair. He grabbed his Frappuccino and took it with him toward the front door.

"I'm glad to see he likes my coffee."

Had he only drunk tea with Marissa to get on her good side? She narrowed her eyes. "Honestly, who drinks a cold drink on a cold day? I find that very fishy."

"Maybe he's bringing the drink for someone who is warm and cozy inside." Tandy ducked when he looked their way. "Winifred drank an iced coffee on her last visit."

"He's here to steal another wig." Marissa pictured him wearing long blonde curls. "Or maybe not."

Tandy pushed her door open and stood. "There's one way to find out." She swung the back door wide for Marissa since it took her a moment to climb off the floor of the car.

They kept themselves hidden behind vehicles as long as they could before running under the portico to the sliding glass doors. Marissa's gaze lit on Austin's dark beanie at the front desk on the far side of the massive lobby as they entered near a black and orange balloon arch.

Her rubber boots made a small squeaking sound, but Tandy's combat boots clomped like horse hooves. She might as well have worn a yellow trench coat with as much attention as she'd draw their way.

Austin turned from where he'd been talking to the front desk manager as if he were going to look back their way. Marissa panicked, shoving Tandy behind one side of the balloon arch before taking cover on the other side. She stood stick straight and pressed her body against the latex, knocking the hat off her head. The top strands of her hair lifted to stick themselves to the balloon arch with static electricity. Hopefully, both her hair and the hat remained hidden.

Tandy was hidden, but with her dark hair braided, she didn't have the same static electricity problem. She just rubbed a shoulder and sent Marissa a mock glare.

Maybe Marissa had pushed a little too hard. "Sorry," she signed by circling her fist around her torso.

Unfortunately, her extreme measure would be for naught, because the glass doors slid open once again and the owner of Grace Springs Manor blew in, dressed in a navy three-piece suit. Joseph Cross was sure to give their hiding place away. He stopped before crossing under the balloon arch.

"Good morning, Mr. Cross," said the clerk from the front desk. "Is there anything I can do for you today?"

Cross stroked his meticulously trimmed silver beard. "No, no." He motioned toward the desk. "Please, continue helping our guest."

"Yes, sir."

Marissa brushed her hair down and peeked around the arch to ensure Austin had returned to his conversation and had his back to them once again. She bit her lip and looked to Mr. Cross. Too bad he didn't know sign language too.

The man's tanned forehead wrinkled above dark eyebrows that either he had colored or they'd never turned silver. He looked from Tandy to Marissa then back, obviously curious as to what they were doing but almost hesitant to find out. After a pause, he shook his head, waved away his questions, and kept walking.

It kind of reminded Marissa of that scene in *The Apple Dumpling Gang* where Don Knotts and Tim Conway were trying to rob a bank, but the townsfolk waved them off as harmless. She might be offended if not for the fact that Cross's indifference kept them from being discovered by her cousin.

Tandy pointed after Mr. Cross and bugged her eyes as if to say, "That was weird." Marissa shrugged in an "I dunno" sort of way.

The echo of Mr. Cross's footsteps faded enough for her to make out Austin's conversation. The employee said, "I'll page the activities' director for you."

Her cousin was in cahoots with Yvette! Marissa covered her mouth to keep from gasping. So that's why the woman was so mad about her suggesting to Archibald that Austin might be the perp. Because he was. And she knew it.

Tandy's mouth fell open. She pointed Austin's direction then made a heart with her hands before straightening her fingers to turn the shape into a triangle. She was saying Birdie had been right about a love triangle including Yvette and Hubert, it just hadn't included the old woman.

Marissa wanted to nod, but the love triangle was hard to imagine. Even if she looked at her cousin objectively, he was a big step up from Hubert. Plus, she'd seen some of the women he'd dated. They were never as short or round as Yvette.

But it did make sense that if the activities' director was involved somehow, there had to be another criminal running around town in a hockey mask. And what other reason would these two have for meeting up?

A door buzzed open from the memory ward. Marissa peeked through a couple of black balloons, her hair returning to stick to them like a magnet. She smoothed the strands in order to see Yvette breeze into the lobby. Today her duster was sleeveless and forest green, and it flew behind her like the cape of a super villain. How had Marissa never seen this before?

Yvette strode to the counter. "What are you doing here?"

Marissa held her breath to hear Austin's response. It would tell her everything.

Unfortunately, Yvette seemed to be every bit as focused because she totally missed Farmer Pete catching the door to the memory ward before it closed behind her. He was going to successfully sneak out.

The man wearing his trademark suspenders and a John Deere hat gave a toothy grin and headed Marissa's direction. His funny walk turned out to be a tiptoe with as quiet as he was able to keep his cowboy boots. Tandy lunged in front of the entrance to block the doors with her body, but her movement only made the doors slide open.

Austin and Yvette were too wrapped up in whatever they were talking about to notice her, but if Tandy stayed there, they would. Marissa plowed Tandy from her spot and back into her hiding place behind one side of the balloon arch.

Pete drew closer.

Tandy gripped Marissa's shoulders. "We can't let him escape," she whispered.

"We can't let Austin and Yvette see us either," Marissa whispered back. Though they were totally missing the mismatched couple's current conversation, they needed to see what happened next.

"We've got to get them to see Pete and stop him then." Tandy looked around as if for help. "If we throw something his direction, it would make a noise, and they'd look up."

Marissa's hair glued itself to her face when she let go of it to search her pockets for a coin or anything she could throw. Empty. There had to be something. Pete was getting closer. She slid her hands down her body for whatever she could find. Without another thought, she ripped off a red rubber boot and hurled it blindly toward the door to Memory Care.

"Your shoe?" Tandy questioned, but it was too late. They watched the boot fly through the air, big, red, and rubbery.

It landed softly, with a gentle whisper. Marissa looked toward Yvette and Austin to see if they noticed. Nope, they hadn't even looked up.

"Ugh." Tandy let go of Marissa's shoulder and squeezed at a balloon. "I don't have fingernails. Help me pop this."

If only Marissa had thought of that before tossing her boot. She gripped a balloon and flexed her fingers to curl her nails into the latex, but her new acrylic nails were too thick to be sharp. If Pete got any closer, before the balloon popped, they'd be sure to be discovered. Marissa pressed the sides of the balloon together, bracing both feet on the floor to engage her entire core in her efforts.

The sock on her right foot slipped sideways. If she didn't catch herself, she'd end up doing the splits directly under the balloon arch, which would be even more conspicuous than red rubber boots.

Grabbing hold of the balloons for balance, she shifted her weight to her booted foot and pulled her right foot back in. The arch swayed forward with her force.

Tandy dove to grab onto the frame of the balloon arch and hold it up, but she must have unhooked the bottom from whatever it was attached to. The whole thing sprang forward, shooting balloons across the room like bubbles. At least enough of the balloons remained to cushion Marissa's landing on the tile floor-until they popped like popcorn.

Her body jolted with every loud bang.

She looked up through her floating hair from where she'd sprawled to find Yvette and Austin gawking down. Is this where Yvette or Austin pulled a gun on them? That's usually what happened in these situations.

How well could Marissa run from the killers without one of her boots? She could cry for help, but residents like Birdie might call the police but then forget why they called.

"My balloon arch." Yvette reacted to the shock of seeing Marissa sprawled in the middle of the room with a burst of laughter. Which was no shock.

Austin leaned against the lobby desk with an elbow and crossed one ankle over the other. "Hey there, Cuz. What's up? Besides your hair. It looks like you're auditioning for a horror movie."

Marissa rolled from the remaining balloons and pushed to her feet. She felt a little off kilter, but the dastardly duo didn't seem in a hurry to catch her, so maybe she could get her boot back on before she had to run for her life.

Yvette chuckled then charged forward. Oh, no. She was going to give chase. It had just taken her a moment for her fight or flight response to kick in.

Marissa tensed, ready to defend herself.

Yvette ran right past Marissa without touching her. She must have considered Tandy the bigger threat. Marissa whirled to help her friend.

Tandy stood in front of the door, legs spread, arms wide like she assumed Yvette was going to run away, not attack.

Oh, wait. Tandy wasn't blocking Yvette. She was blocking Pete from escaping like she'd tried to do in the beginning.

Yvette merely corralled Pete and herded him back toward the memory care wing, laughing all the way. Apparently, she wasn't too angry at Marissa anymore. And she cared more for her residents and her balloons than she did about being spied on by amateur sleuths.

As for Austin, he seemed even less concerned with a smirk that told her he thought she was the one who should be embarrassed. But if that was the case, then what was he doing here?

Tandy surveyed the mess they'd made. Yvette walked Pete toward the memory ward, pausing when Marissa's red boot stood in their path. She looked back at Marissa's feet for a moment before continuing around the shoe with the older gentleman.

Black and orange balloons bounced freely around the grand entryway. Well, the ones that Marissa hadn't popped anyway. Tandy was almost surprised that Archibald hadn't mistaken the sound for gunfire and shown up to protect Birdie.

But no. It was only Austin. Looking as arrogant as if he'd known they'd been following him the whole time and drove to the retirement center to lead them on a wild goose chase. Now he had another humiliating story to tell about Marissa. Tandy needed to step in as maid of honor.

She stood tall, hoping her appearance was formidable enough to distract Austin from watching Marissa put her boot back on. "What are you doing here?" she demanded. Let him try to come up with a good excuse.

Austin motioned the direction Yvette had disappeared. "I came to talk to the woman who confronted Marissa yesterday.

I thought maybe I could smooth things over and do some sleuthing to help get Connor out of jail."

Tandy's puffed-up stance deflated like a balloon arch in Marissa's way. Austin was the nicest of Marissa's cousins, though that didn't say much, but trying to get Connor out of jail when the rest of the family had turned on the groom was almost valiant. *If* Tandy had reason to believe this guy.

She narrowed her eyes to study him closer. "How did it go with Yvette?"

Austin took a sip through his straw. "You weren't listening?"

Marissa had reached her missing shoe and was now hopping on one foot to pull it on, her hair floating around like Medusa's snakes. "We tried to, but we were distracted with keeping Pete from escaping."

Austin's smirk spread into a full-blown smile. He ran a hand over his face as if trying to wipe it away. "Is that what you were doing?"

Tandy crossed her arms. She wasn't used to being the butt of jokes like Marissa. "Yeah. Now tell us more about what you were doing. What did Yvette say?"

Austin looked the direction the woman had gone. "She said she's worried about Birdie with Archibald missing, and she's upset that you didn't use the opportunity to bring him in when you could."

Tandy grimaced and swiped her business partner's hat off the floor. If Marissa had talked Archibald into turning himself in, this might all be over.

Marissa finally tugged the boot on and found solid footing.

Tandy tossed her the hat she needed to get her hair back under control. Yeah, Dick Tracy had a more noticeable outfit than Marissa's, but she bet he never made as dramatic an entrance.

Marissa caught the hat and set it on her head like a crown. In between her klutzy moments, she had the panache of a beauty queen. "Austin, you may be my cousin, but you've been in all the wrong places at all the wrong times. Including now. I'm going to question Yvette to see if your stories match up."

Chapter Sixteen

TANDY MARCHED TOWARD THE DOOR TO the memory care wing and punched in the numbers Yvette had given her when Archibald went missing. She didn't have to wait for the front desk clerk to page Yvette like Austin did, which gave Austin's story some credit. If he really was in cahoots with Yvette, wouldn't she have given him the code too?

The lock buzzed. Tandy held the door open for Marissa.

Marissa sailed through. "How'd you know that code?"

"Yvette gave it to me." Tandy entered and waited for the door to swing shut behind her. She didn't want to have to worry about any other escapees.

Marissa studied the warning sign about Pete printed on a piece of paper and stuck to the glass. "Yvette should have been more careful not to let Pete escape."

"Yeah." Tandy looked at the photo of Pete's big smile before leading the way down the hall to find the activities' director. Was the woman just slacking on the job, or was she involved in something more sinister? Speaking of sinister... "You'd think Birdie would be the one trying to bust out of here with all her spy experience."

"Well," Marissa shrugged, studying the decorated doors they passed. "Pete is the one who sold the farm to Connor's family. His kids pressured him and used the money from the sale to put him in here. He used to come drive the tractors for the pumpkin patch until his memory started to go. Then it got too dangerous."

That made sense from what Tandy had seen, but how sad for Pete. Also, how sad for Connor if they couldn't get him released from jail. He'd lose his chance to drive tractors while he was still young. Along with everything else.

Tandy scanned the hallway, wondering if she could figure out which door decoration belonged to Pete. The brown door on her right had been given a giant face that looked like it was stitched on. A fake floppy hat covered the top of it, completing the look of a scarecrow's head.

That was a possibility for Pete, but so was the door across from it with a silhouette of Snoopy sitting in front of the moon and surrounded by pumpkins. She'd check the rest of the hallway to make sure there were no doors with tractors before she knocked on any of them.

Birdie's door up ahead on the right was cracked open slightly. Maybe Yvette had gone in to check on the woman while she was down this way. Tandy pointed. "That's Birdie's room."

Marissa gasped, hand to her heart. "Oh, no! I hope Birdie is okay. Is the sheriff here?"

Tandy frowned at the dramatic response and worried she was missing something that should indicate danger. Why wouldn't Birdie be okay? Oh. The yellow crime scene tape. "Yeah. That's her door decoration."

Marissa's hand dropped to her side. "Whew. Scared me there."

Tandy held a hand to her lips and snuck closer to the door. If Yvette was inside, maybe they could eavesdrop and see if the activities' director was worth eavesdropping on.

What sounded like a witch's cackle came from the room. Yep. Yvette was inside, and she seemed pretty happy about it. Maybe the activities' director really did care about Birdie. She could be like a mama bear, her anger at Marissa the day before was only her protecting her babies—letting Pete escape was an oversight.

Tandy stepped to one side of the door. Marissa positioned herself on the other side. They both turned their ears towards the opening.

"Birdie." Yvette spoke firmly but kindly as if addressing a naughty kindergartner, and Tandy could totally picture her as a teacher. "Just because the tea shop owner mentioned wanting to bake a file into a cake to take to her fiancé in jail doesn't mean you should hide your fingernail file in a Ding Dong."

Tandy pressed her lips together to keep from guffawing at the image...and to keep from correcting Yvette on the difference between a Ding Dong and a cupcake.

Marissa's mouth fell open. Her eyes sparkled in a way Tandy hadn't seen for a while.

Tandy had to look down to keep from laughing with her friend, though Yvette probably wouldn't even hear them over her own howling.

"Sweetie, how were you going to get this to the jail anyway?"

Birdie was the cutest. But she could end up a jail *birdie* if she tried to help Connor with a jailbreak. "I was going to ask you to take the cupcakes to him," the older woman responded. "Or I can drive the bus."

Tandy remembered the children's book *Don't Let the Pigeon Drive the Bus*. She imagined the author being inspired by this very situation, except he hadn't wanted to use Birdie's name.

"Aww..." Yvette softened enough to turn serious. "The teashop owner is out front. I'll see if I can catch her, and I'll ask her to take the rest of this Little Debbie's package to Connor if you want me to."

"That would be delightful, dear," Birdie warbled.

Tandy tensed, ready to step away from the door before Yvette came out. Marissa looked around as if wanting a place to hide.

The door swung open. Yvette's eyes startled wide then her mouth opened wider. Laughter spilled out. "I should have known you two would be here." She wiped her eyes. "But why snoop when you can come on in? Look who is here to see you, Birdie."

"My lands. I'm so glad you're here." Birdie waved the women in and pointed to a little brown cupcake with the plastic handle of a metal fingernail file sticking out one side. "I heard you say you wanted to bake a file into a cake. I don't have an oven in here for some reason, so I couldn't bake one, but I have these cupcakes, and I have a fingernail file. Yvette was going to see if you'd take it to your fiancé for me."

"Oh, wow." Marissa eyed the cupcake then Tandy as if unsure how to respond.

Tandy nodded her approval to make Birdie feel good. "I'm not sure Connor will be able to use that kind of file, but I know another guy who likes to get his nails done." She glanced at Yvette to see how the woman would respond. Did she know Austin had gotten a pedicure in Tandy's place the other day?

Marissa's lips made an O. "Yes." She nodded a little too enthusiastically. "My cousin Austin."

Yvette's jolly smile didn't fade even a little as she watched Birdie interact. She stood with her duster flared out to the side so she could place one hand on a hip.

Tandy tried to keep the joviality going as she asked Yvette her questions with the hope she didn't come across as suspicious of the activities' director. She didn't want to anger the woman. "I'm glad you got Pete back to his room without trouble."

Yvette gave a little nod. "Yeah, his favorite show was on TV. I had been headed to turn on *Mud, Sweat, and Tractors* for him when I got paged to the front counter anyway."

"Hmm." Tandy tried to nod with sympathy. "I'm really sorry about the balloon arch."

Marissa backed Tandy up. "We were trying to keep Pete from escaping when we accidentally knocked it over."

Tandy looked up to meet Marissa's gaze, new respect blossoming in her heart. Her friend spoke the truth without revealing their actual intention to spy.

"Thank you for your help." Yvette glanced down at Marissa's galoshes as if wondering how her boot could have come off in the balloon debacle. "I thought the balloons would be fun, but they do get in the way. I should probably head back down to help the janitor clean them up."

Tandy stepped toward the door to keep Yvette from escaping. "We can help too." She eyed Marissa and tilted her head toward the door so they'd be on the same page.

"Of course we'll help." Marissa jumped to attention, knocking the illicit cupcake to the floor, frosting first.

Yvette laughed.

Tandy was not as surprised. "Or maybe I'll just leave Marissa here to clean up this new mess."

Marissa cringed. "Sorry."

Tandy opened the door for Yvette, and called back to Marissa, "I'll see you out front when you're done." Marissa gave a thumbs up, and Tandy trotted after the bustling activities' director. "Did we interrupt a meeting? It looked like when we knocked over the balloon arch, you were having a discussion with Marissa's cousin."

Yvette glanced over her shoulder and shrugged. Even though she was short, the woman was hard to keep up with. "He said he felt bad that I'd been so upset yesterday. He wants to help me find Archibald and asked if he could talk to the residents around Archie's room." She laughed again. "He also told me an interesting story about Marissa putting salt in his milk as a prank when they were kids."

Tandy's eyebrow arched. If Austin was really trying to help Marissa and Yvette the way he claimed, then why was he telling stories that made it sound like he might still have a vendetta against her? Though it didn't sound like there was any connection between him and Yvette. Austin was doing this all on his own. She just didn't know what he was doing.

Back through the security door, they found janitors trying to catch balloons and pop them. They also found a gaggle of elderly women in modest bathing suits, swim caps, and towels herding the balloons toward the janitors with brightly colored pool noodles. They joked and competed among themselves as if they were playing croquet at a lawn party.

And Tandy hadn't thought anyone could make a bigger scene in the lobby than Marissa.

"Oh, my." Yvette cackled. "They must have been on the way to water aerobics. I'm going to have to get them back into the swimming pool before they slip, but this gives me an idea for an activity later. When everyone is dressed."

She bustled toward the older women and shooed them to a side door. A couple of them waved their pool noodles at Yvette like they were ready for a duel.

It seemed like Grace Springs Manor was a great place to live. Except for the drugs and murder part, of course. But that she was going to help solve, even if it meant Marissa's cousin was guilty.

"Yvette, did you give Austin permission to investigate on the premises?" she called.

Yvette's head cocked like she was shooting the elderly women a warning look, even while she laughed. She might have been laughing too loudly to hear Tandy's question.

A throat cleared from the front desk at Tandy's side. Mr. Cross stood there, arms folded, watching the chaos without as much amusement. "Did you and Marissa knock down the balloon arch?"

Tandy quirked her lips. Talking to Cross always made her feel like she was back in the principal's office. "Accidentally."

"Well, I should hope it wasn't on purpose."

"We're just trying to help figure out who killed Hubert."

The hard lines of his face softened slightly. "I know about Connor going to jail. That's why I allowed the reporter to question residents."

Tandy froze. Did Cross think Marissa's cousin was a reporter? Is that what Austin told him? Highly suspicious.

Should she let the owner of Grace Springs Manor know he'd just let another one of their suspects have free range of the premises? Mr. Cross had been the one to let Hubert stay on as an employee even though he was suspected of stealing...if Yvette's story was to be believed. "Did you know about Birdie's claims that Hubert stole from her?" she asked.

"Yes." Cross kept his rigid stance, the only movement coming from his eyes as they narrowed. "Birdie's claims are not always accurate. And she's the one known for her sticky fingers around here."

Tandy's experience didn't give her any arguments in the old woman's favor. "She's a sweetheart though."

"Yes, she is." Cross made a sound between a huff and a sigh, which was probably as sentimental as he got. "Archibald would do anything for her, and I suppose that's what he did."

"Hmm..." Tandy couldn't yet agree with his belief. Especially with Austin running around pretending to be a reporter. "Do you mind if I go see if Austin has discovered anything?"

Cross looked from her toward the pool party. "If you're done doing damage to my property for the day."

Marissa found tissues in the bathroom and used them to scoop the smashed cake off the floor. She tossed it in the garbage then turned on the bathroom sink to rinse off Birdie's fingernail file in the stream of cool water. "I'm going to let you keep this, Birdie. I don't think it's the kind of file that would have cut through jail bars anyway."

Birdie appeared in the bathroom door, her face as sweet and wrinkly as a dried apple. The line between her innocent and immoral sides seemed to be about as clear as her memory. She probably didn't realize that if Connor got released legally it could be because her husband was arrested. "I was just trying to help, dear."

"I know. Thank you." Marissa set down the file and dried her hands. "But we're going to get Connor out without a jailbreak."

"Do you visit him?" Birdie asked like it was the most romantic thing in the world. Hopefully, she wouldn't have to find out for herself how depressing jail visits really were.

Marissa's chest constricted tight and tingly at the memory of Connor in handcuffs. "Yes."

"Then you can still take him these." Birdie wobbled away.

Marissa stepped out of the bathroom to see what other illicit gifts the woman had in mind. But she was only taping the box of cupcakes closed again. "Eating a sweet always makes me feel better."

"Me too." Marissa's tongue watered at the thought of rich chocolate. She didn't know if she could take anyone cupcakes in jail, but if not, she could stuff her face with them. It had been too long since her last stress-eating session. "Thank you."

She took the box and tipped forward to wrap the frail, little woman in a hug. She smelled of cinnamon and sunshine.

Birdie patted her on the hand. "You'll bring your beau around for a visit?"

Marissa closed her eyes and imagined such a scene. Her own parents might not welcome him in their arms like this, but Birdie would. "I'm sure he'd be delighted to meet you, Birdie."

"Good, good. Thank you for stopping by."

Marissa released her hold and stepped back. "It's been my pleasure."

She smiled wistfully at the crime scene tape as she closed Birdie's door and headed down the hallway. She didn't want Birdie's husband to be guilty of killing Hubert, but she didn't want Austin to be guilty either. And she certainly didn't want Connor to go to prison. So where did that leave her?

A cleaning lady buzzed her through the door into the foyer. Where she expected to find Tandy and Austin, she found Mr. Cross overseeing a bunch of janitors jumping on balloons. She peeked outside to the parking lot and saw both Tandy's bug and Austin's SUV sitting empty, so she figured she'd try Winifred's room. That's usually where Tandy seemed to go.

She lifted a hand to hide her face so she didn't have to see the blame in Mr. Cross's expression over the mess she'd made as she passed. A balloon popped, the sound causing her heart to jump. Her hand dropped as if to hold it in her chest, and she accidentally met Mr. Cross's stoic gaze.

"Oh, hi," she gushed like she hadn't seen him standing there all Godfatherly. "I bet you've never had such a sight in your lobby before."

One corner of his mouth curved upward. "One would think."

Whatever that meant. "Do you know where Tandy went?"

Mr. Cross pointed towards a back hallway. "She's with the reporter who is questioning Archibald's neighbors. Archibald has the undecorated door."

Marissa nodded thanks and jogged the way he'd pointed, just glad to get away from him and his rigid demeanor. She'd like to accuse Mr. Cross of making her feel like a kindergartner, but she *was* wearing rubber boots and carrying Little Debbie's.

Too late to reconsider her appearance in order to make a good impression on the reporter. With any luck, the journalist would find some clue that they'd missed. Something more than conjecture and speculation. How convenient that she and Tandy happened to follow Austin here at the same time the journalist decided to investigate.

She blew out her breath and looked for Tandy's camouflage sweatshirt. The woman might be easier to find if so many residents hadn't decorated their doors like the outdoors. Oh, there by a sunflower door. With Austin.

Marissa joined the two and looked around for the reporter. "I'm glad to hear a reporter is investigating Hubert's death. Where did he go?"

Tandy just glared at Austin.

"I'm right here," he stated.

Marissa frowned into her cousin's unconcerned eyes. Why did he always try to make everything about him? "I know you're right here. I'm asking about the reporter."

"I'm a contributor to *Realtor Magazine*."

Marissa blinked. "What does that have to do with anything?" Was he just trying to distract them from their sleuthing? Why had Tandy allowed him to tag along? Marissa looked to her friend and held her hands wide in question.

"*He's* the"--Tandy made air quotes with her fingers— "reporter. Or that's what he told Mr. Cross anyway."

"What?" Marissa's tone leapt to great heights. "Real estate has nothing to do with the investigation of Hubert's death."

Austin sipped the straw to his stupid coffee until it gurgled empty. "I never said it did."

Marissa set her jaw. Was he looking for more ways to annoy them? "If you're here to help us out by investigating, as you claim to be, then why are you just sipping coffee in the hallway?"

Austin knocked on a door with sunflowers. "I'm trying to interview Archibald's neighbors, but nobody is answering their doors."

Marissa sucked in a breath. With Archibald's disappearance and the crime scene tape on Birdie's door, she dreaded finding out any more residents were missing.

"Winifred would answer for *me*." Tandy pouted. "She probably doesn't want to talk to *you*."

Austin's expression remained nonchalant. With his sisters, he was used to being ridiculed this way. "Winifred is the one with the wigs?"

Tandy eyed him warily before answering. "Yes."

"It was her wig found in the alley then." He lifted his chin like he'd discovered a clue. "You don't think she's avoiding us to hide from the law?"

Marissa wrinkled her nose. They'd considered the possibility that Yvette was involved even though she couldn't have been the person they'd chased into the alley. There was the same possibility for Winifred. Could she and Archibald be working together?

"No." Tandy wouldn't even consider it. "She's taking a nap. Or her television is turned up too high for her to hear us."

"If she has nothing to hide…" Austin paused dramatically. "Then why does she wear so many wigs? Are they disguises?"

Tandy rolled her eyes as if she and Marissa had never jumped to such ridiculous conclusions. "She's a performer," Tandy argued.

Austin held up a finger. "Aha! And perhaps you are her audience?"

Marissa tilted her head at Tandy. They should at least consider it a possibility. From where Winifred filmed Connor in the corn maze, she'd been close enough to hit Hubert with the shovel. "We should ask her," Marissa suggested, like a mediator. "If she doesn't answer the door, we can get Yvette to unlock it to check on her. With all that's been going on around her, it would be good to make sure she's safe and healthy."

A wheelchair rounded the far corner. An orderly pushed Winifred down the hallway toward them.

Today Winifred wore a velvet, burgundy turban. It reminded Marissa of the curtains that used to go up in a theater before a movie. Winifred always seemed to be putting on a show. In fact, as soon as she saw them waiting for her, her countenance changed. She sat up straighter, shined like royalty, and opened her arms with welcome.

Tandy sent Austin a warning glare before turning to smile at the old woman. "Winifred. You've been missing all the fun. Where'd you go?"

"Tammy, you brought your friends. I'm so glad you're all here. I was at chemotherapy. You could visit me at the hospital next time if you want. Me and the other ladies like to play Pinochle."

Chemo? Winifred had cancer. Which was why she wore wigs. She wasn't a suspect. She was a patient.

Chapter Seventeen

TANDY COULD PUNCH AUSTIN. FIRST, FOR lying about being a reporter. Second, for presuming he could help their investigation. But mostly for suspecting Winifred when what the woman needed was support.

Instead of making a fist, she pointed toward the lobby entrance and narrowed her eyes. She dared him not to leave.

He didn't even have the decency to hang his head. In fact, he smirked and introduced himself to Winifred, but with the excuse that he needed to get back to family. Like his relatives even wanted him around. The guy had to wear a fake wedding ring.

Marissa clasped hands with Winifred. Her other hand carried a box of Ding Dongs. From Birdie, Tandy presumed, hopefully sans any fingernail files.

"Here comes the bride..." Winifred sang in a deep vibrato.

Marissa's smile faltered. "I'm going to go make sure Austin finds his way out of the building all right."

Tandy nodded her approval. "Good idea."

She didn't want Austin wandering around, slurping melted ice, claiming to be a reporter, and accusing cancer patients of murder. But she also didn't want to leave this cancer patient by herself. As for Marissa, she probably felt like she was going to throw up every time someone mentioned her wedding.

Tandy grasped Winifred's key and unlocked the door. Then she nodded to the orderly. "I'll take her from here."

"Tammy, you are such a good girl. Have you found the thief who stole my wig yet?"

Tandy rolled Winifred through the doorway and positioned the wheelchair next to her recliner before locking the wheels in place. "Not yet. I see you're not wearing a wig today. You didn't have them all stolen, did you?" She peeked into Winifred's room to make sure no other wigs were missing from the wig tree. Though if there was another one gone, they'd know what to look for.

"No." Winifred sighed. "I always wore Sheena to play cards in. My other wigs are all too long and the strands get in my way when I look down."

Of course that had to be the wig the thief stole. It was one thing for the perp to ruin his own life by dealing drugs but messing with Winifred's card game took the crime to a whole new level.

Tandy circled the wheelchair to stand in front of Winifred. "I'm sorry. Is there anything else I can do to make you comfortable? How do you feel after chemo?"

Winifred relaxed into her seat. "I'm sleepy right now. Tomorrow is when I'm going to feel like I got hit by a bus. Too bad I didn't consider that when planning for Marissa's bridal shower."

Tandy backed up and sat on the arm of the couch in contemplation. "You're still planning the shower? I thought the whole idea of it was to help Birdie remember her love for Archibald. And Archibald isn't even around right now." Not to mention the video Winifred showed Sheriff Griffin that was evidence that kept Marissa's fiancé in jail.

Winifred smiled dreamily. "Archibald has been calling Birdie, you know. Maybe the bridal shower will help her remember who he is when he calls, which will lure him out of hiding."

Tandy tilted her head. If the plan worked, and Archibald confessed to hitting Hubert with the shovel, Marissa's wedding wouldn't have to be canceled. But that was a very big if. "Have you heard or seen Archibald lately? Have there been any noises coming from his room or anything?"

"No." Winifred gripped the armrests of the wheelchair and shifted her weight forward to place her feet on the floor. "If Archibald doesn't want to be found, Archibald won't be found. He may be old, but he knows what he's doing."

Tandy didn't doubt it.

Winifred's breathing grew heavier. "Will you be a dear and help me into bed. I just want to lie down."

"Oh." Tandy jumped to her feet and rushed forward, but then she stood facing the large woman, unsure of how to support her.

"Let me hold onto your arm."

Tandy turned sideways and crooked her elbow. It hurt to see Winifred so weak. She was a charismatic, natural leader, full of joy. She brightened a room just by being in it. Tandy didn't know much about cancer, but it was obvious the treatments dimmed Winifred's light. Worse, if the treatments didn't work, her light could be snuffed out far too soon.

Who would remember her then? She had no family to carry on her legacy.

Tandy let Winifred cling to her, and they took baby steps toward the bed. The woman needed to rest. "Don't worry about throwing Marissa a bridal shower tomorrow. We had a couple's shower at our shop a few weeks ago. She's all set to wed." Or she *was*. Back when she had a groom. "As for Archibald, bringing him in is the sheriff's job. Your job is to take care of you."

"I..." Winifred paused mid-sentence to catch her breath. Tandy pulled down the quilt and satin sheets. "Will you help me undress, sugar?"

Uh... If the woman had trouble breathing while walking to her bed, she certainly would need help with disrobing. But this wasn't a job Tandy had prepared for.

"Wait until you see my unmentionables. You're gonna love them."

Tandy bit back a smile. The comment reminded her of how she'd had special underwear with ruffles on the butt when she was little. She'd always insisted on wearing them backwards so she could see the ruffles. Not that she'd ever admit to Marissa that she used to like ruffles. "Now I'm curious."

"When you're my age, your unmentionables have to be something pretty special."

Tandy's smile escaped, and she could feel the other woman's joy deep inside as she helped Winifred undress. Winifred did so in the same way she did everything, with flair. She kicked surprisingly hard for her condition, sending red, polyester pants with the elastic waistband sailing underneath the dresser.

Winifred pointed to a hook on the back of the door. "My nightgown is there."

Tandy retrieved the light blue cotton gown with buttons up the front. It wasn't any more special than the nude granny panties Winifred had seemed to think would so delight her. She lifted it above Winifred's head.

"Breast cancer turns everyone into a flasher," Winifred said with her head still inside her pajamas. Her face popped out, headwrap askew. "I'm always stripping for the doctors."

Up close, Tandy got an even better view of Winifred's penciled-on eyebrows. Now she knew why they were penciled on. She sobered, guiding the gown down Winifred's body so she could see the woman's whole face again. "I'm sorry to hear you have to deal with that."

"Hobble-dee-gobble-dee." Winifred sank gingerly onto the bed. "If you're going to have cancer, breast cancer is the best one to have. Very treatable. And the pain of treatment doesn't last forever."

Tandy helped her swing her feet up and recline. She pulled the covers to Winifred's shoulders. It tugged at her heart to know this woman was dealing with such health issues on her own since she had no family. "The few times I met you, I never would have guessed you were in pain. You always seem so joyful."

"Oh, I *am* joyful." Winifred tugged her turban on tighter, eyes still beaming, even in her weariness. "Every day is a gift and sharing my gifts with others is what brings me joy."

Tandy swallowed. What a different world this would be if everyone had the insight that seemed to come with fighting a disease. Instead, it was like humanity had a cancer. They fought against themselves. Was there a cure?

Marissa forced Austin out to the parking lot. Of course, he claimed he wanted to help her, and his story seemed to align with Yvette's, but then he lied to Mr. Cross.

She marched him to his SUV. "What did you really come here for?" she demanded.

Austin stuck his hands in his pockets and studied their surroundings from the large brick structure to the lush foliage and river in the background.

A thought bubbled to the surface. Marissa crossed her arms. "Does this have to do with your real estate business? Are you wanting to sell this property?"

"I want to sell every property, but it's not for sale." Austin laughed lazily. "I'm really trying to help you, Cuz. You're just suspicious because you know that after the way you used to treat me, you don't deserve my help."

He was too much. Learning Winifred had cancer was too much. Having Birdie stick a fingernail file into a cupcake was too much. Though, now that she had those cupcakes...

Marissa pried a piece of tape off the cupcake box with her French tips and stuck a hand inside. The packaged cupcakes wouldn't compare to her chocolate turtle cupcakes baked with homemade caramel sauce. But chocolate had tryptophan in it, which would help her brain make serotonin and hopefully trick her into feeling happy. Well, not *happy*-happy, but less stabby. Austin was lucky she didn't still have Birdie's fingernail file with her.

"Maybe you're still pulling pranks on me," he said. "This time by framing me for murder."

Plastic wrap crinkled under her fingers.

"Are my sisters in on this too? Could they have been running around in masks and black clothing when they know I'm around, so I get pinned for their crimes?"

Marissa pinched at the plastic to retrieve a cupcake, but her fingers closed on something smooth, cool, and hard.

"Ashlee did give me the black clothes to wear underneath the clown suit Amber picked out."

Definitely not a cupcake.

"Honestly, they are more likely to have killed Hubert than anyone else I know. They've always loved breaking hearts."

Tandy strode up behind Austin. "Nice family you've got here, Marissa."

Marissa struggled to register the fact that Austin was throwing his sisters under the bus. All her focus was on what she felt inside her cupcake box. She pulled out a phone for all to see.

Tandy frowned at the device. "You dropped your phone in the box of cupcakes?"

"No." Marissa turned over the device. It was a smartphone, but not one of the expensive ones. "This was in the box Birdie gave me."

"She misplaced it in the box?" Austin shrugged. "You'd better return it. I can go with you."

Marissa lifted her eyes to Tandy to try to read the other woman's thoughts. If Birdie was capable of sticking a fingernail file in a cupcake, was she capable of trying to hide a burner phone? She'd asked Marissa to give the box to Connor.

Tandy's mouth formed an O shape, as if she too was not prepared to voice her assumptions either.

Austin leaned against the truck's tailgate. "What are you girls not saying?"

Marissa cringed. The phone in her hand felt as explosive as a bomb. Dare she try to disarm it?

Tandy took the box of cupcakes and peeked inside. "These cupcakes are from Birdie to be delivered to Connor. In jail."

Austin guffawed. "You think she was trying to send him a phone? What for?"

Marissa pressed the side button on the smartphone to look at its home screen. The background lit up with standard kaleidoscope wallpaper behind icons for basic apps. She turned the phone for the others to see. "If this is Birdie's phone, wouldn't it be more personalized?"

Tandy tilted her head, eyes squinting. "Not necessarily. My grandma didn't grow up with cell phones, so she only used hers for the basics."

Marissa's grandma hadn't even texted, but Birdie wasn't the normal grandma. "Yeah, but didn't you say Birdie was a former spy. She would have more knowledge about technology."

"A forgetful spy."

"Whoa-whoa-whoa." Austin set down his plastic cup on the bumper and held up his hands. "Are you guys saying you think a former spy is trying to sneak a burner phone to a guy in jail?"

Tandy scratched her head. "She did try to sneak him a file."

Marissa couldn't help wondering if the nail file was a ploy. It might have been a diversion to keep Marissa from seeing the phone Birdie had hidden. She swiped her thumb across the smooth face of the device to check for a lock screen.

Nope. She had full access.

Of course, that didn't prove this wasn't Birdie's personal phone either. With as forgetful as the woman seemed to be, she wouldn't want a password preventing her from calling anyone.

"Who did she call?" Austin asked.

Marissa checked contacts. Only Archibald's name came up. She tapped to find out their history. "She called Archibald this morning at six."

Austin pointed emphatically. "Call him back."

Tandy stepped forward to see the numbers for herself. "Yvette made it sound like Birdie didn't have a phone. If Birdie had this, why would Archibald have called Yvette to talk to his wife?"

Marissa checked for text messages and email. No other communication appeared. "This could be a new phone."

"Hello?" Austin asked like he was the one receiving a call. "Archibald could probably answer those questions for you. And you've got his number right there. Why don't you ask him?"

Marissa stared at the phone. "Did Birdie hide the phone in the box and forget, or was she trying to sneak this to Connor? Did she want Connor to call Archibald?"

Tandy smooshed her lips together and wrinkled her nose. "As much as I hate to say this, we should probably take the phone to Griffin as evidence."

Back at the police station, Marissa handed the box of Ding Dongs to Griffin.

He looked at the picture on the front of the box. "If you're trying to bribe me, cops prefer donuts."

Marissa wondered for a moment if bribery would work. She had a recipe for really good blueberry glazed cardamom donut holes. But no. That's not why she'd handed him the box. "These cupcakes came from Birdie, Archibald's wife. She gave them to me to give to Connor."

Griffin's gaze flicked from her to Tandy and Austin behind her. "That's sweet. I'll have my deputy check them and pass them along."

Tandy spoke up. "You might want to check them now, Sheriff."

Griffin paused. "Okay?" He tilted the box upside down above his desk. Plastic wrap rustled as a few cupcakes rained down followed by the thunk of a phone.

Griffin froze them with another stare before snapping on a pair of gloves. "You haven't touched this yet, have you?"

"I did." Marissa wrinkled her nose. "But I was just trying to eat a cupcake. I didn't expect a phone to be in there."

Griffin picked it up and powered it on. "You didn't go through it though, right? You brought it straight to me?"

"Well…"

"Marissa." Griffin rolled his eyes to the ceiling. "We've talked about fingerprints. With your fiancé arrested over them, I'd figure you would be a little more cautious."

Chapter Eighteen

MARISSA'S HEART SWELLED LIKE A TEABAG, steeping trepidation. She was at the police station because she was trying to help. She didn't need any more problems.

Tandy stepped forward to defend her. "We were just trying to figure out why there was a phone in the cupcakes. With as forgetful as Birdie is, we weren't sure if she realized it was in there or not."

Griffin swiped the screen. "And what did you determine?"

"We think it's new," Marissa rushed to explain. "It only has Archibald's number on it. Maybe he slipped it to her when he kissed her goodbye the other day."

Griffin snapped at Romero. "Find out what cell phone carrier covers this device and get them on the phone. Now that we have a number, we can triangulate Archibald's location."

Marissa took a deep breath. They were finally getting somewhere. She didn't know if Birdie or Archibald were guilty of anything, but if the police could at least bring him in, they would get some answers. She needed to share this hope with her other half. "Can I see Connor while I'm here?"

Griffin glanced at his watch. "I've got a few minutes. But if you want me to be able to track down another suspect and get him out of jail, you should keep it short."

Marissa nodded. No need wasting any more time. The sooner she saw Connor, the better for both of them.

Griffin led her toward the hallway. Tandy took a seat in a plastic chair by the wall and gave her an encouraging smile as she passed. Austin watched, as well, and Marissa wondered if he'd be there when she came out. She still wasn't sure of his motives.

In the cement block visiting room, Marissa took her seat in a cold metal chair and clasped her hands together. Her pulse throbbed in weird places like the joints of her elbows and knees as she waited for Connor to join her.

She was used to telling him all the tiny details of her day. Used to processing her thoughts with him. Used to depending on his feedback for direction. Without him, she wasn't sure she was seeing the truth around her clearly, and if she couldn't see the truth, she might never be able to get him out.

Was this how Archibald felt without Birdie by his side? Was this why he'd started making poor decisions? If Connor went to prison, would she go as crazy as the old man on the run?

Her heart jumpstarted back to life when he entered the room, and she didn't let him make it to his chair. They embraced in the middle of the room again and stood that way for a while. But she needed to offer him the possibility of release.

"I think we found Archibald."

He pulled away to see her face. His gray eyes silvered with hope. "What do you mean, 'you think'?"

She smiled to encourage optimism. Both his and her own. "Birdie tried to sneak you a phone in a box of cupcakes, and it had the number for Archibald's burner phone. Griffin is tracking him down now."

He let her go, but only long enough to bring his hands to her face. His mouth followed, hungry for the possibility of a future together.

She kissed him back, her heart aching for more time to do it right. Touching had become a luxury. Expensive. So she'd take her money's worth.

The door whooshed open. A throat cleared.

She tried to pull away, but Connor wasn't ready to let her go. She returned for one more kiss then forced herself to put space between them.

His fingers slipped away, but his gaze locked on hers, searing even hotter than his hold. "I've been praying, and I really believe the next time we kiss, we'll be man and wife."

She wanted to believe him—wanted to promise to prove him innocent. But he wouldn't let her make promises like that the last time she'd been here. Was his prayer and the confidence that came with it really from God?

Would God love them enough to both be their enough as well as give them more?

"I'm sorry to interrupt." Greg's voice finally pulled Marissa's attention away from her fiancé, but she gripped his fingers to keep their connection. Connor squeezed, and even that small movement overwhelmed her senses, making it hard for her to focus on his lawyer.

It was Greg's pink tie that caught her attention. What did Tandy think of her boyfriend wearing pink? He still looked manly and professional but with the kind of style that would attract Barbies, not biker chicks.

"Nice tie, man," Connor said for her, and she loved him for it.

Greg straightened the shiny strip of fabric. "I'm supporting Breast Cancer Awareness Month."

"A good cause, but not very manly." It was a wonder Connor was able to keep his sense of humor in prison. Maybe it's what helped him keep a grasp on normalcy. Maybe it was this growing faith he seemed to have in God. He'd probably had a lot of time to pray lately.

Greg tilted his head, playing along. "Tell that to the Cincinnati Bengals who are wearing pink gloves, shoes, and wristbands for all their games in October."

"Touché."

Marissa smiled. Both Connor and Tandy would excuse the color pink for raising awareness of breast cancer. Especially with what she'd just found out about Winifred.

Greg blocked her view of his tie by lifting his briefcase. "I really don't want to interrupt, but I have to be in court within the hour, and I wanted to go over a couple things with my client really quick."

Connor released her hands, and she shivered from the cold air that took his place…and from the fear that she might have to get used to cold air. Sensing her change in temperature, he gripped the edges of her scarf and tied them to bundle her up. Then he pulled on the edges to tip her toward him and lean his forehead against hers.

She looked down at his scrubs then closed her eyes again to block out their surroundings. She imagined him free from jail, wearing a tie like Greg's at their wedding. Except it wouldn't be pink.

"Greg's job is to get me out of jail, not yours," Connor said softly but sternly. "I don't want you risking your life for me by trying to track down the real killer."

Of course he didn't. And she wasn't risking anything. Hanging out at an old folks' home wasn't dangerous. If Austin turned out to be the killer, he was her cousin. They used to share a bunk bed at family reunions. Even though she'd short-sheeted him once, she wasn't afraid of him.

"You understand?" he asked when she didn't respond quickly enough.

If she never responded, could they stay like this forever?

Probably not since she could hear Greg walking to the chair she'd abandoned and snapping open his briefcase. She nodded her understanding, rocking his head against hers. That didn't mean she wasn't going to investigate. It simply meant he didn't need to worry about her.

"This worries me," Griffin said to someone on the other end of the phone as he stared down at the deputy's computer screen on his desk at the back of the room. The deputy had taken Griffin's place, guarding Connor when Greg arrived so the sheriff could come take a look at a map the phone company had emailed him.

Tandy sat straighter, wondering if she could get close enough to see the map pulled up without Griffin noticing her. Austin had gone outside with Kristin for her smoke break. Tandy wasn't sure if he smoked or he just wanted to talk to Kristin, but it left one less person to stop her from getting to the laptop. She needed to take a closer look to find out Archibald's location. And why it was "worrisome."

She squinted in concentration. It didn't help her make out the lines on the screen any better, but it heightened her other senses to hear Marissa's boots clip-clopping down the hall.

Marissa could make a great distraction. She was legendary for it. But how could Tandy get her to fall without hurting herself? If they were successful in getting Connor out of jail, Tandy wouldn't want Marissa to have to wear a cast in her wedding ceremony. Maybe she could communicate with Zam's sign language.

Tandy leaned sideways to get a better look in the hallway, but Marissa had her eyes on the floor and didn't notice her. The fact that she was watching where she stepped also made it less likely that she'd fall on her own. Of all the times for the klutzy beauty queen to pay attention to where she was going...

Tandy rolled her eyes and her gaze landed on the first door in the hallway. A sign marked it as the evidence room.

Her stomach lurched, and she let her guts take the lead. "No, Marissa," she almost shouted.

Marissa froze in place. Her eyelids lifted, widening her dark eyes with panic.

Tandy gave an apologetic shrug then continued the charade. "I don't think you're supposed to go in the evidence room!"

Marissa looked around in confusion, but she was around the corner from Griffin, so he couldn't see her react, though he spun around to look.

"I'll have to call you back," the sheriff said into his cell while glowering at Tandy. He slammed the phone down. "Marissa?" he called in a commanding tone.

Tandy pointed him down the hallway like she was trying to be helpful.

He stalked forward with heavy strides, hands fisted. As soon as he passed, Tandy scrambled for the computer. Black lines made a grid on the screen in what would be the downtown area of Grace Springs. A flashing red beacon pinpointed Archibald's location outside of town, closer to the river. She traced the roads with her finger, imagining how to get to the right spot. It seemed to be close to the retirement community.

Her finger stopped short, and she sucked in a breath. Archibald was in the corn maze.

Marissa's voice defended herself in the distance. "I wasn't going into the evidence room."

A doorknob wobbled. Tandy's heart felt just as wobbly as she scurried back toward her chair.

"See?" Marissa triumphed. "It's locked. I couldn't have gone in."

Tandy dropped silently into her seat, gripping the edge with her fingers to release anxiety. She forced her feet to swing like she was an innocent schoolgirl. She might have even whistled if she knew how.

Griffin stomped back out into the main office, glancing suspiciously from Tandy to his computer. Marissa followed behind him, her narrow eyes also asking questions. Tandy would answer Marissa later.

Griffin crossed his arms. "Anything I should know before you girls take off?" he asked.

"Nope." Griffin already knew that if he didn't do his job, they'd do it for him. But just to put some pressure on, she asked, "Anything we need to know before we head out to The Farmstead to finish setting up for Marissa and Connor's wedding?"

Griffin lifted his chin so he could look down his cute little nose. "That's a crime scene, and the groom is a suspected criminal."

Marissa stepped between them, probably even more confused than before but wanting to defend her groom. "Griffin, you released The Farmstead for business yesterday. This is the busiest time of year for Connor's family. As for Connor, I'm trusting you to bring in Archibald and arrest the real perp."

Griffin's gaze now ricocheted between the women as if trying to figure out how much they knew about Archibald's location and what he could say without giving it away.

Tandy scooted forward in her chair to plant her feet and stand. She had places to go, things to do, perps to catch. "If you close The Farmstead now, it wouldn't look good for you," she said. "Like you thought you'd missed some evidence. Or like you thought someone was hiding there." She strode to the door and held it open for Marissa.

Griffin's smooth jaw dropped. He held up a finger as if he had something to say, but no words came out. He probably knew he had to leave The Farmstead open to do business as usual if he didn't want to scare off Archibald. The old man had already outwitted Griffin a couple of times. The sheriff's pride would keep him from coming out and saying that Archibald was indeed hiding on the farm because that would require admitting that Tandy was right.

Marissa sailed through the doorway, but her head swiveled to keep her confused stare focused on Tandy. "Is Archibald hiding in the maze?" she whispered as she passed.

Tandy didn't answer right away but kept holding the door open for a tobacco-scented Kristin to return to work followed by Austin, hands in his pockets. Apparently, he didn't smoke but wanted to be near the woman who did.

Leaves skittered across the sidewalk in a cool breeze. The clouds had dissipated in time for the sun to sink low in the sky, casting long shadows in its golden glow and offering the promise of starlight for the evening Tandy had planned. She waited for the door to click shut before explaining it to Marissa, though Marissa had already guessed it.

"Yes, Archibald is hiding in the maze."

Marissa pulled on mittens. "How do you know this?" she asked.

Tandy pulled out her keys and clicked the fob to unlock her car doors. "Oh, I got a look at the map on the computer when Griffin was preventing you from sneaking into the evidence room."

Marissa crossed her arms and popped a hip. "A little warning would have been nice before you made me the star of that scene."

"I wanted to alert you in sign language, but you weren't looking at me." Tandy quirked her lips to one side. She should be sensitive to her friend's emotions. "How'd it go with Connor?"

Marissa's chin puckered. Oh, no. Was she going to cry? Tandy hadn't meant to initiate the water works. She wasn't good with emotional stuff.

Marissa lifted her chin as if stubbornly refusing to tear up. "Connor said he'd rather spend his life in prison than to let anything happen to me."

"Oh. That's...that's...really sweet." Tandy had to sniff to keep her nose from running. She usually wasn't mushy, but Connor's sacrificial love had the power to find a part of her heart not protected by armor. "Good thing he won't have to go to prison, since we now know where to track down Archibald."

Marissa didn't move except for her nose scrunching. "Why aren't we leaving the hunt to Griffin?"

Tandy's eyes wandered back toward the police station. Through the window she could see Sheriff Griffin stuff a chocolate cupcake into his mouth. He didn't seem too concerned about Connor. She probably would have had better luck with him if they'd actually bribed him as he'd joked. "Archibald seems open to talking to you. Even if we can't find him in the maze, he might come to you if he has the opportunity."

Marissa's eyes lifted toward the deceptively sunny sky. "I know Archibald called me, but what if he was trying to get us to investigate someone else instead of him? He really could be the killer."

178

Tandy sighed. That was a strong possibility. In which case, they shouldn't put themselves in harm's way.

Through the window, she watched Greg walk down the hallway and address Griffin. He wouldn't want to take them to investigate, but he wouldn't have to know what they were doing. He may wear pansy pink ties by day, but he'd started taking martial arts classes at night. If something went wrong, he could defend them. "We'll take Greg with us."

Marissa followed her line of sight. "I suppose."

Greg headed their way. He disappeared from view for a moment before the door swung open. He stopped when he saw them standing there. His dark eyes met Tandy's before he peeked cautiously at Marissa. As if satisfied to find her holding up okay under pressure, he turned back toward Tandy. "Everything okay?"

She'd start by addressing him as Connor's defense attorney. Keep him from suspecting that they were taking Connor's release upon themselves. "What are Connor's chances of getting out of jail by Saturday?"

"Well, there are no guarantees." He peeked at Marissa once more. "But if Griffin can track down Archibald the way he thinks he can, then it certainly improves our chances."

Tandy reached for Marissa's hand. "We're going to be optimistic about moving on with the wedding planning then. Do you want to go with us out to The Farmstead for one trip through the corn maze before it gets harvested?"

Greg glanced at his watch. Good. He wasn't suspicious. "I guess I'm off now. Though I'll want to run home and change."

Tandy bit the inside of her cheek. "We should probably go shut down Caffeine Conundrum too. Shouldn't take us long."

Marissa relaxed her stance, obviously more at ease with having Greg's help. "When it gets dark, they have actors dressed like zombies running around and scaring people."

A corner of Greg's lips curved up. "That's my favorite part. And it would be a good break from the stress you've been dealing with, huh, Marissa? I'll pick you both up after the shop closes."

Tandy didn't want to waste any time, but at least now they'd have a full moon to help them with their search.

Chapter Nineteen

GREG'S GOLD MERCEDES PULLED TO THE curb right as she flipped the shop's open sign to closed. When he climbed out of his car and stood, she admired his black leather jacket. Yeah, he wore it with a plaid shirt and khakis, so he was still kinda GQ, but her kind. She pulled on her own leather jacket and beanie then grabbed her purse to join him.

He kissed her cheek then opened the passenger door. "No Cocoa?"

Tandy smiled at memories of Cocoa yapping up a storm last year when trick-or-treaters came to her door. "No. Zam took him home for the night. Cocoa can't handle people in masks."

"He'd probably try to protect you from them, huh?" He closed her door and headed around the hood.

That was true about Cocoa trying to protect her. Maybe she should have brought him. But he was such a little guy. She was better off with Superman.

As for Marissa, she'd gone home to change her clothes, as well. Said she wanted to wear running shoes in case they had to run. Tandy got the impression Marissa wanted to be prepared to escape danger, while Tandy was ready to give chase.

It took a while to find parking in a field near the corn maze, then Greg and Tandy had to walk through the makeshift lot to get to the entrance. Their breath crystalized in visible white puffs, but the brisk temperature didn't deter visitors. A line for tickets wound along the fence. Marissa met Greg and Tandy at the ticket booth and waved to an employee who allowed them in without tickets.

Marissa had gone for the entire sporty look with her purple puffy jacket and ponytail through the back of a ballcap. Tandy should have known her friend wouldn't want to run from any shovel-wielding killers without looking stylish.

Firepits lit gathering spots, and the scent of burning logs filled the air along with the familiar cinnamon scent of the donuts Birdie stole on the day they'd met. Children bounced in bounce houses and slid down slides on potato sacks. Hydraulics hissed from the apple shooters, and pumpkins thunked down after being shot from pumpkin slingshots. A barrel train full of boisterous children chugged by.

"I've never seen it this busy." Tandy hadn't expected a crowd since she'd only been thinking of finding Archibald. Would he still stick around with so many people present? Had Griffin already looked here for him? She'd think the sheriff would have let her or Marissa know if the man had been found.

"Oh, yeah." Greg grinned like a kid on a field trip. "I always loved pumpkin patches when growing up. Did you two want anything to eat before we head in?"

The kettle corn did smell invitingly sweet, but Tandy had a bridesmaid dress to fit into in a couple of days.

Marissa turned her back on the field. "I need a corndog."

Tandy lifted an eyebrow. Her friend didn't seem too concerned about fitting into her wedding dress, but that could be because she was more concerned about having a wedding. As a stress-eater, the week before her wedding could be considered her Superbowl—sans the tackling.

"My treat." Greg walked backward toward the one concession stand that didn't seem too busy. "You don't want anything, Tandy?"

She'd be hungry later if she didn't eat. She shrugged. "I'll take the chili fries."

"You've got it." He pointed toward a couple leaving a bench by a firepit. "Warm yourselves up, and I'll be right back."

Tandy trudged after Marissa and sank onto a wooden bench cold enough to feel wet. She rubbed a hand over her rear to make sure she hadn't sat in a puddle. Nope. Dry, but she could use some hand warmers to stick in her back pockets. This wasn't how she'd imagined their search.

She extended fingers toward the fire to reach its warmth. "You think Archibald is still here?"

Marissa scanned the activities. "The maze is a good place to hide, but I'd expect him to be by the apple shooters."

Tandy glanced at the row of rifles firing Granny Smiths like bullets. No old men aimed at targets, only middle school boys who had to be freezing since none of them wore jackets. In fact, one even had bare legs sticking out from basketball shorts.

"Hey." Marissa pointed toward the maze. "Is that who I think it is?"

Tandy's gaze followed the invisible line from Marissa's finger toward the maze entrance. She tensed, expecting to see Archibald's red hunting cap, but instead she saw a man dressed in black. Adrenaline zipped up her spine.

The figure looked like the one they'd chased down the alley during their pedicure appointment, except he wasn't wearing a hockey mask this time. Or Winifred's wig. It was hard to tell the color of the man's hair under a black beanie. "You found the drug dealer!"

"No, it's my cousin."

Austin? "He looks like—"

"I know."

"What's he doing here?"

"Maybe he's looking for Archibald too."

Tandy narrowed her eyes. It was a possibility since Austin was at the police station when Griffin had the map on his computer. But he could also be using the search for Archibald as an excuse for some other shady activity.

He headed toward the maze. Tandy stood. She had to see what he was up to.

"Are you following without Greg?"

Tandy glanced over her shoulder to see how far away her boyfriend was, but she didn't see him in the crowd. "I can't let Austin get away."

"We should wait." Marissa stood and grabbed her arm. "We brought Greg to keep us safe."

Greg stepped into the flicker of firelight, corndog in one hand, chili fries in the other, and a big grin on his face. "You want me to keep you safe from zombies?"

Tandy twisted her lips. How much should she tell him?

"Actually," Marissa answered for her, "Archibald is hiding out on the farm."

Tandy grimaced as she waited for Greg's response.

He didn't disappoint, splaying his hands wide and almost stabbing a stranger with the corndog. "What?"

The stranger dodged just in time, but a few of Tandy's chili fries toppled to the grass. She rescued the overflowing paper container.

Greg let go of the fries but shook his head at her. "Why would we come if Archibald is here?"

It was hard to focus on her boyfriend while keeping an eye on the man in black behind him in the distance. Thankfully, there was a line to get into the maze, and Austin had to wait. So she took time to explain. "If Griffin could find Archibald, he would have picked him up by now. But I think the old guy will come out of hiding for a chance to talk to Marissa. He seems to want to help her."

Greg lowered his chin and his tone. "Tandy, he's a suspected killer. Marissa would be stupid to...no offense, Marissa...put herself in danger like that."

"No offense taken." Marissa plucked the corndog out of his flailing hand and took a bite. "Tandy is the one trying to put me in danger."

Tandy rolled her eyes at the idea of putting her friend in danger. She honestly couldn't see the old guy killing a good person. Archibald had been a soldier. He was trained to take out bad guys. So maybe Archibald would have killed Hubert if Hubert was stealing drugs, but he wouldn't hurt Marissa. "You forget Marissa is engaged to a suspected killer. How stupid is that?"

Marissa's eyes slid Tandy's direction and scowled. "Offense taken."

"I don't mean you're stupid, Marissa. I mean it's stupid we have to prove Connor innocent." Tandy brushed off Marissa's disapproval. Another fry bit the dust, leaving a trail of chili on her fingers. She licked off the spicy smear then dug into the container for more. The mixture of zesty meat, tangy tomatoes, and crispy shoestring potatoes filled her belly with satisfaction.

Greg didn't look as satisfied. "*My* job is to prove Connor innocent, but that doesn't include escorting two naïve women through a corn maze of zombies in search of a possible murderer. That's how horror movies start." Now that he had free hands, he was able to cross his arms. "Do you know how angry Connor would be at me for doing this? Angrier than when I beat him in fantasy football."

Marissa pointed the corndog Tandy's way. "He makes a good argument."

Of course he did. He was a lawyer. Tandy sighed and looked back toward the cornfield, unwilling to wave the white flag. Her gaze snagged on Marissa's cousin disappearing into the maze. "If we leave hunting Archibald to the sheriff, will you at least follow Austin with us?"

Greg arched an eyebrow. "The same Austin who happened to be wearing black the day that guy ran from you down the alley?"

Tandy shoved a few more fries in her mouth so she could toss the container in the garbage and give chase. "Yeah, he's wearing black again."

Marissa trotted after Tandy and Greg, trying to swallow the rest of her sweet cornbread and run at the same time. She'd finished the snack, but she'd keep the stick to use as a weapon as needed. The idea came from Connor who always called her favorite chick flicks "corndog movies." He joked that he needed to eat a corndog while watching them with her so he could use the stick to poke his eyes out when he finished eating. She bet he wouldn't mind watching a chick flick with her now.

As for her stick, she didn't know if she could actually poke someone, but she could always threaten. *Freeze, or I'll poke you in the eye with my corndog stick.* Yeah, she was probably better off praying that Austin wasn't a bad guy.

"Maybe Austin just likes to wear black," she called up to Tandy between huffs and puffs. "Or maybe he dressed like the Dread Pirate Roberts for Halloween."

Greg's eyebrows dipped at her reference to *The Princess Bride.* Apparently, he wasn't a fan of chick flicks either, though

The Princess Bride couldn't really be called a corndog movie. It had pirates in it.

"We'll find out." Tandy charged past the line of paying customers into the mouth of the maze.

An employee dressed like a zombie bride with a "bloody" dress and white face reached out to stop her.

Marissa waved at the employee as she ran through. "They're with me."

The girl stepped back. "Oh, sorry. I didn't see you, Marissa."

"It's okay." Being Connor's bride came with privileges, though if she didn't get Connor out of jail in time for the ceremony, she was going to feel dead like a zombie bride.

She smiled at the employee then faced forward again, realizing too late that Tandy and Greg had come to a stop at a T in the maze. She let up her pace and tried to dig her feet into the soft dirt, but it didn't look like she was going to be able to slow in time. She held up her hands, careful to turn the corndog stick so that it wouldn't jab Tandy when she ran into her.

"Watch out," she called. Pinching her eyes shut, she tensed for the upcoming crash.

A hand hooked her elbow and pulled her to a stop. She opened her eyes to find herself inches away from Tandy's back. She looked over at Greg holding her elbow. Wow. He had good reflexes.

Tandy turned to find them arm in arm like they were ready to skip down the yellow brick road. She tilted her head. "While you two might be afraid of lions, tigers, and bears, I'm afraid I've lost Austin."

Marissa looked right and left. The right trail was empty, but on their left, a zombie cheerleader waved pom-poms robotically. "Eat 'em up. Eat 'em up. Raw, raw, raw!"

"I'm afraid of *her*." Or perhaps the fear was Marissa's leftover PTSD from 8th grade cheerleading tryouts. She'd executed the perfect toe touch but somehow didn't get her feet back underneath her for landing. Her pride had been even more bruised than her tailbone.

Tandy headed toward the ghoulish girl fearlessly. Of course, the brunette had probably never tried and failed to make the rally squad. "Have you seen a guy dressed in black come through here?"

The cheerleader broke into a clap. "Hey, hey, what do you say? The guy in black went that-a-way." She struck a pose with one pom-pom pointing deeper into the maze.

Tandy nodded at Greg and Marissa. "Let's go."

Greg unhooked arms and jogged after his girlfriend.

Marissa followed, but eyed the creepy cheerleader as she passed. How did they know she was giving them actual information and not playing a part? Marissa opened her mouth to question Tandy when two hands reached from between cornstalks.

She screamed and waved her corndog stick like a magic wand. So much for using it as a weapon.

Attached to the hands came another female zombie. She wore a ripped gown, tilted crown and sash that read Dead Beauty Queen.

Marissa screamed louder and stomped her feet to make the nightmare stop. The zombies were mocking her life, which was worse than haunting. First, she hadn't made the cheer team. Then she'd fallen off the stage at the Miss Ohio pageant. Would she never become a bride either?

Greg appeared at her side, fists lifted. "What happened? Are you okay?"

Tandy had been wise to bring him along. If fight or flight syndrome was really a thing, he was a fighter. Though, what did that make Marissa? The saying really should be—fight, flight, or freak out.

She freaked. "No. I'm *not* okay."

Tandy joined Greg's side, looking her up and down to figure out what the problem was. It made Marissa feel even more absurd. But also angry.

She wailed. "I don't want to become a zombie bride."

The girl wearing the crown backed up like she was the one who had something to fear. "I'm just going to go…" She pointed down the maze for a moment then took off running.

Tandy wrapped an arm around Marissa's back, which was especially sweet since Tandy hated emotion. Marissa's friend's concern made her want to bawl even more.

Tandy patted her side stiffly. "I'm here, because as your maid of honor, I'm not going to let that happen."

Marissa wiped at an eye to keep from crying and a laugh escaped. "Because you don't want to be a zombie bridesmaid?"

Tandy lifted a shoulder. "I wouldn't mind it so much. I mean, my dress is already black."

Then they were both laughing. Greg eyed them with apprehension, though he lowered his fists.

"Marissa?" Another male voice spoke her name. This one deep with an audible smirk. Austin strutted down the path. "I thought that was your hysterics I heard, Cuz."

Marissa straightened, her mirth vanishing like her cloud of breath. He was the reason she'd had to face her failures in this maze of doom, and he wasn't even dressed in a pirate costume. Just a black jacket and joggers. "What are you doing here?" she demanded.

"Why the tone?" He stuck his hands in his pockets. "I'm trying to help you. Like before."

She narrowed her eyes. "You're trying to find Archibald?" Even if he was, it could be to plant incriminating evidence on the old man.

He quirked a brow as if surprised by the question. "Is that what *you're* doing? Because you'd probably have more luck if you stayed a little quieter."

She folded her arms. If he wanted to help, he could start by not making fun of her.

Tandy glared. "If you're not looking for Archibald, what *are* you doing here, Austin?"

Austin glanced from Tandy to Greg and shook his head like they were all idiots. Finally, he pointed up.

Marissa eyed Tandy who was already looking up before she lifted her own chin. A pair of old sneakers dangled from a power line by their shoelaces. Where had she seen that before?

"A sign for drug dealers." Tandy made the connection first.

That's right. There had also been shoes hanging above the alley where they'd chased the guy in the hockey mask. "How'd you know those were here?" she asked. Because she couldn't be sure Austin wasn't the drug dealer.

A group of giggling teenagers pushed past. Greg watched them, like he was ready for one of them to pull a shovel out of their back pocket.

"Kristin," Austin answered once the group was out of hearing range.

"Griffin's receptionist?" Greg challenged, still watching the teens.

"Yep." Austin looked around as if bored by their speed of sleuthing. "She's not only a receptionist. She also maps out crimes so Griffin can find a pattern and predict where a criminal might strike next."

Marissa wrinkled her nose. She'd always thought the lady was simply a gossip. "I didn't know that."

"Well," Austin gave a smile that might be considered charming if he wasn't such a jerk. "It helps if you talk to her sweetly."

A rogue teenager raced by to catch up with her friends. Greg positioned himself between their group and the pathway like a guard dog.

Tandy clicked her tongue. "Are you saying Kristin mapped this location for drug deals, and you decided to check it out?"

"That's exactly what I'm saying."

Ironic that Archibald picked this same spot to hide out. Unless he was also looking for the drug dealer.

Greg's fists rose in front of his chest. "Have you seen anything since you've been here?"

Austin huffed. "I might have if not for the commotion you three decided to make."

Marissa curled her toes in mortification. Her fit about not being able to solve the mystery could be what kept Connor in jail.

Tandy blinked slowly as if she thought Austin the idiot. "Don't listen to him, Marissa. It's not likely something was going to happen tonight anyway. It's too busy right now for anyone to try to get away with a crime."

"Or..." Austin wiggled his eyebrows. "It's the perfect night."

As if on cue, a guy in a rubber zombie mask burst out of the corn. He charged, axe wielded overhead.

Marissa's heart lurched, and she heard herself shriek. She wanted to run, but every neuron in her body exploded with tingles, preventing the message from traveling between her brain and muscles.

Greg, however, reacted at warp speed. His fist swung through the air, connecting with the mask's pockmarked nose.

Marissa was still on her first shriek when the attacker landed flat on his back. They all stared down in shock.

Austin glanced up from the body. "You can stop screaming now, Cuz."

Marissa closed her mouth and the silence that followed sounded even eerier. They were about to crack the case like the ending of a Scooby-Doo cartoon.

The man on the ground pulled up his own mask. With all the blood on his face, it took a moment for Marissa to recognize him as Vince, the farm employee who'd chased down Pete after he'd commandeered the tractor.

Vince touched his face then glared at Greg. "What did you punch me for, man?"

"You came at us with an axe." Greg shook his fist out from the punch then swiped Vince's weapon. The axe practically bounced out of his hand, and his eyes widened. He lifted it in front of his face. "It's fake."

"Of course it's fake." Vince groaned. "I get paid to pretend to attack people with it. That's my job."

He was pretending? Marissa winced.

Tandy covered her mouth at the realization her boyfriend had struck an innocent employee.

Marissa dug into her pocket for the little package of tissues she kept handy for Connor's allergies this time of year. She'd help Vince stop his nose bleed, then hopefully they could all laugh about this.

"As for you." Vince motioned to Greg before taking her tissue. "You're not allowed to touch employees."

Greg's face went slack. "I didn't mean to."

The teens returned in time to overhear Vince's claim. They weren't giggling anymore.

One pointed at Greg. "You had your fists up like you were ready to fight."

Oh, no. He had.

A family crowded in from the opposite side, faces pale. They were all witnesses now.

Vince touched his face, smearing blood across his cheek. "I can report you for assault."

Marissa's lips parted in despair. Greg couldn't be arrested for this, could he? He didn't deserve that. And also, if Connor's attorney went to jail, who was going to defend him in court?

Chapter Twenty

"I'M SO SORRY." GREG'S HANDS HUNG limply at his sides.

Tandy rubbed his arm. He'd only been trying to protect them, which is exactly what she'd brought him for. Of course, they'd been a little jumpier than most of The Farmstead visitors. And yeah, Greg was proud of his new ninja skills, but he never would have wanted to display them by beating up a fake zombie.

He dropped to his knees next to Vince and pulled off his jacket then his plaid flannel shirt. Being the GQ kind of guy he was, he wore a white t-shirt underneath, but he still had to be cold as he wadded up the flannel shirt for Vince to use as a handkerchief. The man had already bled through all Marissa's tissues, though she rummaged through her purse for more.

Austin watched from above, hands in pockets. "Have him sit up and lean forward to keep the blood from going down the back of his throat."

Greg reached to help Vince, but Vince held up the hand he wasn't using to plug his nose. "Don't touch me anymore, man," he said in a nasal tone.

Greg lowered his hands, looking to Tandy for help. She stepped forward to trade places with him and stooped down. Scooping an arm behind Vince's shoulders, she leaned her weight sideways to rock him up into a seated position.

An unbroken stream of blood poured onto Vince's jumpsuit that was already spotted with fake blood. Teenage girls giggled nervously, and a middle-aged woman moaned at the sight.

As if dizzy, Vince closed his eyes and dropped Greg's shirt in order to prop himself up with a hand to the dirt behind him.

Tandy grabbed the flannel shirt and held it up to catch the flow of blood before it had time to splatter. "Pinch the bridge of your nose."

Vince lifted his free hand. It looked rough and dirty, but it did the job.

"Here." Marissa squatted, offering something white and gauzy in her palm. "Tampons."

Vince opened his eyes to scowl. Austin chortled.

"It will absorb the blood," Marissa reasoned. "Just stick the ends in your nostrils."

Vince took the tampons slowly. "This better not end up on YouTube."

One of the teens pocketed her phone.

He growled but tucked the ends of the cotton tubes up his nose. Crisis averted. Now they wouldn't have to call 9-1-1.

"What's going on here?" a familiar voice boomed. The group of teenagers parted for the sheriff.

Tandy cringed and peeked at Greg. Who had called him, and how had the law officer arrived so quickly? Had he already been there searching for Archibald?

Greg took a deep breath and met Tandy's gaze. He would accept responsibility for his actions, so she'd play his defense attorney, because his motives were right. And because assault wouldn't look good on his record.

She handed Greg's shirt to Vince in case he wanted to use it to wipe himself off. Then she stood. "Greg accidentally punched one of the zombies."

Griffin hooked his thumbs in his belt loops and looked from Vince to Greg. "How do you accidentally punch someone?"

Greg ran a hand across his face. "Reflexes?"

"You came in here ready to fight," claimed the teen that had noticed him with fists up earlier.

Greg couldn't argue, so Tandy placed a hand on his shoulder in solidarity. "Vince jumped out of the corn and scared us."

"Yeah, and you got angry at me for getting too close, so you punched me." Vince looked up, tampons sticking from his nose, and Tandy had to bite her cheek to keep from laughing. She knew the situation was serious, but it sure looked funny. "This farm has been here for over ten years, and never before has a zombie gotten punched in the face. Visitors are even warned not to touch the entertainers."

He was certainly entertaining. The teenage girls began giggling again.

Griffin pressed his lips together as if he were also fighting amusement. "Sir, are you okay?" His low tone only cracked once.

Vince pushed to his feet and ripped the swollen, red, feminine products from his nose. No more blood rushed out, but the damage was already done. "No, I'm not okay." He pointed at Greg. "This guy probably broke my nose. And this lady"—he motioned toward Marissa with the tampons in his hand --"made it worse."

Marissa held a hand to her heart. "I was trying to help."

"By traumatizing me emotionally?"

Now the guy was taking his victim act a little too far. "Okay." Tandy sliced one hand down on the other palm in sign language for "stop" and stepped forward. "Greg said this was an accident, and he apologized. What more do you want?"

Vince narrowed his eyes at her before turning toward Greg. "I want you to try to convince a judge because I don't believe you."

Tandy's heart crashed into her ribs. "Are you serious? You want him arrested?" She balled her fists. If Greg was going to get thrown in the slammer for assault, she'd go with him.

Greg's fingers circled her upper arm, holding her back. How was he the rational one here?

The sheriff adjusted his belt and glanced uneasily at Greg before focusing on Vince. "Now, sir, you can press charges if you want, but—"

"But Greg's a lawyer," Tandy finished for him. "He'll get himself off."

Vince wiped dirty hands on his coveralls. "He's not above the law. You can't just go around punching people. Even if it was an accident, so is manslaughter."

Marissa shook her head. "You're not dead. You only look like it."

If looks could kill, Vince would have ended her life right there.

Marissa wrinkled her nose at the realization she wasn't helping, though Tandy personally appreciated the inadvertent insult.

Yeah, Vince was hurting, but whereas his injury had been unintentional, he was striking back on purpose.

Greg blew out a long breath. "It's okay, ladies. He's right that I'm not above the law. This is how the justice system works, and I'll support the justice system even when I'm the one being accused."

"But you're not guilty," Tandy cried. "This is injustice." Blast him for being such a decent human being.

"Enough," Griffin barked. "Greg, I'm going to have to take you in. You have the right to remain silent—"

"I know." Greg reached in his pocket and pulled out his car keys to hand to Tandy.

Her heart sank. She took the hard, jagged keys from him, but there had to be something more she could do than drive his car home. It was her fault he was even here. "I'm so sorry."

"It's not your fault." He gave her a sweet and steady smile and held out his wrists for Griffin to cuff. "At least Connor and I will be able to listen to football games together again."

She didn't deserve him.

The crowd murmured. The teenager's phone came back out. This time definitely in camera mode.

Marissa slid next to Tandy's side and circled a supportive arm around her waist. She also knew the helpless, heart-in-your-throat, righteous indignation of watching someone you love get arrested unfairly. Yeah, Tandy loved Greg. Not because of all the things he'd done for her, but for what she wanted to do for him.

"All right, folks." Griffin addressed the growing audience. "I'm going to get this gentleman out of the cold while my deputy takes statements from each of you."

Greg caught her eye and gave a don't-worry wink before Griffin ushered him out of the maze. How could he be so calm and confident? He hadn't even been able to get Connor out of jail yet, and he was a lawyer.

Tandy had thought she and Marissa were in this mess together before, but now Connor's release rested completely on their shoulders. Getting Connor out of jail had also become even more personal. She needed him to fire Vince if the guy didn't drop his charges against Greg.

Marissa leaned her head on Tandy's shoulder as they watched Griffin lead Greg away with Vince hobbling along behind. Was she hugging her friend tight to support Tandy or because she needed support now that her fiancé's lawyer was going to be cellmates with him?

Austin joined them, though his presence was as pointless as Charlie Brown waiting for The Great Pumpkin. "Drama follows you everywhere, doesn't it, Cuz?"

Marissa refused to look at him. "We followed you in here, *Cuz.*"

He chortled. "So I'm at fault for this?"

"No." Tandy groaned, more woeful than wronged. "Though it's extremely convenient."

Austin turned sideways to face them and stroked his smooth chin as if intrigued by the insinuation. "How so this time? Before you blamed me for a crime, but I clearly wasn't the one punching employees tonight."

"Employee, singular," Tandy corrected.

Marissa crossed her arms, hugging away the cold night and the chill from Austin's attitude. "He might not have punched anyone if we hadn't felt like we needed protection when following you into the maze."

Austin shook his head. "What did you think I might do that scared you so much? Wait for you to fall asleep, then draw a moustache on your face with permanent marker?"

The image of ten-year-old Austin sporting Sharpie facial hair flickered in Marissa's brain as if from a vintage recording. "I forgot we did that to you."

"No wonder you have issues," Tandy deadpanned.

Marissa scrunched her face in shame for the part she'd played.

Tandy lifted an eyebrow and pointed at the shoes hanging overhead. "Could one of your issues be dealing drugs?"

Had Marissa's childhood prank wars sent Austin down the wrong path? Was she liable for an alleged drug addiction because she once removed the cream from his Oreos and refilled them with toothpaste?

Austin huffed. "If I was the one having clandestine meetings under a pair of sneakers, you think I really would have pointed them out to you?"

Tandy lifted her chin, getting some of her old spark back. "Yeah, I think you're that arrogant."

A smirk spread across Austin's face, proving Tandy's point. "I'll take a drug test if you want me to, but if you're looking for convenience, you should talk to the deputy." He nodded toward Romero. "What exactly were he and Griffin both doing here tonight?"

Marissa bit her lip. Was Austin trying to sidestep their suspicions, or was he onto something? She'd wondered about the sheriff's sudden entrance, though she figured he probably could have heard her scream from back at the police department.

Tandy nodded. "We'll take you up on your offer of drug testing, *and* we'll talk to Romero. My guess is they were here looking for Archibald."

That made sense. Though Marissa still found Romero creepy, and she'd had enough scares for one night. "You can talk to him."

Tandy lifted a shoulder before heading to join the deputy and his witnesses. "I guess that's what a maid of honor is for, right?"

"Right." Who else was there to ask police questions when both the groom and best man got arrested for crimes in a corn maze? Marissa watched her friend stride away and found herself alone with her cousin once again.

Austin kicked at a rock. "You still think there's going to be a wedding?"

Not wanting to answer, she set her jaw. Why did her cousin act like it was okay for him to cause trouble then pretend he wanted to help? "If not, I can always put on a fake wedding ring like you."

Austin's eyes snapped up at that, flashing with a shadow of the pain she remembered from their childhood. Then they cleared, and he was looking down his nose once again. "May my fake wedding ring be a reminder that your life could always be worse. At least you have someone who wants to marry you."

Marissa blinked from the impact of his words. Maybe she wasn't the one who'd hurt him the most in life. Maybe the bride who jilted him caused him to turn to drugs. "What do you mean?"

He brushed the air with the back of his hand and strolled away. "Don't worry about it," he casually tossed over his shoulder.

Marissa frowned after him. Tandy considered him a suspect, but he didn't scare her. If he'd gotten himself into trouble, she couldn't help but think it was an attempt at finding love. Could she blame him if he'd started taking drugs to numb his anguish? It did hurt to be alone.

With that thought, she realized how deserted she'd become there in the dark cornfield by herself with only the silver glow from moonlight overhead. Tandy still spoke with Romero at the spot where the maze had come to a T, but the stalks around Marissa could conceal more predators.

She listened for danger over the crescendo of her heartbeat. What had made her ever want to get married in this terrifying place?

"Marissa?" a gruff voice hissed.

Her body froze. All except for the tiny hairs along her neck, which stood on end like cornstalks. She slid her eyes side to side, looking for the owner of the voice.

"Marissa, it's me, Archibald."

Her eyes bulged, searching for a glimpse of the old man, but she couldn't tell from which direction his voice came.

She wasn't afraid of Archibald either, only afraid they wouldn't catch him. She'd try to get Tandy's attention or tackle the old man on her own, but first she needed him to say something else so she could pinpoint his location. "The police are looking for you."

"That's a bunch of hooey." He grunted. "Those whippersnappers almost caught me. Thankfully, you screamed and drew them away in the nick of time."

She closed her eyes. Griffin had been so close to arresting Archibald, and she'd messed it all up. "Why don't you turn yourself in?"

"Bull pucky." He snorted. "Then Hubert's murder would never be solved."

Her lungs expanded with hope. "Have you solved it?"

"I was about to."

The voice came from her left. She turned her head to comb the rows of darkness for a glimpse of the senior snoop.

"Don't look at me. I don't want to draw attention."

She could keep looking and yell for help, or she could finish listening to what he had to say first. She glanced at her feet to keep from attracting attention. Good thing she'd worn her *old* running shoes since they were covered in mud. "What do you mean you were about to solve the murder?"

He coughed, and she wondered if his health was at risk. It couldn't be good for his immune system to be sleeping out here in the cold.

"This is the spot where Hubert sold the drugs he stole. So I'm watching to see who shows up."

That was Austin's excuse too. "Who showed up?" Marissa studied the footprints around her feet. Could one of them be from the killer? Did the drug dealer wear flat soles or shoes with lots of tread?

"There was a teenage twit hangin' out here like she was waitin' for someone. I don't think she's the new drug dealer, but I think she was waitin' for whoever it was."

Could that have been the teen who filmed Greg's arrest? "You didn't see who met her?"

"That's when the cops started sniffing around. They must have found my number from the burner phone I gave Birdie then triangulated my location."

Marissa's eyebrows arched. He was good.

"I had to skedaddle before I saw if the twit met up with anyone or not. But whoever it was, they had to be nearby."

A heavy sigh fogged the air in front of Marissa, but she saw Austin's face in her mind. He'd been nearby. Again. At least he'd agreed to get a drug test. She'd hold him to it. Even schedule it for him tomorrow.

"I believe you, Archibald," she said. And she really did. He was on her side, and she wanted to be on his side. "Can you please come with me to tell your story to the police? I know you don't trust them, but even if they put you in jail for the time being, you'd have a warm place to sleep."

He coughed again then cleared his throat. "I've lost toes to frostbite before. This is nothin'. Just part of the hunt."

Marissa tried not to imagine the man's feet. "Archibald, you're coughing—"

"Give Birdie a peck on the cheek for me."

Marissa's expression softened. He may be a cranky old man, but he loved his wife. "Come in and kiss her yourself."

"I want to, but I'm doing somethin' even more important for her. I'm makin' the world a better place for our heirs."

Stalks waved and fallen husks rustled. He'd disappear if she didn't try to stop him. If she alerted the creepy deputy, it would be for Archibald's own safety. She knew he was trying to do the right thing, but she had to make the right choice as well.

Archibald would hate her for it, and it could even destroy her only chance of having Connor proved innocent, but that's what love did. It did what was best for others even when it didn't feel good.

She shook her head and jogged toward Tandy and Deputy Creeperson. "Archibald is here."

Chapter Twenty-One

TANDY TOOK OFF THROUGH THE ROWS of corn in the direction Marissa pointed. Surely, she could catch the old man. Then he'd have to reveal what he knew. Or maybe even confess to Hubert's murder.

She flicked the flashlight on her phone and alternated from pointing the beam in front of her to shining her light through the cornstalks, looking for movement. So far, nothing.

Romero followed, static crackling on his two-way radio. "Romero to Griffin, come in."

She slowed before stepping onto an open path. She checked to make sure the area was clear and Archibald hadn't found another shovel, though she had trouble believing he'd use it on a girl. He was old fashioned that way.

Detective Romero burst into the clearing beside her. "This is police business," he scolded her. "You need to exit the maze immediately."

She didn't have time to argue if they were going to catch Archibald. She watched the top of cornstalks to see if any were moving more than others. There.

She dove into the amber waves once again. "You guys just arrested my boyfriend. I'm going to do what I can to get him out of jail," she called back.

Romero's footsteps pounded after her. "Your boyfriend was trying to protect you. He wouldn't want you out here, chasing a suspect."

Greg didn't have much of a choice now. The two of them had reconnected last year when he'd helped her get out of jail, and she still owed him. Romero's words would only push her harder.

Static crackled from the deputy's radio. "What is it, Romero?"

The deputy explained their chase between huffs and puffs. Tandy's own breath grew louder as she continued on in the still night.

She made it to another path. A group of teens screamed at her sudden appearance. She pushed through them. "Did you kids see an old guy in a hunting cap come this way?"

"What kind of zombie are you?" asked one of the boys.

Romero joined her. "I'm the kind with the authority to shut down this corn maze. You all need to leave immediately. After you answer the question about an old man."

One teen laughed. "Is this part of the entertainment? I love it."

"No." Tandy could almost hear the deputy ground his teeth. She turned in a circle, scanning their surroundings. They didn't have time to wait for answers.

Floodlights flashed on from the four corners of the field. The teens shrieked. Tandy raised an arm to shield her eyes from the sudden brightness.

A voice boomed from a bullhorn in the distance. "This is the police. The Farmstead is being shut down. I need everyone to exit in a quick and orderly fashion."

"Dude," yelled one of the teens. "This is awesome."

Tandy wished Greg was there to punch him. She jumped to see if she could get a better view from higher up. She didn't see Archibald, but she caught a glimpse of Marissa's purple jacket from the top of the metal bridge. She'd have a good view of the maze from up there.

Tandy jumped again to see which way Marissa was looking.

Marissa caught her eye and pointed toward the pumpkin patch at the back of the maze. "He's getting away," she shouted.

Tandy grabbed the deputy's arm and tugged. "This way."

With the lights overhead, she was able to run without the aid of her flashlight. Having a direction to head helped too. Her ankles threatened to turn on the mushy ground, but she pushed harder, picking up pace. Cornstalks rustled behind her as Romero followed.

They burst into the pumpkin patch to find people everywhere. Families laughed and chatted as they roamed through the vines, picking gourds to take home. Apparently, the announcement of shutting down the place hadn't reached their ears. Perhaps because they'd been riding on a trailer of hay bales behind a noisy tractor.

Sheriff Griffin rounded the corner of the field to join them. He lifted his bullhorn to his mouth. "The pumpkin patch is now closed for a manhunt. If you don't want to be searched, return to your hayride immediately."

The crowd quieted then murmured among themselves. None of them moved very quickly.

Tandy jogged to the middle of the patch, checking every person she passed for a buffalo checked cap or jacket. Archibald had to be here. Her eyes caught on a body in red at the far end of the field. It hid, partially in a ditch and behind a pumpkin.

"Look!" She pointed and checked over her shoulder to make sure Griffin and Romero saw the person too.

"This is not a drill." The sheriff's voice echoed through the night. "I need the pumpkin patch cleared. Hurry."

The crowd did not hurry. They moseyed, mouths agape.

Romero drew his gun.

They screamed and ran, stampeding past Tandy.

Griffin nodded to her. "Stay here."

Tandy froze, eyes focused on the guy hiding in the distance and the police moving in on him. She could feel the rumble of the tractor engine behind her. Her heart continued to thump loudly even when the sounds of the hayride faded. She wiped perspiration from her forehead, not cold anymore despite the crisp air.

The cops took positions on either side of Archibald's hideout, Romero behind a sign and Griffin behind a pyramid made out of hay. They both crouched low, guns pointed at their target.

Tandy wondered if she should take cover, as well. There weren't many hiding spots in the wide-open space, so she simply squatted to make herself smaller. She'd run if she had to, but hopefully Archibald would turn himself in peacefully.

"Archibald," Griffin called through his bullhorn. "We have you surrounded. Come out with your hands up."

No movement.

Griffin motioned to Romero. Romero nodded. They moved in together.

"Last chance, Archibald."

Tandy held her breath. *Come on, Archie.*

The man stayed hidden.

Something cool touched her hand. Tandy's heart jumped like a kid in a bounce house. But it was only Marissa beside her, come to watch the takedown.

Marissa gripped Tandy's fingers. "Lord, don't let him do anything stupid. Keep them all safe."

"Amen," Tandy whispered.

Griffin nodded. The men charged. Archibald's coat didn't move, from what Tandy could see. The two men stood above him, guns pointed.

Griffin nudged Archibald with his foot. Romero lowered his weapon.

Marissa covered her mouth. "Is he okay?"

Griffin bent over and picked up a scarecrow wearing Archibald's coat and hat. This was the second time his coat had led them astray.

Tandy groaned and turned to look in the direction the hayride had gone. "He's more than okay." He'd had plenty of time to escape.

Marissa rubbed the grit out of her eyes the next morning and stared from the warmth of her bed at the antique drum ceiling light decorated with a crystal flower bud design. Today was the eve of her wedding. Or what should have been the eve of her wedding if she were to have a wedding. It would be kind of hard to do a rehearsal with the groom in jail.

Last night, they'd come so close to catching the drug dealer and then Archibald. But not close enough.

Her phone vibrated on the nightstand. It would be Mom. Or her wedding planner, wondering if she was ready to call it quits.

And she didn't have an answer.

She reached for her phone to see what Tandy had to say but her hand bumped the soft leather of her little pink Bible. Maybe that's what she should have been reaching for.

She gripped the spine and held it up to stare at. "Do you have any answers for me, Lord?"

The Bible said *love never fails*, but that wasn't a guarantee Connor would get out of jail. It wasn't a guarantee that if he married her, they'd live happily ever after. So what kind of guarantee was it?

She flipped open the cover and leafed through thin crinkly pages, finding I Corinthians 13, the love chapter they'd been studying in premarital counseling. Verse seven jumped out at her.

It bears all things, believes all things, hopes all things, endures all things. Love never fails.

Her heavy heart didn't know if it could bear anymore. It had been through too much.

Maybe that was the point. With all the disappointment and pain in life, it was easier to stop believing. It seemed prudent to quit hoping. Smarter to give up.

But then, what would that get you? Nothing. It was a vicious cycle.

Marissa had heard that one of the greatest regrets of the elderly was that they hadn't taken more risks. Going for the gold didn't guarantee you would win, but *not* going for the gold guaranteed you *couldn't* win.

Pete had lost his farm, but his attempts at driving a tractor brought a huge smile to his face.

Winifred sang through cancer.

Birdie was losing her memory but that didn't stop her from sneaking donuts and trying to bust an innocent man out of jail.

As for Archibald? Whether what he was doing was right or wrong, he was doing it out of love for a woman who didn't even remember him.

They weren't letting pain get them down. They weren't giving up hope. They weren't protecting their hearts from disappointment. The old folks at Grace Springs Manor broke through their pain with the love of life.

Even if they didn't get what they were after, they went for it. The way God went after her.

God's love was the only guarantee. His love didn't fail. And He was going to be her example.

She would choose to bear all things, believe all things, hope all things, endure all things. Connor may not get out of jail in time to attend the wedding she'd planned, but on the slim chance that he did, they could only have a wedding if she continued to plan it. So that's what she'd do.

If he wasn't released, she'd marry him in front of a justice of the peace, because that's what she told him she'd do. And love never failed.

Even when it made a person look crazy.

Tandy would normally hate decorating for a wedding, but today she hated it with the kind of passion that turned brides into bridezillas. And she was only the maid of honor. How was Marissa able to be so level-headed about table placement and linens? She was usually the crazy one.

Marissa planted her hands on her hips and tilted her head, completely absorbed in the barn décor. She'd even dressed in the white leggings and a long, cream, cowlneck sweater she'd bought for her rehearsal dinner. "What do you think, Tandy? Should we put the long table for the wedding party at the front or along the side?"

Tandy shivered and crossed her arms. "Just put it next to the propane heater." At least Connor's family owned this venue, and they wouldn't be out too much money when he didn't show up for the ceremony.

Marissa looked up with a sweet smile. "Good idea."

Tandy forced herself to smile in return though she probably more closely resembled a zombie from the corn maze than a bridesmaid. "Is your mom coming to help?" she asked in place of, *Does your mom know you're about to lose your sanity and are going to need her to rock you the way only a mom can rock a crying baby?*

"Yep. Mom and Aunt Linda are finishing up the personalized lanterns she made for centerpieces. They're bringing them over with lunch."

Lunch would reveal how stressed Marissa really was. Tandy bet she'd stuff all the cookies in her mouth before the sandwich wrap was even opened.

"Hey, Marissa." Vince stuck his head in the barn door, his nose a little crooked between the dark bruises under his eyes.

Tandy squeezed her short unmanicured fingernails into her palms, ready to reenact last night's fight scene. Why hadn't the farmhand been fired yet?

Marissa did a double take, her brown eyes flickering with wariness on second glance. "Yes, Vince?"

Tandy forced herself to be still and wait. Maybe God had worked a miracle and the jerk was dropping charges.

"The rental company just delivered your tableware," he said. "I signed for it for you."

Tandy narrowed her eyes. How did he have the gall to show his face and act like everything was normal with the wedding planning when he'd just put the groom's lawyer in jail? If the wedding got canceled, all the guests should take their dinnerware and throw it at him.

Glass shattered, and it wasn't until Marissa ran toward the door of the barn that Tandy realized the sound was coming from real life and not her fantasy. She blinked and charged after her friend.

"Oh, no..." Marissa stopped short, and Tandy almost trampled her.

She caught herself in time to see Farmer Pete driving the big, green tractor over boxes set on the ground. Vince ran and jumped on the side of the tractor, forcing Pete to slow down and stop.

Tandy's heart sunk. She was afraid to look at her friend. Afraid the scene was going to serve her simply one too many shots of espresso.

Chapter Twenty-Two

MARISSA STARED AT THE MANGLED CARDBOARD and shards of white porcelain spilling out from underneath tractor tires. Her heart felt every bit as shattered, her face just as pale.

"No," she said. This wasn't happening. She couldn't believe it. Pete couldn't have escaped Grace Springs Manor again. Vince couldn't have left the tractor available for him to climb into again. The old farmer should have had too much experience with tractors to accidentally run over a pile of boxes.

If she accepted that this was happening, would she be able to move forward? One did not simply order a second set of dishes from a rental company when the groom was in jail.

Tandy squeezed her shoulder. "I'll get it cleaned up. Then we can...uh...go buy paper plates. The thick ones. Those are kind of classy, right?"

"No," Marissa said again. Both refusing to believe her dishes were ruined and that there was any kind of paper plate acceptable for use at a wedding. They might as well go buy red plastic cups and dispense iced tea from a bright orange beverage cooler. They were definitely going to have to serve cupcakes after she smashed her wedding cake into Vince's face. With her luck, he would press charges, and she would get to spend her wedding day in jail too. "When does my cake arrive?"

Pete headed their direction, skinny knees leading the way. His trademark smile had slipped to reveal wrinkles she hadn't noticed before. "Boy howdy, Miss Marissa. I didn't see those boxes there. I came over looking for you."

Should she laugh or cry? Or both?

Vince followed behind him, phone to his ear. "Yes, Pete escaped again. I need you to come pick him up from The Farmstead. He crashed into some things needed for Marissa's wedding."

Marissa covered her mouth, holding back a sob at the reality Vince's words forced her to face. Though it wasn't really the dishes she would mourn. Her fiancé was the only thing needed for her wedding.

Vince shoved his phone in his jacket pocket. "I'm sorry too, Marissa. I left the keys in the tractor when I hopped down to greet the delivery man."

Marissa huffed, unable to form actual words.

Tandy didn't share the problem of being speechless. "Are you saying accidents happen, Vince?"

Vince touched his nose and looked away.

"Maybe Marissa should press charges against you for negligence."

Vince crossed his arms. "I'm not the one who ran over the boxes."

Pete took off his hat, regret marring his forehead and dampening his light brown eyes. "I was hoping you girls would take me back home."

Marissa's eyebrow dipped. What was it with the men of Grace Springs Manor wanting to hang out with her? First Archibald, now Pete.

Tandy's voice snagged her thoughts. "Are you serious, Vince? You're throwing a senior citizen under the tractor?"

Marissa closed her eyes. Playing the blame game wouldn't help anyone. She felt like throwing dishes, but they'd already been smashed. She took a deep breath of sweet earth and pungent tractor exhaust before forcing herself to face the chaos in front of her. "Please. Both of you. Help me clean up this mess."

Tandy jutted her stiff jaw Vince's way before turning her back on him. She grabbed an empty rain barrel next to the barn and dragged it toward the broken dishes. Though she always took her attitude with her, Tandy could be counted on to do what was needed.

Vince followed suit, thank goodness. He shrugged out of his navy barn jacket and hung it on one of the white folding chairs lined in front of the barn before climbing back onto the tractor and moving it out of their way.

Pete found a shovel from somewhere and used it to start scooping the shattered dishes into the barrel.

Marissa frowned at the shovel. If she was going to blame anything for destroying her wedding, it should be the shovel. If only murder weapons like that weren't so readily available on farms. She doubted Pete was the murderer, but still, seeing a shovel in his hands made her shiver a little.

Of course, that's when Mom's Jaguar full of female relatives rolled up. The twins climbed out of the backseat.

Amber tossed her beautiful hair. "What happened here? Are those your dishes?"

Ashlee actually laughed. "I knew you were clumsy, Marissa, but I never imagined you could destroy a hundred table settings at once."

Aunt Linda gasped. "Oh, honey. Maybe this is a sign."

Mom opened her door, alarm separating her perfect red lips.

The group stilled, waiting for her response. Marissa looked from face to face. Aunt Linda's concern was genuine, not fake like that of her daughters who kept glancing at each other smugly. Mom appeared torn between wanting to look good and wanting to support her daughter, which was an improvement for her. As for Tandy, her cheeks simmered pink, a teapot ready to boil.

But the face that mattered most was locked behind bars. Connor was the one she was doing this for. And she'd keep doing it. No matter what. "We're getting paper plates."

Aunt Linda guffawed. The twins snickered.

Mom met her gaze, the flash of conflict in her eyes dimming with determination. Perhaps pride. She gave a small nod. Half a smile. "Get back in the car, ladies. We're going to buy paper plates."

Marissa watched them drive away, even more amazed at Mom's response than when Pete ran over her dishes. This is what it felt like to have her mother on her side. To feel worth fighting for. Such a little gesture could be life-changing for them.

Porcelain crashed into the rain barrel, drawing Marissa's gaze back toward Tandy and Vince, cleaning up shattered dishes.

Tandy watched her with wary eyes as she worked. "You okay?"

Marissa stood still, taking stock of her feelings in the same way she often did after a fall. Where did it hurt?

No panic rose up. No dread. No wild desperation. It was weird. Like that time Connor tried to teach her how to ski, and she'd lost control, tumbling dangerously down a mountain. As she'd lain in the snow, questioning her ability to get up or even walk again, she realized she'd been protected by her thick winter gear as well as the snow itself.

"I'm okay," she said in wonder. Perhaps that was how God's unfailing love worked. It insulated from the damage of life. Because, believing in His resurrection power meant no matter how far she fell, she'd be able to get up again.

Tandy lifted a crystal goblet that had lost its stand in a mock toast before dropping it into the rain bucket.

That might be the only toast Marissa got from her maid of honor, but it was enough. She smiled her thanks then bent to pick up shards of glass that had been strewn across the lawn.

A short black bus painted with the sweeping blue logo for Grace Springs Manor crunched over gravel. Yvette's red curls bounced from her spot behind the steering wheel. Marissa could tell the woman's mouth was open in laughter before she even cut the engine and opened the door. Sure enough, her amusement greeted them first.

Marissa still wanted to be angry at the activities' director for ruining her breakfast with her family, but it was hard to be angry at someone who had such a contagious laugh.

Yvette's face radiated sunshine even as she apologized. "I'm so sorry he got out. We're training a new CNA at the retirement community, and she didn't realize she hadn't closed the door to the memory ward all the way." Joy punctuated each sentence until Yvette got closer and realized the mess being cleaned up was caused by her escapee. "Uh-oh. Your dishes."

Marissa wrinkled her nose. At least Yvette felt bad about it. She must not have anything personal against Marissa anymore. Her earlier anger had to be the strain from her job.

Marissa shrugged a shoulder at the broken dishes. What was one more loss? "Mom went to pick up paper plates."

"Pete!" Yvette scolded.

Pete dropped his shovel and lowered his head.

Marissa held up a hand. "It's okay. Really."

Vince took the shovel from Pete. "Here. I'll take that. Let's get you in the bus, Pete." He dumped the shovel's contents in the rain barrel with a puff of glass particles.

"Thank you." Yvette wrung her hands, continuing to apologize as Vince propped the shovel against the rain barrel with a plinking sound and marched Pete away. The activities' director giggled a couple times, but not with happiness. More like she was trying to force Marissa to laugh along.

Marissa continued picking chunks of glass out of the gravel with the hopes that Yvette would see she had both moved on and had more to do. "I'm just glad Pete wasn't hurt," she said. He mattered more than a bunch of dishes that could be replaced with paper.

"Yes. Yes." Yvette walked backwards but kept talking. "It could have been much worse. I'll have a talk with the CNAs and make sure he's watched more carefully."

Marissa smiled and nodded, letting more dish fragments tinkle into the barrel and drown out Yvette's yammering. The woman finally turned, and Marissa squatted to pinch at smaller pieces of glass, careful not to cut her skin.

She reached for a white shard when an amber piece caught her eye from behind the shovel head. She hadn't ordered any amber colored glass, had she? Maybe Mom had snuck in a special set of dishes for the bride and groom.

She leaned forward to retrieve the piece. It gave in her fingers as she pinched it, more flexible than glass. She pulled it from its hiding place, and a beam of sunlight turned it orange. She lifted the round cylinder to discover a white cap, and her heart hitched at a sticker with lettering. This was a prescription bottle.

Had Vince dropped it? She'd heard a plinking sound when he set the shovel down. She glanced at the bus to see if he was looking her way, but from her squatting position, the farm hand wouldn't be able to see what she held.

She bit her lip and turned the bottle over. *Roberta Clack.* Who was *that*? The delivery driver? Could she have dropped her pills in the box of dishes?

Clack sounded familiar. Clack. Clack...

Archibald Clack!

Roberta had to be Birdie.

Marissa gasped. There was one person who could have dropped Birdie's prescription drugs in that spot. Vince.

"Did you cut yourself?" Tandy asked.

"No." Marissa held up the bottle so only Tandy could see it. "I just found a bottle of Birdie's prescription drugs that Vince dropped."

Tandy's gaze flicked to the name on the bottle. *Roberta Clack.* Though she hadn't known Birdie's given name, she had no doubt Marissa was right. She squinted to read the name of the drug. *Diazepam.* She'd never heard the name before, but she bet if it was close to the field where alleged drug sales had taken place, it had to have some street value.

As for Vince? He'd been in the corn maze last night in the exact same spot where a pair of shoes had hung overhead. The teen could have been waiting for him, but Greg punched him in the face before he could make a sale.

Or maybe Vince wanted to get punched in the face, so he could get rid of Connor's attorney since Connor had taken the fall for Hubert's murder. Which only made sense if he was the murderer.

Archibald had been so close to catching Vince. And she'd been close to catching Vince in the alley and the pharmacy.

But how did he get Winifred's wig? Could he have stolen it off Hubert when he'd attacked him with the shovel? Stolen these drugs as well?

Her pulse tapped a Morse code warning: Vince was nearby. There was a shovel right in front of her. If they confronted him, they could get whacked.

"What do we do?" Marissa hissed.

Tandy grabbed the shovel for defense and held it up like the weapon it was. She glanced over her shoulder to see where Vince had gone. Still in the bus, helping Pete. Or perhaps, trying to steal more drugs.

"Real subtle." Marissa pocketed the pills, staying crouched in her hidden spot.

Tandy set the shovel on end and stood tall like the farmer with his pitchfork in *American Gothic*. That would look more natural, right?

"I'll call Griffin." Marissa pulled out her phone.

Tandy twisted her lips. "You think he'll believe our claims against Vince? Your fingerprints are all over the bottle. It will seem like we're out for revenge since the guy put Greg in jail." She peeked at Vince in the bus again, confirming her memory that he'd been wearing work gloves. "He might not have left any fingerprints. And he could claim he's never seen these pills before. Maybe even blame us for stealing them. I mean, we've been in Birdie's room, while he hasn't."

Marissa ceased dialing and looked at her phone helplessly. "What do you think we should do then?"

Tandy frowned down at her friend. They needed more evidence before they called Griffin. Something that proved Vince had a connection with Hubert.

Her gaze flicked to the bus once more. The man sure was taking his sweet time, but it could work in their favor. He'd left his phone in his jacket pocket, which hung on the white folding chair right behind her. She set the shovel down.

"Watch Vince for me. Let me know if he looks this direction." Tandy's pulse rapid fired like it was laying down cover for her to move in a shootout. Did Birdie get this rush every time she swiped something?

Marissa's eyes bulged at Tandy before she turned to peek over the rain barrel. "He's laughing with Yvette."

Tandy creeped backwards toward the jacket, hooking her hands behind her. This way if Vince glanced over, he wouldn't suspect her of rifling through his things. Her fingers connected with a soft corduroy collar. She walked them down to stiff canvas then reeled the side of the jacket upward to reach the pocket without bending over.

"You know what this means?" Marissa asked.

Tandy felt an opening in the material. She slid her hand inside. Empty. Her heart shuddered in disappointment. "Birdie was right about her drugs being stolen?"

"And…" Marissa glanced her way. "Austin is innocent."

Tandy released the wrong side of Vince's jacket and side-stepped to the other side of the chair to repeat her process. "Were you worried?"

"Yeah." Marissa sighed. "His sisters weren't the nicest to him, and I'd joined in their tricks sometimes. I failed him as a cousin."

This side of Vince's jacket felt a little heavier. That had to be a good sign. Tandy worked her fingers past cool, round buttons. "People fail each other all the time," she reasoned absently. Her hand slipped under the flap concealing an opening. "What matters is that we don't stop trying."

"He's coming."

Tandy's breath hitched, and she dug into Vince's pocket with a jerk. Her fingers clutched the smooth, solid rectangle inside. She released the jacket and slid Vince's phone into her back pocket in one smooth motion.

Gravel crunched. The bus roared to life.

Tandy glanced Vince's direction without looking directly at him. Sure enough, he was sauntering their way. She scrambled toward the barn. "Let's go."

Marissa popped up from behind the rain barrel like a Jack-in-the-box. She stared awkwardly at Vince for a moment. "Can you finish cleaning this up?" she asked robotically. "Tandy and I have to keep setting up tables."

"Yeah. Sure." Vince shrugged.

Tandy exhaled. Though Marissa wasn't the best actress, she'd given Vince a distraction that would keep him busy for a while. They'd have time to go through his phone before he realized it was missing.

She watched from the shadows of the barn door as Marissa ran her way. Unfortunately, she didn't bring the shovel.

"You left him a murder weapon," she hissed when Marissa rounded the corner of the wide barn door.

Marissa stopped in her tracks, hands hanging empty by her sides. "He needs it to scoop up broken dishes."

Hopefully, that was all he'd use it for. "Fine. I guess I'll just have to be fast." She swiped a thumb across the phone screen and they both stared down at a lock screen with a keypad for entering numbers. Tandy shook her head, unsure where to begin with code cracking. "Birdie could do it."

"Maybe we should take the phone to Griffin," Marissa suggested.

If only. "Police have to use warrants and stuff. Otherwise evidence is inadmissible in court."

"Okay, *Greg*. Now what?"

Tandy didn't have an answer. If Vince was a drug dealer, his phone would be the most incriminating piece of evidence.

If only his lock screen was controlled by facial recognition. Then they could knock him out with the shovel and hold his face in front of the device to gain access. Though she didn't see either of them capable of hitting him with a shovel. Could they sedate him with drugs? That would be ironic. Except there was no facial recognition feature on his phone. They needed a passcode.

The phone buzzed in her hand. She jumped and almost dropped it.

"Incoming call." Marissa jogged in place with excitement. "This could be the evidence we need. Who's calling?"

Tandy read the name flashing on the screen. "It's Yvette."

Chapter Twenty-Three

MARISSA FROZE MID-JOG. OF ALL THE people calling to buy drugs, she'd never expected Yvette. "Why would Yvette have Vince's number?"

Tandy stared at the screen. "She could have gotten it when she was here."

Marissa wrinkled her nose. That didn't explain why Vince would have her number programmed in, though it did make sense that the activities' director would want to stay in contact with The Farmstead since Pete kept sneaking over and driving the tractor. But… "She was just here. Why would she need to call now?"

Tandy's thumb hovered over the answer icon. "I could ask her."

Marissa leaned backward for a peek out the door at Vince. He was still shoveling broken dishes, so he hadn't missed his phone yet, but he would. "What if we go ask her? That way she doesn't know we…uh, borrowed…Vince's phone, and he won't know either. He may think he dropped it like he dropped the drugs."

Tandy smooshed her lips together. "I do like the idea of getting away from him and his shovel."

Marissa looked around at her half-decorated wedding reception venue. So much still to do, but if she was going to have a groom, she needed to follow up on every lead. "Let's go."

They snuck to Tandy's Bug and took off before Vince could stop them. Marissa twisted in her seat and watched him shrink in the rear window. "We need to hurry before my mom returns."

"We will, though your mom is a toughie." Tandy slowed to turn onto the main road. "As for your cousins, I feel sorry for anyone who crosses them."

Marissa flopped forward with a sardonic laugh. "Maybe we should have brought them with us. They could be our bodyguards."

"At an old folks' home?" Tandy buzzed along the river toward the huge brick estate. "Who are you more scared of — Winifred in her wheelchair or Birdie and her cookie snatching?"

"A cookie sounds good." Maybe she'd see if Birdie could snatch one for her.

"I knew you were stressed."

Marissa leaned sideways against the cool window. She'd been imagining her wedding since she was a little girl, but she'd never imagined it like this. "I'm at peace with having my wedding canceled, but that doesn't mean I have to like it."

Tandy pulled into the parking lot, her gaze sliding sideways to eye Marissa. "Your wedding isn't canceled yet, and if it's up to me, it won't be."

Marissa appreciated the support, but she didn't want to get her hopes up. As soon as Tandy shifted into park, she popped her door open and headed for the entrance. "It's okay, Tandy. Let's just focus on finding the real killer, whether it gets Connor out in time for our ceremony or not." She'd thought she'd had direction from God on continuing the preparations, but that could have been to give her mom a chance to step in and be the mom Marissa had always wanted her to be. Or for them to find Vince's stolen drugs.

Tandy threw on her little black backpack and pocketed her keys. "Are you sure?"

Marissa paused outside the entrance, waiting for Tandy to catch up, so she could give her a side hug. "You've been a great maid of honor. But I don't want to think about the wedding anymore." She turned to enter the sliding glass doors together. "This isn't about me."

"Surprise!" yelled a group of grandmas.

Marissa jolted to a stop in the entrance. Her eyes roved the foyer from the balloon arch that had been replaced with pink balloons to the table holding a two-tiered cake to the semi-circle of chairs filled with little old ladies. The doors started to slide closed on her automatically, but she took a step and her weight triggered them to whir open a second time.

She glanced back at Tandy. "Did you know about this?"

Tandy's eyebrow arched high in just as much surprise as Marissa felt. "I knew they were talking about a wedding shower, but I didn't think they'd really go through with it."

Winifred rolled forward, an actual shower cap on her head in place of a wig. "I helped Pete escape so he would go to the farm, and you'd have to bring him back here."

So that's why Pete had been looking for her. If only Winifred's plan hadn't also ruined her dishes. Was it really the thought that counted? She tried to keep her cringe from showing.

Winifred beamed. "When Yvette picked Pete up, I didn't know how we were going to lure you over."

Was that why Yvette called Vince? Marissa's cheeks burned with all the effort she had to put into smiling. While Winifred had her intentions in the right place, she'd surely lost her mind.

Winifred's voice dipped. "Were you onto us?"

Marissa pried her lips from their frozen smile. "Not at all."

Winifred leaned forward. "So what brought you here?"

Marissa shook her head slowly. She couldn't blurt, *We swiped Vince's phone after we saw he had drugs stolen from Birdie, then Yvette called him so we suspect her of being involved.* But she had to say something. "Yvette."

Winifred's drawn-on eyebrows dipped low. "Yvette?"

"Yvette?" echoed Birdie with pink frosting smeared across her face.

"Birdie!" Winifred bellowed. "The cake is for Marissa. Could you not wait five minutes?"

Birdie smiled innocently.

Winifred sighed. "Marissa, will you wheel me over to the cake? We might as well cut it now."

Marissa wasn't in the mood for celebration, but Winifred must have gone through a lot of trouble to put the event together, and cake always helped. "Okay."

Tandy hitched a thumb toward a back hallway. "I'll go talk to Yvette."

"Okay." Marissa wrapped her fingers around the handles to Winifred's wheelchair and pushed her past the line of older women she'd never met before. They called out congratulations and complimented her youthfulness, though they all were acting younger than she felt. Would Connor still be in jail when she was old enough to move into a place like this?

Tandy didn't find Yvette in her office, so she headed toward the memory care wing in case the activities' director was still getting Pete settled in his room. Sure enough, the door with the tractor decoration stood open. Pete sat at a small table facing her way. It looked like he was supposed to be working on a jigsaw puzzle of a farm, but Tandy had all his attention.

"Howdy, Miss Tammy." He gave a big wave. "You made it."

"I'm here." With as many people as Winifred had calling her Tammy, she might be better off changing her name than correcting them.

Apparently, Pete had known of the plan to trick Marissa into showing up at the wedding shower. Had Yvette? Tandy scanned the room, but one only needed to listen for the woman.

Gushing water in the bathroom shut off, though Yvette continued to laugh. "Now, Pete. You must take your medication to keep you from…" Her voice faded when she appeared in the doorway, cup in one hand, pills in the other. "Oh, hey, Tandy. Are you here to check on Pete?"

"Yes." She wasn't going to discuss drug theft and murder in front of the old man. "I'm glad Vince was able to call you right away." At the time, she'd figured he must have googled the retirement community, but now she knew he had Yvette in his contacts list.

Yvette continued her mission to administer meds, giggling once again. "Again, I'm sorry Pete escaped, but he's in good hands now."

Pete took the small plastic cup from Yvette and shot Tandy a toothy grin. "Vince and I traded places. He used to work here, and I used to drive tractors. Now I live here, and he works on the farm."

Tandy cocked her head. Had she heard him correctly? Vince used to work at the retirement community? That could be where he got access to Birdie's drugs and Winifred's wig. "How long ago was that?"

"He was here last harvest season," Pete recalled. Though how reliable was his memory?

Yvette gave a sad chuckle. "Remember when I said Mr. Cross didn't want to let another employee go... for a certain reason?" She tilted her head toward Pete, inferring that she wasn't going to discuss drug theft in front of him.

Tandy didn't blame her. She'd put the pieces together best she could and wait for when Yvette could fill in the rest. "Yes," she answered. "Was Vince the one fired?" It explained why he had Yvette's number. Didn't explain why she'd called though.

"He was." Yvette watched Pete take his pills then patted his hand. "Enjoy your puzzle, Pete. We'll come get you for lunch in a bit."

Pete shot Tandy a thumbs up. She gave him one in return and preceded Yvette into the hallway. How sad that so many employees took advantage of the elderly. The residents she'd met had been a pure joy.

Yvette led the way back toward the lobby where Marissa's shower was probably in full swing. The grandmothers might not be the wildest partiers, but they could give much marriage advice from their personal experience.

"So," Tandy wondered. "Is that why you called Vince a little bit ago? Because you suspected him of being involved in this with his previous drug theft?"

Yvette paused, hand on hip. "I called Vince, but he didn't answer. How do you know that?"

Tandy imitated Birdie's expression of innocence. "I saw your name pop up on his phone and wondered."

"Yeah." Yvette turned, her laugh dryer than before. "After speaking with him at The Farmstead when picking up Pete, I started wondering if there was any connection between him and Hubert. I wanted to talk to him before sharing my concerns with Sheriff Griffin."

A surge of hope made Tandy's heart tingle. Yvette would be a better witness than either she or Marissa because she didn't have a significant other in the slammer. Yvette had no reason to point fingers, so Griffin would be more likely to listen. Preferably before Marissa's scheduled wedding ceremony. "Since Vince didn't answer your phone call, maybe you should call Griffin right now."

"I guess you're right. Especially since I might have messed up Marissa's wedding by attacking her in front of her family." Yvette tapped in the door code from inside the memory care ward. "I'll head back to my office and do that now."

Tandy couldn't wait to tell Marissa. Vince would get arrested, and Connor would be set free. Her toes curled in anticipation.

Yvette pulled the door open to reveal a frosting covered Birdie, blocking their path. The activities' director wrapped an arm around the old woman's shoulder to turn her back toward the party. "Let's get you a napkin for your face."

The woman didn't turn. "I need to use the powder room."

Of all the times…

Tandy scanned the entryway for an employee who could help. A lone woman in scrubs laughed and joked with Marissa over by the cake table. Probably an old friend of the bride. Marissa knew everyone in town.

As maid of honor, Tandy needed Yvette to make that phone call to save Marissa's wedding, but she didn't want to interrupt the shower to do it. "I'll take Birdie," she offered.

Yvette laughed her thanks. "What a crazy day, huh?"

"No kidding." Tandy held the door open and motioned Birdie through. She'd assist her to her own bathroom.

Birdie toddled down the hallway. "Did you deliver my cupcakes to Marissa's betrothed?"

Tandy strolled next to her, too lost in thought to really focus on conversing. "Um… You mean the cupcakes with your phone inside?"

"Oh, you found it."

Tandy lowered her chin and gave Birdie a soft scowl. "Yes. You shouldn't have done that."

"It's okay." Birdie pulled another smartphone from her pocket. This one had a rose gold glitter case. Yvette's. "I have another phone."

Tandy rubbed a hand over her face. Had Birdie swiped the phone right in front of her? Yvette had given her a side hug. Was that all it took? Tandy shoved her hands in her pockets to double check that she still had her keys and Vince's phone. She was safe. But Yvette needed her phone back to call the sheriff.

"Birdie," she admonished. "That's not your phone. You can't even get into it. How do you plan to use it?"

Birdie pressed the power button then clicked a couple icons to reboot in "safe mode." The phone restarted, and her tiny, veiny fingers flew, deleting a third-party app that provided the lock screen. Once more, she restarted the phone, this time with no passcode needed. She tapped on a little old-fashioned telephone icon to open the phone app. She was in.

Tandy blinked and shook her head. She should still scold, but she couldn't help being impressed. She pulled Vince's phone from her pocket. "Can you do that on this phone?"

"I can try." Birdie traded her.

Tandy looked down at Yvette's phone where the redhead smiled in her selfie with Hubert. She needed to return the phone to the activities' director, but she couldn't pass up an opportunity to get into Vince's text messages. And Yvette could always call Griffin from a land line.

Birdie repeated her process. "There." She held the phone out proudly.

Tandy still wondered what all the old woman remembered. She had the skills to work a phone better than the younger generations, but she didn't remember her own husband. It was sad, but ironically, her abilities might be what brought Archibald home. That was if Vince's phone revealed what Tandy thought it would.

"Thanks." She clicked on history, and Yvette's phone number popped up on the screen multiple times. Yvette had only mentioned calling him once. "That's weird."

"It *is* weird," Birdie agreed. "I thought she was dating Hubert. They talked about going on a trip together."

Tandy glanced up, still unsure how reliable Birdie was as a source. "You mean the group vacation to Costa Rica?"

"Yes." She nodded once before shuffling into the bathroom.

Tandy frowned back down at the two devices in her hands. She didn't quite understand their connection, but she'd ask Yvette when she returned the woman's phone. By now Griffin should be on his way, and he could take it from here.

Chapter Twenty-Four

TANDY WALKED BIRDIE BACK TO THE party then continued on to Yvette's office. She found the woman pulling her pockets inside out and rifling through her purse and piles of paper on her desk.

"You call Griffin?" Tandy asked to be sure he was on his way.

"Yeah." Yvette peeled with laughter. "But I had to do it on my office phone since my cell went missing. I know I had it with me when I picked up Pete. Like I said, I called Vince from it."

Tandy's fingers curled around the phone case in her pocket, but the mention of Vince stilled her. Birdie had jumped to the conclusion that Yvette called him because they had a romantic entanglement. It certainly didn't make sense that Yvette would have called him so many times if she'd just now suspected him of stealing. Could she be in on the theft?

Tandy released Yvette's phone and stepped toward the desk. "I'll help."

"Thanks." Yvette tugged at drawers and rifled through their contents. "I wonder if I left it in Pete's room."

Tandy's eyes scanned the catalog of medical supplies and brochures for Costa Rica, looking for something out of the ordinary. A love note? A bank deposit slip for cash? She lifted the brochures and her gaze landed on plane tickets. To Costa Rica. Except there were only two names listed. Yvette Foster. And Vince Foster.

The memory of the drug store being robbed by a perp with a white strip where a wedding ring should have been played in her mind, and everything made sense. Vince was Yvette's husband.

Marissa stared at the last space on the Mad Lib wedding vows she'd been instructed to fill out as part of her geriatric wedding shower. "Period of time," she read from underneath the blank.

"Two minutes." Winifred hooted first. But she'd already come up with answers for many of the other spaces. And "two minutes" really didn't bode well for wedding vows.

"Forever," called Birdie.

Marissa wrote down *forever* in the sentence, and her heart squeezed in her chest. *I look forward to the next forever of our lives.* She and Birdie were in the same boat with that one. Their forevers affected by uncontrollable circumstances.

The rest of the vows didn't make any sense. She read them aloud for the enjoyment of those who'd helped her write them. And to keep from crying. "I, Marissa, take you, Connor, to be my *fluffy* wedded husband. In the presence of *gypsies* and our *trees*, I offer you my *cranky* vow to be your *joyous toilet...*" and so on.

The ladies rocked with laughter. But it wasn't nearly as loud as it would have been if Yvette had been there. Hopefully, Tandy was getting some good information from her.

Marissa took a deep breath to finish. "I look forward to the next *forever* of our lives." Her voice broke.

The room quieted.

Winifred interrupted the silence by bursting into song. "I'm forever your girl..." Her arms splayed wide like she was performing opera, not Paula Abdul.

Marissa gave a sad smile. She'd take a *fluffy wedded husband* over no husband any day.

Winifred rolled into action, literally. Marissa's old friend from high school, now a CNA, pushed the large woman toward the cake table. Winifred reached underneath and retrieved a package of toilet paper. "All right, ladies. We're going to cheer Marissa up by making her a gown. Birdie and I have another surprise planned, but first you must make her look beautiful."

Marissa stood where directed, and toilet paper spun around her like it was magic in a room full of fairy godmothers. She got puffy sleeves, a full train, and even a butt bow. It may not have been her dream dress, but at least when she broke down in tears because her groom didn't show up, she'd have a place to wipe her nose.

She looked for Winifred to thank for the sweet gesture, but she'd disappeared. The woman said they had another surprise for her, but what else could there be?

Tandy's fingers trembled as she picked up the one-way tickets to Costa Rica. First, they should have been booked for roundtrip. Second, there should have been a lot more than only the two tickets there. Third, Vince shouldn't have been booked at all.

As activities' director, it would have been Yvette's job to collect thousands of dollars from each resident for the trip. It would have been her job to secure hotels, schedule outings, and book flights. Tandy did the math based on what Marissa said they'd paid for her honeymoon. If Yvette pocketed the five thousand dollars from even half of the two hundred residents for their vacation, that was half a million dollars. A lot to live on in Costa Rica. Was the woman really capable of running off with such stolen cash?

Tandy inhaled, her eyes darting up to view Yvette in this new light. The woman held a gun on her. Apparently, she was also capable of murder.

Tandy's heart froze, sending ice through her veins. "How long have you been planning this?"

Yvette chuckled. How could she still be laughing? "Since Mr. Cross fired Vince instead of getting him the help he needed."

Revenge. But not warranted. "You said he'd stolen drugs. Was he not guilty?"

She laughed. "He couldn't help himself. I'd hoped that working at the farm would keep Vince away from drugs, but then we hired Hubert who still supplied him. I threatened to fire Hubert, but by then Vince had already told him our plan for Costa Rica."

The pieces fell into place. Birdie had been mistaken about Yvette having a relationship with Hubert, but she'd probably heard them talk about the Costa Rica trip. "Hubert wanted in."

"Yeah. And there was no way I was going to take along the devil feeding Vince's addiction."

"So *you* killed him." Tandy stared at the woman with the gun. Did she not see the irony of calling the person she'd killed 'the devil'? Or maybe all killers had to twist truth in such a way that they thought themselves the good guys.

Speaking of good guys, Yvette had most definitely *not* called Sheriff Griffin. And she looked very willing to commit another murder.

Tandy took short sips of air, mentally measuring the distances between doors and different hiding places, trying to pick her best route for escape if bullets started flying.

Yvette shrugged. "I didn't plan to kill him. But then I realized he'd brought more pills to The Farmstead for Vince. When I tried to take them away from him, he was stronger than me. So I hit him with the shovel. We both ran when we saw Connor coming, but thankfully Connor followed him, and I got away with the drugs and his phone. I'm sorry Marissa's wedding is going to be ruined, but I need her fiancé to take the fall."

"How convenient." Tandy grimaced. "But do you think Vince is simply going to quit taking pills because Hubert died? We know he robbed the pharmacy because of the white strip on his finger where a wedding band used to be. When did you two get married?"

Yvette glanced at her bare ring finger. "We'd just eloped when Cross fired him. Naturally, I decided to keep it a secret while planning our getaway."

"Naturally." Tandy narrowed her eyes. "But Vince didn't need to hide his ring since he worked on the farm. That is, until you killed Hubert there and had to cover up your connection."

"Something like that."

Yvette wouldn't be revealing this info if she wasn't also planning to get rid of Tandy. "What about my body, Yvette? Are you hoping to be out of the country before anybody realizes I'm missing?"

Yvette huffed. "If only you two baristas hadn't been so snoopy. I tried to warn you off, even turning Marissa's family on her. But she kept digging."

Yvette circled the desk. Coming closer for a better shot? Tandy should have taken Greg's martial arts class with him. Then she'd know what to do in this situation.

Yvette continued her narrative. "Marissa's wedding shower is going to prove too much stress for her, and she's going to flip."

Tandy's eyebrow arched. Marissa had been more peaceful today than she'd seen in a long time. Surprising but fitting at the same time. "No, she's not."

Yvette cackled, the sound no longer cute or contagious. "That's what I'll tell police anyway when they ask questions about your death. Two birds, one stone."

Tandy stiffened. She didn't want to die, but even more, she didn't want to leave her best friend responsible for her death. Marissa had already been through so much. And she was as sweet and innocent as they came.

Marissa appeared in the doorway then, dressed like a mummy for some reason. She struck a pose to show off the toilet paper. "Old folks still like to TP things at Halloween."

When Tandy didn't crack a smile and the activities' director didn't giggle hysterically, Marissa's eyes flashed in confusion and she glanced from Tandy to Yvette. They all knew the exact moment she spotted the gun because her body slammed backwards against the door.

"Yvette?" she squeaked.

"Mrs. Vince Foster," Tandy corrected.

Yvette used her gun barrel to wave Marissa next to her friend.

Marissa cooperated, though her round eyes questioned reality.

"They're taking off for Costa Rica with all the vacation money from the residents," Tandy explained.

Marissa gasped. "Then why don't you just go, Yvette? Why do you have to kill anyone?"

Yvette huffed. "That had been my plan. But people keep getting in the way."

"Yeah, we're the bad guys here," Tandy quipped. She'd like to punch things, but she'd settle for sarcasm until she had a better opportunity for attack.

Yvette kept the gun trained on them as she sidestepped close enough to the door to peek out. With the coast clear, Yvette motioned them into a hallway and towards a metal door marked with a neon EXIT sign.

Marissa glanced at Tandy as if for instructions on what to do next, but Tandy was still working on it. Maybe once they got outside, they could run. She nodded for Marissa to follow orders then led the way toward the exit.

Tandy slammed the push bar in, hoping for an alarm. No such luck. And there was nobody out back to sound an alarm either. Only a large strip of grass separating them from the murky river.

She could slam the door on Yvette and pray her bullets didn't pierce metal. Or they could run for the riverbank and risk their lives by jumping into the icy water.

She'd stall while she considered their options. "Yvette, you said you were going to pin my death on Marissa."

Marissa pressed a hand to her heart. "I would never murder you, Tandy."

Tandy smiled at her dear friend. They'd both wanted to kill each other when they'd first met, but they'd come a long way since then. "That means a lot, Marissa. Thanks."

Yvette snorted. "Well, it doesn't matter now because I'm going to have to kill you both."

Tandy ground her jaw. "And who are you going to blame our deaths on?"

Yvette squared her body towards them, steadied the gun with both arms, and aimed their way. "Archibald, of course. He likes guns."

Marissa gripped her hand. Yvette could get away with this.

Chapter Twenty-Five

A CHUGGING SOUND INTERRUPTED THE STANDOFF. Yvette paused in her attempted murder to assess where the sound might be coming from.

A bright green tractor rounded the corner of the building, driven by Pete. He must not have swallowed his pills that were supposed to keep him out of trouble.

But even more important, he pulled a flatbed trailer where Archibald stood on a pyramid of hay. The old man aimed an apple shooter Yvette's way, resembling Rambo with a bazooka.

Yvette had been right. He did like guns.

A row of apples shot through the air, the first hitting Yvette off balance. It knocked her sideways so that none of the others hit their target, but it also kept her from firing back.

Archibald reloaded. "You girls gonna keep lollygaggin' or jump on?"

Tandy jolted into action, tugging Marissa with her.

A bullet pinged off the metal flatbed in front of them, and they dove for cover behind a bale of scratchy hay. The trailer rumbled forward, but it wouldn't be fast enough to keep Yvette from catching them. Tandy lifted her head to peek over the haybale and see how much time they had before the mad woman found her balance and caught up.

Red hair flew wildly as Yvette tried to shoot and run at the same time, but another round of fruit arced through the air, pummeling her backwards to the ground. She rolled over, flipping to face them and staying low. The barrel of her gun aimed their direction.

Tandy ducked as gunfire rang out and a corner of the haybale puffed into the air. Adrenaline zinged through her, relief warring with horror.

The apple shooter's hydraulics hissed above. Archibald laughed louder than Yvette ever had. "Pete, take us back to the farm lickety split!" he called.

Yvette jumped up but ran the other direction. Was she giving up that easily?

Marissa lay flat on her back with a moan, but Tandy watched to see where Yvette went. Even if the woman wanted to run away, she would still need to pick up her husband, and Vince was probably at the farm.

Yvette scrambled for a black Lexus, which was a pretty nice vehicle for someone in her position. Tandy had never noticed it before because she'd always been in the company bus.

"She's been launderin' money through activities at Grace Springs Manor," Archibald announced like he'd been the one to crack the case and save the day. "She was good at it too. I only figured it out because the guy she was in cahoots with made some really poor choices while doped up on pills." Okay, Archibald had been the first one to put it all together. And thank goodness he had.

Marissa pointed at the road. The black car raced parallel to them. Yvette's window slid down. "Duck!"

Both she and Tandy dropped their heads behind the hay bales once again before the crack of gunfire. But Archibald's grunt was not followed with return fire. In fact, he stumbled down the hay pyramid and fell to his knees in front of them. A red liquid patch spread across the sleeve by his shoulder.

Tandy's heart plummeted. This man had saved them. She had to return the favor.

She ripped off her jacket and flannel shirt the way she'd watched Greg do the night before for Vince. If only they'd known the farm hand was a bad guy then. Because they hadn't, she now had to stop Archibald's blood. She balled the shirt and pressed it against the seeping wound.

He gritted his teeth, but no sound came out. He was an animal.

"Oh, no," Marissa whispered. "Yvette turned down the drive to The Farmstead."

"Stop, Pete," Tandy called. They had enough problems with Archibald's gunshot wound. She'd rather the tractor driver not deliver them directly back into the hands of the shooter.

But the tractor continued to rumble forward. Past the farmhouse and toward the corn maze. Pete probably couldn't hear her. And even if he could, he'd never willingly stopped the tractor without someone jumping up and stopping it for him.

They needed help, but Tandy couldn't let go of Archibald to call the police.

"Do you have your phone?" She eyed Marissa's TP wedding dress doubtfully.

Marissa looked down and patted the pockets underneath the strips of soft paper. "I don't."

Tandy kicked her jacket toward her friend. "I've got both Yvette and Vince's phones in there. Call Griffin."

Marissa scrambled through the pockets, glancing over her shoulder for Yvette. The Lexus kicked up dust, but Yvette hadn't parked yet. They'd have time to get through to Griffin before the killer reached them, but they'd need to find somewhere to hide until the police showed up.

Marissa pulled out Vince's phone then dropped it to keep searching for another.

"What are you doing?" Tandy shouted. "Call from that phone."

Marissa retrieved Yvette's shiny phone. "What about the lock screen?"

"Birdie removed them."

Archibald closed his eyes and smiled through his pain. "Birdie is the bee's knees."

Yvette's tires screeched to a halt.

"Call now." Tandy measured their distance to the corn maze entrance. "We'll jump off into the corn maze as Pete passes it. Then…"

A shovel smashed down, knocking the lifeline from Marissa's hands. Vince stood over them, eyes wild. "I wondered what happened to my phone."

Marissa screeched and scooted backward away from the same kind of tool that had started it all. If Vince hadn't been there, they might have had a chance. But now they didn't have time to escape into the maze with a wounded old veteran, and even if they did, Griffin would not be on his way to help.

To make matters worse, Pete picked that moment to stop the tractor and take off toward the petting zoo with his gangly gait and one-track mind.

Marissa glanced over her shoulder at Tandy to see if her friend had any more tricks up her sleeve. But no, she was focused solely on Archibald's sleeve. Blood seeped through his shirt, and though he seemed to be trying to resist the pull of gravity, his head listed to one side, only lifting when he coughed. His usual scowl had gone slack.

"We need to get him to a hospital," Tandy stated.

The lump creeped higher in Marissa's throat. She turned to face off with Vince. "Your wife planned to kill us and blame it on Archibald. Are you going to let her keep killing people to cover up your crimes?"

Vince wielded the shovel like a baseball bat, though his dark eyes jittered, studying them nervously. It was bottom of the 9th. Bases were loaded. Three strikes, and he'd be out.

Marissa wound up for the pitch. "If Archibald dies too, who are you going to blame our murders on?"

A car door slammed by the barn. Yvette pointed her gun and strode over. "We'll blame it on your cousin. You suspected him and requested a drug test, right? Just in case, I laced his Frappuccino with fentanyl at the coffee shop this morning on my way in to work."

Marissa's jaw dropped hard enough to pull her whole body forward. "He got another coffee?" The traitor.

Tandy growled. "You did what?"

And Marissa refocused. One problem at a time.

Yvette shrugged. "Is it really any worse than when Marissa put salt in his milk as kids?"

"Yes," she shouted. Though shame wrapped itself around her heart, boa constrictor style. She not only used to prank Austin, but she'd given him a complex that could be used as a motive in court. And all he'd been doing was trying to help.

"Yes," Vince echoed Marissa's answer, frowning at his wife. "You don't mess with opioids. You can get him addicted."

Like addiction was worse than going to jail for murder.

"Don't worry." Yvette shooed Vince back to standing guard. "If we make it look like he killed these three, the attorney boyfriend will see he's put in prison for life."

Tandy's eyes bugged at Marissa. Archibald's eyes closed. Now what?

They were dealing with a couple who had some serious issues. Maybe Marissa could use their marital woes against them. "How did *you* get addicted to opioids?" she asked Vince.

He grimaced. "My mom had painkillers for her cancer. When she passed, I took them to deal with my grief."

Memories of Winifred's pain scrolled through her mind. If Vince had compassion for cancer patients, how could he do such a thing as steal painkillers from them? And how could he kill anyone, knowing it would cause their loved ones the same pain he went through?

Yvette looked around then motioned toward the maze. "Let's finish them in there where there won't be any witnesses."

Marissa eyed the stately barn with rows of white chairs waiting for her wedding tomorrow, and somehow that same strange peace she'd felt about not being able to wed Connor also settled over her at the thought of death. God's love never failed. No matter what these people did to her, she was going to get to spend eternity in heaven. That's where all wounds would be healed, from cancer to dementia to heartbreak. She just didn't want to leave Connor behind to face the pain of grief.

She squared off with Vince once again. "You realize that the pain you felt when you lost your mom will be inflicted upon everyone who loves us, don't you?"

Vince hesitated, shovel drooping. He wasn't the heartless one here. He felt trapped by his addictions. And those addictions weren't going away unless he turned himself in and got help. Unless he broke the vicious cycle and chose a love that never failed. "I know you are trying to guilt me, but I don't think I could feel any worse than I already do."

Yvette laughed wildly. "Let's go. Corn maze now."

Marissa sucked in the icy air so quickly it stung her gums. She didn't want to obey, but the corn maze might offer their only escape. She scooted toward the edge of the trailer and looked back at Tandy who had to loop one of Archibald's arms around her neck to help him move.

Oh, no. Marissa would have to help with Archibald too. He wouldn't make it without them, and they could never leave him behind. She reached out and hooked his other arm around her.

The old man grunted. He'd been the one to figure out whodunit and come to their rescue, but it was all for naught. Marissa hadn't even gotten to tell Birdie how much he loved her the way he'd requested.

They scooted his feet to the ground, and the extra weight made Marissa wobble. At least her boots had flat soles this time.

"Got him?" Tandy asked.

"I think so."

Archibald smelled of cinnamon, like he'd been living on stolen donuts. His prickly beard stubble snagged on the toilet paper wrapped around her arms.

His eyes blinked open long enough for him to ask, "What in tarnation are you wearin'?"

She looked down at the irony of her outfit. After a life committed to fashion, she was going to die while dressed in Charmin Ultra. "It's a wedding gown made out of toilet paper. Winifred and Birdie threw me a shower, and this is what women do at showers."

"Peculiar. But at least I got to spend my life with my love." His eyelids drooped once again, tugging her heart down with them.

Connor.

"Move," Yvette barked.

The three of them hobbled as one. Marissa scanned the farm a last time before the cornstalks would block her view. There had been no farm hands around to witness their disappearance, but maybe somebody would hear her if she screamed. She was good at screaming.

Tandy caught her eye, her glare more determined than desperate. "Archibald," she whispered. "Do you have a real gun on you?"

Marissa's breath caught. If he said yes, did Tandy know how to shoot? Because she sure didn't.

"Good grief." He harrumphed. "I left it in my jacket that I put on that scarecrow."

Figured. Marissa inhaled, preparing to scream.

Archibald pinched her neck for her attention. "When we get into the maze, I want you to drop me and skedaddle different directions."

Leave him behind? After he came to their rescue?

"No," Tandy refused before Marissa could even squeak the word.

"I need to know that Birdie is taken care of, and these yahoos aren't going to do it."

He would lay down his life for the wife who didn't even remember him. That was love. The world could learn from such sacrifice. Starting with her.

"There's got to be another way," Marissa whispered. Her guts churned even more now at the idea of losing Archibald than they had at the thought of personally taking a bullet.

"My life is almost over anyway. You young things have too much life left to give up," Archibald argued. "There's no other way. Unless God himself sends an angel—"

Police sirens wailed in the distance.

Tandy turned at the sound of sirens. They all did. Including Yvette.

"Lucky for you, Archibald..." Hope surged, leading the way. She wouldn't leave the man to run, but she'd leave him to fight. "I survive on coffee and Jesus."

In a quick twist, she ducked under his arm and hooked it across Marissa's chest to her other shoulder. She continued her momentum to dive at Vince's legs. She'd wanted to take him out yesterday, and this was her chance.

Vince startled and swiped his shovel her direction, but her arms encircled his legs first, sending him backwards. Greg would claim her strike to be a "weak shoestring tackle," but it did the job. She rolled off Vince, grabbed the shovel, pushed to her feet in one move, twirling the handle like a kung fu master.

The terror in Yvette's eyes betrayed her laughter. Maybe it had been nervous laughter all along. If only they'd known and arrested her in the beginning. She took one look at Vince on the ground, Tandy with the shovel, and a cop car chasing the bus from Grace Springs Manor down the dirt road, then she darted into the maze.

Tandy let her go. Griffin could take it from here. Especially since Yvette's evil laugh would make her easy to track down.

She did a double take at the bus. Greg's grim face peered through the windshield from behind the steering wheel.

Her mouth fell open. The man was all about law and order, so what possessed him to escape from jail, commandeer someone else's vehicle, and lead the cops in a high-speed pursuit?

The bus braked in a cloud of dust. The doors whooshed open, and Tandy could almost hear the theme song for *The Dukes of Hazard* as Greg jumped out. Connor followed.

Greg reached her first, but he couldn't wrap her in his arms like a normal reunion because she wielded a shovel. He stepped behind her as if daring Vince to try to take them both on.

"And I thought you needed rescuing," he quipped.

Connor's charge came to a halt as well since Marissa was already in another man's arms. "Archibald's hurt?"

"Yes," Marissa struggled to stay upright.

Connor stooped to scoop the man from her grip.

The sheriff jogged up behind them and cuffed Vince. "Romero, call for an ambulance," he barked. "Though I came here to take Connor and Greg back to jail, it looks like Vince is the real criminal."

"Vince stole the drugs." Tandy tilted her head toward the cornstalks where Yvette's laughter grew louder then quieter as she zig-zagged her way through the maze. "But his wife, Yvette, is the killer."

Griffin drew his gun. "I guess I'm going after Yvette." He took off into the corn maze, chasing the woman who had no choice left but to surrender.

Archibald, on the other hand, scowled at being carried by Connor. "I just want my Birdie."

"I'm right here, Archibald," a voice wobbled. Birdie gripped the handrail to the bus and tottered down. "My lands. What kind of trouble did you get yourself into this time?"

Tandy gaped, dropping the business end of the shovel into the dirt. Not only did the woman with dementia remember her husband, but she'd apparently taken off with the bus to break Tandy's man out of jail.

Greg stepped beside Tandy, wrapping an arm behind her back. "That little lady could write the book on trouble," he said. "She just appeared with the key to our jail cells. We weren't going to let her bust us out until Winifred told us Archibald believed it had been Vince wearing her wig. Connor realized you two could be in danger here on the farm."

Winifred rolled onto the platform for lowering wheelchairs. She waved her arms, doing justice to a Whitney Houston song on her ride to the ground.

Tandy arched an eyebrow. "You broke the law based on words from a lady wearing a pink shower cap?"

Greg turned to face Tandy, gripping the collar of her leather jacket. His coffee brown eyes darkened to the color of espresso. "I care about the law because it was created to protect the people I love. If it doesn't allow me to do that, then I'll break the law to protect them...to protect you...and I'll serve my time in prison."

She stared up at him in wonder. He wasn't just a good man. He was a good man who loved her. Griffin better not put him back in jail. She dropped the shovel to hug him tight.

With her cheek against Greg's shoulder, she watched Connor set Archibald down on the picnic table. It's where they'd all been when Archibald had first asked Tandy to take care of Birdie. Now Birdie took care of him, aware for the moment that this man had kept his vows when he'd declared "until death do us part."

Tears ran down the old woman's cheeks, though her husband beamed like he'd won the lottery, bullet wound and all.

Marissa's mom and company rolled up. Doors slammed and all four blondes stared in shock at the mayhem around them.

"What are you wearing?" mocked Ashlee.

"And what happened?" Mom asked.

Marissa beamed, ignoring the jab. "My groom broke out of jail to save me from the danger I got into when trying to prove him innocent."

Amber gasped. "Now he's even more of a criminal. Why would he do that?"

"Because that's what you do when you love someone." Austin's voice boomed. He emerged from the corn maze, holding Yvette's arm wrenched behind her. "And Connor's not the criminal. She is."

Tandy gaped. Austin had been truly trying to help them all along.

Marissa's Aunt Linda held a hand to her heart. "Austin? What's going on?"

Austin shrugged as if he caught killers every day. "When I tested positive for drugs this morning, I realized the only place I could have been drugged was at the coffee shop where I'd run into Yvette. I just needed to prove it, so I came back to the spot where I knew drugs were sold and waited for this lady to show up."

Yvette cackled in spite of the fact that she was now the joke.

Griffin charged from the maze at the sound of Yvette's laughter, then slowed when he realized she'd already been captured. "Good work, Austin. Thank you."

Wow. The sheriff gave someone else credit.

Griffin holstered his own gun so he could take Yvette's and cuff her hands behind her. As he paraded the woman past them, he nodded to Austin's mom. "Your son is a true hero."

Marissa's aunt's eyes lit on Austin. Perhaps he was finally going to get the respect from his family that he'd longed for.

And it had come from helping out the person who had hurt him rather than try to get revenge the way Yvette had.

Austin shrugged it off. "This isn't about me. It's about Connor being free to marry Marissa."

That's when Connor turned to face his bride directly. His eyes shown as if she was walking down the aisle toward him in a designer gown rather than a bunch of wadded up toilet paper.

Chapter Twenty-Six

MARISSA LOOKED UP FROM HER SUNFLOWER bouquet to the man waiting for her in a charcoal gray suit in front of the barn at the end of the aisle. Yeah, he had shaggy hair because he'd missed his trip to the barber, but he was still as warm and dependable as home. The way he smiled at her in her grandmother's vintage gown made her feel every bit as desired—though he always smiled at her like that.

Winifred, dressed in her Beyoncé wig, belted out the Etta James lyrics they'd been planning to have the DJ play, "At last..."

It couldn't be more appropriate. The moment was hard won and perfect. The paper plates had turned out to be a sign after all. A sign of how she'd stick with this man in any circumstance.

Dad held out his elbow, and Marissa hooked her hand through it. She took a deep breath and hoped out of habit that she didn't trip on her hem as they moved forward. If she did trip, it would be okay, because she was surrounded by people who'd seen her flaws and loved her in spite of them. Well, maybe not the twins, but her mom did now, and that canceled out their patronizing opinions.

Marissa didn't want to be gorgeous and heartless like her cousins anymore. She wanted to be free like Birdie who waved a hanky when she passed. The woman may not fully know who she was, but she didn't let the judgements of others get in her way. No matter where life took her.

Marissa grinned at Tandy as she got closer. Was her tough friend wiping at tears? Nah, she had to be developing allergies like Connor.

As for her groom, his gray eyes sparkled with newfound appreciation for life. She seriously would have married this man in jail, but because she didn't have to, every day spent together would feel like a gift.

Maybe that's how God wanted her to feel about life. He took on the sins of others so she could have a future in heaven, but He didn't stop there.

God was enough—and everything else was a gift.

When they got to the vows, Marissa repeated after Pastor Meade, adding, "I look forward to the next forever of our lives," from her wedding shower Mad Libs. And she meant it.

Connor's brow wrinkled in confusion for a moment before the pastor distracted him by announcing, "You may now kiss the bride."

Connor lifted her veil then leaned his forehead against her as if waiting for her to admit he'd been right about their next kiss being as man and wife. He knew God's love too.

She grinned along with him, savoring the celebration. This moment was well earned.

His face finally tilted, and his lips claimed hers.

Cheers filled the air, and Connor lifted Marissa's hand overhead when they turned to face the crowd. Mom and Dad and their beautiful but snobby relatives. Connor's family of farmers that welcomed Marissa as their own. The townsfolk, including the old folks who now felt like family.

Austin even stood next to Kristin, his wedding ring finger bare as if he was ready for a new beginning. Marissa knew he was capable of moving forward, exactly as she had.

When it came time for the bouquet toss, there were many competitors, though Archibald made sure Birdie didn't think she was one of them. Even with his arm in a sling, he was there for his wife. The beauty of it took her breath away.

In contrast, Ashlee and Amber jockeyed for position underneath the crystal chandelier hanging from the highest wooden arch of the barn.

Tandy stood behind them, arms crossed as if she didn't care whether she would ever get to wear a white dress or not, and maybe she didn't. She seemed to prefer black, but one corner of her lips curved up, and her eyes flashed with confidence.

Greg stood on the sidelines, leaning forward as his hands rubbed together like a football coach. Oh boy.

Marissa grinned at Connor then turned her back to their wedding guests.

The DJ counted down. "3...2...1..."

Marissa whipped the bouquet overhead then spun to see who caught it.

The twins may not have had any shoestrings to tackle, but Tandy dove for their legs anyway. It wasn't so much that she was desperate to be the next bride, she just wanted to save Zam from their clutches.

Both women toppled sideways into the hay, leaving a clear spot for the bouquet to land. Kristin charged in, ready to recover the fumble, but Winifred blocked her by rolling her wheelchair in the way.

Tandy bent forward, gripped the bunch of stems, and stood.

Winifred clapped her hands like a cheerleader, and started chanting, "Tammy! Tammy!"

The wedding guests joined in, despite knowing Tandy's real name.

She smiled and sniffed her sweet yellow blooms before handing the bouquet to Winifred. "You may not have ever gotten married or had kids, but I want you to know I adore you and think of you as a grandmother. I seriously wouldn't be here without you."

Winifred's fake eyelashes fanned as if trying to dry up any wetness underneath. "Oh, sugar," she held out her arms.

Tandy swallowed the lump in her throat and let herself be enveloped in the pillowy embrace. She'd never gotten this from her parents, and she hadn't realized how much she longed for it.

The twins climbed from the hay, brushing themselves off and muttering. Ashlee crossed her arms. "That's not how this is supposed to work."

"Hobble-dee-gobble-dee." Winifred released Tandy to face off with the blonde brats. "Young lady, what do you know about love?"

Amber sniffed, and Ashlee tossed her hair.

"That's what I thought." Winifred gripped Tandy's hand. "Tammy isn't looking for someone to be there for her. She's looking to be there for others. Once you learn that, you'll be able to find the love you've always wanted. The way she has."

Tandy pressed her lips together to keep from laughing. And crying. Rather than gloat over the twins' embarrassment, she smiled at Marissa. This old woman put the twins in their place the way they'd both been wanting to.

"Now somebody bring me a microphone," Winifred called. "Because I'm going to sing a song for Tammy to dance with her sweetheart."

Greg took the cue to swoop in and wrap Tandy in his arms. "Where's this Tammy girl I'm supposed to be dancing with?"

Tandy grinned up at him. "I don't know, but I'm not sharing you. Ever."

"You better be careful," Greg warned, spinning the garter he'd caught around his finger. "Because you might get your wish."

At that moment, the background music for *Single Ladies* roared over the loudspeakers, and Winifred did her Beyoncé wig justice. Greg spun Tandy under an arm, with all the enthusiasm of a guy planning to "put a ring on it."

Marissa and Connor snuck away like Pete to pose for pictures on the tractor decorated with a "Just Hitched" sign before returning indoors for cake. The Mr. and Mrs. mugs from Tandy waited for them at the cake table.

Tandy tapped a spoon on her own coffee mug then took the microphone to offer a toast with one of the red plastic cups Mom had purchased last minute. She took a shaky breath and shot Marissa a smile. "I could make some pretty good jailbird jokes right now. But instead, I'll focus on the lovebirds."

Marissa clinked her mug with Connor's. She'd drink to that.

The crowd tittered. Especially Birdie, who leaned her head on Archibald's good shoulder.

Tandy sighed and her teasing wink melted into a soft smile. "All jokes aside, I just want to say that over the past year, I've seen Marissa's determination in making this wedding day happen. Seriously, there were many times when I doubted we'd live this long."

Marissa squeezed Connor's hand. So many times.

Griffin tipped his hat from his spot at the back of the barn. It was like he still thought they needed him for security, and maybe they did.

Tandy turned from the crowd to face Marissa again, eyes twinkling. "But what impressed me most was the peace I saw in Marissa yesterday when it looked like she was going to have to give up this beautiful ceremony. Connor was her bigger priority. Her love for him was the only thing that mattered."

Marissa bit her lip to keep her chin from quivering. Of course Connor was all that mattered. Okay, maybe she hadn't always been so selfless, but the possibility of losing everything had helped put her values in perspective.

Connor kissed her forehead, and she loved him even more if that was possible.

Tandy lifted her cup. "Won't you all raise your tacky red cups and join me in toasting the kind of love that never fails."

Marissa couldn't keep from laughing at that. She set her mug down in favor of the hideous plastic cup then hooked elbows with Connor to stay connected while each sipped their own drink. She'd never been happier than this moment. Because happiness didn't come from a cup but from a heart that overflowed.

Author Note

Dear Reader,

I remember lying in bed the first night I had the idea of a cozy mystery series starring both a tea lover and a coffee lover. I was so excited I couldn't sleep, and I grabbed my phone to brainstorm with Heather Woodhaven who, lucky for me, is a night texter. That idea stage is always the funnest part of writing a book or series. Then came the actual work, and I realized writing mysteries is HARD.

But here we are. We made it to the end. I've fallen in love with my crazy characters and everything I've learned from them. I hope you have too.

As I started *A Mug of Mayhem*, all I knew was that I wanted to incorporate Grace Springs Manor. My dad, both my daughters, and my best friend work at a ritzy retirement community, and they tell the BEST stories. They really had to deal with a former spy who uses her skills to steal cookies. And there really was a lady who raved about how at her age her underwear has to be something pretty special. Some of their stories I couldn't fit into this book. Like the former plumber with dementia who kept taking apart toilets and causing floods. Overall, I just liked the idea of comparing an elderly couple with an engaged couple, so that's where I started.

The character Pete was inspired by a joyous looking farmer who walked past me in a parking lot at Walmart. I mentioned him on my Facebook group, and Bonnie Earl said he sounded like her dad. So I named him Pete in honor of Bonnie's father. The world needs more people like him.

I doubt the real Pete snuck out of his retirement home, but that was also based on a true story shared by readers in my Facebook group. If you're in my group, you probably already know that having Tandy get mistaken for a cop at the pharmacy came from a real fear I had last Halloween when stopping at a pharmacy while in costume. And you were probably also one of the many who helped me come up with the old-timey sayings I used. My fave was Winifred's "hobble-dee gobble-dee."

I gave Winifred cancer because I wanted to have a bunch of wigs in the story. This idea originated with a friend who went through chemo, and one time when she was out for dinner with her husband while wearing her wig, some friends didn't recognize her and thought her husband was cheating. Thus, whenever I wore my long red wig, I would warn Facebook friends that if they saw Jim with a redhead, not to worry.

I didn't want to make a big deal of the cancer, but I felt like it played well into *A Mug of Mayhem* since October is Breast Cancer Awareness Month. If you want to read more about my cancer journey, check out the acknowledgments at the beginning of this book where I thank everyone who helped me both survive and write this story—it's the first book I wrote after going through chemo. During chemo, I pretty much only wrote diary entries on Caring Bridge, which you could visit here: www.caringbridge.org/visit/angelastrong/journal.

In *A Mug of Mayhem*, it's cancer that draws Tandy (Tammy) even closer to Winifred, which was important for me. I wanted to show how when one chooses not to marry and/or have kids, their life can still be a life well-lived and there is still much love to be had. Some love stories go way deeper than romance.

Tandy needed that relationship with Winifred too. Because while Marissa found healing in her family relationships, Tandy never did. Sometimes that happens in life. But it doesn't mean God's love has failed us. It means He'll send us love in unexpected ways.

That is my prayer for you. May God's unfailing love fill you to overflowing so that you can pour out His love on others like one of Marissa's teapots. And even though this series is over, I'd love to be able to keep pouring love into you through my weekly newsletter. You can sign up at www.angelaruthstrong.com.

Strong like my coffee,
Angela